THE **CHRONICLES** OF A **MALFUNCTIONING MALE**

A E BEM

THE **CHRONICLES** OF A **MALFUNCTIONING MALE**

Copyright © Alexander Bem 2022

The right of Alexander Bem to be identified as the author of this work has been asserted by him in accordance with the Copyright, Designs and Patents Act 1988.

All rights reserved. No part of this publication may be reproduced, stored in a retrieval system, or transmitted, in any form, or by any means (electronic, mechanical, photocopying, recording or otherwise) without the prior written permission of the author.

This book is a work of fiction. Names, characters, places, organisations and incidents are either products of the authors' imagination or used fictitiously. Any resemblance to actual events, places, organisations or persons, living or dead, is entirely coincidental.

Third parties do not have any control over, or any responsibility for, any author or third-party websites referred to in or on this book.

To my wife Sophie, for turning a comedy into a love story

Chapter 1

A E Bem

The Chronicles of a Malfunctioning Male

Hindsight is a wonderful thing, and if I'd had the benefit of it prior to my girlfriend of three years breaking up with me, I'd probably have noticed some warning signs.

Warning sign a): not turning up to my birthday restaurant date due to work commitments, only to come stumbling into my place at 2am the next morning to puke all over my bedsheets.

Warning sign b): she issued me with a direct ultimatum; if I wanted to continue with our relationship, I was to promise that I would sever all ties with my two best (and in her words 'immature and depressing') friends, although knowing my two best friends as I do, I kind of had some sympathy with her over this one.

Warning sign c): she suggested we practice an open relationship *after* I found out she'd slept with her boss.

Even then I held out some hope for us, even when she continued to have regular sleepovers at her friend's house rather than mine because 'she lives so much closer to the office'.

'Are you some kind of fucking idiot?' were my friend Ozzy's bewildered and characteristically kind words when I explained my dilemma whilst flagrantly breaching Warning Sign B as I tried to solve the Rubik's cube that our relationship had turned into in my brain. Ozzy had an excellent point; I was indeed a fucking idiot for even contemplating that I might be able to salvage something from a girl who not only seemed to have fallen way out of love with me but actually seemed to hate most things about my entire existence these days.

And so, as a complex litany of thoughts became increasingly jumbled in my mind as I struggled to come to anything close to a definitive decision, the problem was taken out of my hands when my girlfriend, the beautiful apple of my eye, texted me to say her boss had been offered a promotion and she was moving to New York with him as she couldn't spend her life with someone who was happy to waste his existence messing around with ridiculous friends, working in a dead-end job and pretending that he had hopes and ambitions greater than breaking the world record for the most wanks in a day.

That last jibe really hurt; in all fairness, I was well aware that my chances of breaking any wanking world records had sailed off into the sunset long before I'd bid farewell to my teen years.

Three years, though. Three years of someone feeling like the closest person to you in the world, someone being your best friend, your confidante, the first person you think of when you find a funny meme, the first person you want to tell when someone at work's a complete and utter twat and the only person you want to go to sleep with at night and wake up with in the morning.

But what do you do after a breakup? Do you go out and get wildly drunk over and over again until the alcohol turns to hard drugs and you find yourself leading a brand-new life without your former partner or your former job, but with a new bunch of friends; squatting in a crack den and sleeping on a bare mattress stained with vomit and faeces?

I wonder if my mother would've known what to do? Whether she would've had some words of wisdom for me in this situation? I mentioned it to Dad when I'd popped round to his one weekend and he had visibly tensed up. For all his immense qualities as a father, emotional support probably wasn't one of his strong points. He'd spent too much of his time focusing on making sure I had the necessities to live for him to have any time spare to worry about the softer skills of parenting, maybe that's a common consequence of being a single father.

And does love actually exist anymore? I mean really exist, like in the old days, like it did in those films where war or living on different continents were driving two lovers apart? Is it possible to feel that depth of feeling when people know the last kiss, that last glance merely means having to reactivate several dating apps?

The Chronicles of a Malfunctioning Male

So I did the only thing I could do. After several weeks spent ignoring basic personal hygiene, sitting in my pants for hours on the sofa alternating between pot noodles, masturbation and playing FIFA, I carried on. I kept on getting out of bed every morning, a split second of peace as I opened my eyes before my brain slowly clicked into gear bringing with it the realisation of my lonely existence. I continued to go to work and I continued to meet up with my friends. For a while I existed. Until, gradually, the smiles on my face became genuine, the laughs began to occur with increased spontaneity and the pain I'd felt faded away and became a distant memory.

Chapter 2

The Chronicles of a Malfunctioning Male

You can choose your friends but you can't choose your family. That's what they say, isn't it? Although sometimes, I think particularly for boys, it's not quite true. Boys become friends with kids at school or at a kids' football club, and they tend to stay lumbered for life, tangled together by an invisible web of convenience and habit, almost semi-unwillingly, doomed to walk the earth together with a questionable Pick 'n' Mix bag of toe rags and scoundrels for the rest of their days.

I'd met my best friend Ozzy at Cub camp at the age of nine years old. We were at the same primary school but had always ended up in different classes in the same year and so knew each other but hadn't become particularly close. As a kid, Cub camp was a magical place; two nights away sleeping in the woods, campfires, endless games of football, Had, Bulldog Barrier and any other playground game which involved chasing each other to the point of exhaustion with the inevitability of numerous grazed knees, nosebleeds and asthma attacks to bring their conclusion. There were trees to climb, an outdoor swimming pool to swim in and it was a place where legends were born and folklore was written into fact, to be told to future years of excited and overly eager Cub campers.

Ozzy's older brother's mate, Dean Eggerton, had once climbed up to the top of the big tree down by the outdoor swimming pool, fallen out of it onto his head and gone mad from the impact of the fall, ran away from the first aiders into the woods where he stayed for both nights before coming back completely naked having lost his clothes fighting a pack of wolves. And a kid who was a few years above us at school, Danny Bentley, had got up at three in the morning, slept-walked over to one of the dad's tents, unzipped the front, and wee'd all over the dads in there while they were sleeping. As you can see, it really was a place where the special, magical and the quite frankly downright unbelievable could become reality.

As Dad and I made our way to Cub camp I wasn't sure I'd ever felt as excited before in my whole life. I'd barely slept a wink the night before in anticipation, but any sign of tiredness had been pumped out of my body by the liberal supply of adrenaline that was coursing through my veins. But I wasn't the only one; Dad seemed genuinely excited himself. He'd packed a whole crate of those cans that he sometimes drank in the evening. My backpack was heavily weighed down by the sheer number of sweets I'd chucked into it.

'Now remember what I told you, don't shove all those sweets in your gob the moment you get there, because you'll run around like a madman and be sick, OK?' Dad directed as he manoeuvred the heavy traffic out of Uxbridge towards the camp.

'OK, Dad,' I replied, thinking he hadn't said I couldn't shove most of them in my gob.

'And make sure you share them, yeah? You've got about a year's supply in your backpack so don't go being greedy,' Dad continued with his lecture.

'I will!' I exclaimed slightly impatiently, looking out of the window away from Dad for fear that he'd be able to see the lie in my eyes.

'And, Jamie,' Dad continued further, grabbing my shoulder with his left hand at this point and turning his head towards me while we were stationary in traffic.

'What?' I replied.

'Make sure you have a good time!' he said and I smiled and he laughed and ruffled my hair as the traffic cleared slightly.

That night I stood outside my tent having a wee into some bushes, and I watched as the fire roared in the middle of the campsite and the dads all sat around it, drinking those cans Dad had brought. I looked over at Dad sitting there and saw him chatting animatedly with the other dads around the fire, seeing him laughing hysterically, tears rolling down his cheeks as he reached over and cracked open another can. It was then that I'd thought to myself I didn't really know any of Dad's friends, I wasn't actually sure if he had any. Do dads have friends? When do you stop having friends and become a dad? It was always just me and him with everything we did. Going to the zoo, to the cinema, going over the park, it was always just the two of us. I'd see families with a mum, maybe other siblings, but I'd never felt jealous, or that I was missing out on anything. I thought about Mum. Often, to be honest, always, daydreaming at school, work, on the commute, when lying in bed at night, when in crowded places just wondering: what if she were close. Sometimes I'd study the faces of women as they passed me by, checking to see if their features resembled mine at all.

Watching Dad in that moment, enjoying himself in the company of other adults, to be honest, had felt slightly alien to me, but it had made me feel happy seeing him happy.

'That's beer,' a voice said beside me, startling me slightly as I zipped up my flies. It was Ozzy.

'My dad drinks about ten of those every night, then he falls asleep in his chair and sometimes he wets himself. I tried one but it's 'orrible, I dunno how he can stand drinking so many. Does your dad do the same?' Ozzy had continued, pointing at his dad, a man with dreadlocks who looked older than my dad and who had just at that moment stood up and stumbled towards the fire, several of the other dads jumping up quickly to steady him.

'He does drink those cans sometimes in the evening, but he usually just has one, I think, and I've never seen him wet himself,' I'd replied, thinking it was surely quite strange that a grown man was wetting himself.

Later that night, while desperately trying to stay awake until midnight so that we could have the midnight feast we'd been planning for about the six months prior to Cub camp, Ozzy suddenly jumped out of his sleeping bag and shone a torch towards his crotch.

'Look, I've got a rocket willy!' he shouted excitedly, his pants pointing outwards like a lopsided tent.

And so it was there, that year at Cub camp, that the seeds of our friendship had been sown; a friendship bonded over the mutual bewilderment at Ozzy's little erect penis.

As tends to happen with these things, I very soon grew out of Cub camp and a couple of years later had decided it was 'sad' and only for little kids. To this day I can remember the look of disappointment in Dad's eyes when I told him I didn't want to go to Cub camp anymore. It's funny the things you remember which at the time seem extremely insignificant but when you grow older and understand the gravity of these situations, take on an entirely different meaning.

Gary, meanwhile, we had met on our first day at secondary school. We'd not really meant to befriend him, it just seemed to be the case that in every class we were in, one of us seemed to be paired up with him, and so at breaks and lunchtime; he seemed to just appear everywhere we were, saying very little and following almost a step behind, a gormless expression fixed on his face. Initially not particularly wanting him around but simultaneously not having the heart to tell him where to go, he gradually became part of the group and we became a somewhat unlikely trio of friends. We also discovered during class that it was particularly handy to be teamed up with Gary as he seemed to have an uncanny ability to recall facts and to grasp any new concept, be it Maths, Chemistry or Physics, almost annoyingly easily.

'Three pints of lager please, Vijay,' I said as Gary and Ozzy settled down in a booth in the corner of the Prince Albert one unseasonably warm April's evening in Acton, a habit we'd fallen into every Thursday; initially to cheer me up when my relationship had ended several months back, and carrying on like a tradition since then.

'No problem, my friend, you take a seat, I bring over,' Vijay responded.

Vijay was the head barman at the Prince Albert and given the regularity with which we frequented the bar, he'd seemed to come to view himself almost as part of the friendship group. In his forties and still retaining a heavy Indian accent as a result of his childhood spent in Calcutta but often prone to using Cockney phrases, presumably due to the number of years spent in London, he had a habit of involving himself in any private conversations we were having when he was able to discreetly make his way over to our table to lurk during quiet times at the bar.

The pub itself had an aged, traditional feel to it, with comfy booths and an imposing wooden bar area with a wall of spirits behind it.

As I sat down, Gary and Ozzy were deep in discussion. Ozzy turned to me. 'Gary is saying how he doesn't like listening to the song Gangnam Style because it reminds him of when him and Hayley first met.'

'Oh right,' I replied, 'that makes sense, I suppose, is that because it was played a lot around the time you met?'

'Yeah. That and the fact it was our first dance song.'

'Oh god, of course, how could I forget?' I replied

'Yeah, how the fuck could you forget, everyone's been ushered over for the first dance and all of a sudden this dickhead is shuffling along the dance floor like a demented cowboy with Hayley looking on with a face like thunder!' Ozzy cut in.

'Yeah, that first dance slash present thing really was quite a spectacularly bad idea, Gary,' I said, hoping to express some form of sympathy by placing a hand on Gary's shoulder, but also wanting to be clear that it was a shockingly bad piece of decision-making.

'Your first dance is meant to be romantic, slow, so you can have a little dance and have people at the side watch you whisper into each other's ears before breaking into small bursts of cute laughter before you invite the rest of the guests to join you. Why on earth did you think Gangnam Style was a good idea?' I asked, remembering my bewilderment and embarrassment for Gary as he proceeded to perform the whole dance routine to Gangnam Style in front of his new bride, not even once inviting her to join him on the dancefloor.

'Anyway, that's what I was saying,' Gary responded in his defence. 'Songs can sort of take you back to a particular time, give you a particular feeling. And when I heard that song it reminded me of when Hayley and I met, and I remember on our sixth date, I said to her, this song reminds me of you. So I thought she'd remember me saying that and think it was romantic. And she used to really laugh at me when I copied the dance moves. I thought it would be perfect.'

'Yeah, I can see a sort of strange logic in there somewhere, Gary, I can see that your intentions were good,' I replied, 'but in future, I really would suggest running ideas like that past Ozzy and I, because that was a big risk you took there and it really backfired when Hayley threw her drink over you at the end of the song and stormed out of the venue.'

'Yeah, it wasn't the reaction I'd hoped for, to be honest. Lost my deposit on the hire suit as well.'

'Plus you must remember, Gary, that not everyone has a memory like yours where they are bizarrely able to recall the time and place of literally any minute piece of extraneous detail that should happen to occur in their daily life,' I continued, hoping that Gary would see my point.

'Anyway, enough of all that shit, you still got this charity auction with your work?' Ozzy asked.

'Yep, coming up very soon. Operation Win Colette Over will be full steam ahead!'

'You mean Operation Pay For A Girl Who Doesn't Like You To Go Out With You will be full steam ahead?'

'No! Well, yes. Well, no, not at all, actually. One of the charity auction prizes is two tickets to see *Swan Lake* at the Royal Albert Hall, and the other day I was making a cup of tea in the office kitchen when she walked in with Miles.'

'He's the pompous twat, yeah?' Ozzy asked

'That's the one, yeah. Well, the two of them were talking about the auction and she said she'd absolutely love to go to the ballet at the Royal Albert Hall, so I thought why not win the tickets at the auction and then, very casually, like really cool like, ask her if she wants to accompany me to it, and then finally she might get to know the real me and maybe our friendship—'

'Not sure you're friends, are you? Colleagues would be more accurate,' Ozzy cut in.

'No!' I responded emphatically. 'We are more than colleagues, we have definitely developed a friendship!' I insisted.

'Oh right, so you see each other outside of work then, as friends?' Ozzy continued facetiously, knowing full well what my honest answer would be.

'We're friends alright!' I said, louder than expected in frustration at my inability to prove Ozzy wrong without clearly lying.

'Great, so we'll be expecting to see her when you celebrate your birthday, and I imagine she'll probably pop down and join us sometimes when we're at the pub, like friends do?' Ozzy continued, evidently very much enjoying how much he was winding me up.

'Just…fucking…shut…shut the fuck up.' I finally managed to spit out, just wanting to end an argument I'd been destined to lose from the moment it had started.

Chapter 3

The Chronicles of a Malfunctioning Male

The next morning I'd awoken, groggy and confused. As the neurons in my brain very slowly began to fire, the cloudy haze hanging over my head slowly lifted, my consciousness awakened and my mood began to lift as I remembered that today I'd reached the grand old landmark of thirty years of age.

Upon wandering downstairs, I'd been pleasantly surprised to see a hand-addressed letter on my doormat! Perhaps Dad had remembered, or maybe it was from a secret admirer I thought, suddenly brimming with excitement at the possibilities that would bring.

I picked up the letter and felt the card within. I slowly opened the envelope, wanting to savour the excitement of the unknown for a little while longer and removed the card, a picture of a cartoon lion adorning the front. 'Have a Roarsome Day' said a lion in a giant speech bubble with an actual furry mane protruding from the card. I'd been forced to admit to myself that it was an unusual choice for a thirtieth birthday, probably more suited to a toddler, or perhaps the sort of novelty card one might buy their pet cat on its birthday, but maybe my admirer had a thing about lions? Maybe she was comparing me to a lion? Big, strong, hairy, feared by all! Hmm…on reflection I thought this probably unlikely. I opened the card and saw the message was completely written in type except the 'Jamie' which had been scribbled on at the top in blue Biro.

Jamie,
Have a wonderful time on your birthday
Best wishes from

And it was there that I saw that the card had come from an unexpected source, a father figure of sorts I suppose, and someone with whom I'd certainly developed a fruitful relationship with over the past few years.

A E Bem

Papa Giuseppe
Pizza

I eyed the doormat again, lifting it in case of the extremely unlikely event that numerous other cards had been dropped through the letterbox but had somehow been blown under the mat by a freak gust of wind, originating from where I have absolutely no idea. No, this is definitely the only card I've received, a thirtieth birthday card from Papa Giuseppe's pizza, but no thirtieth birthday card from my actual, biological papa. To be honest, I've been a good customer to Papa Giuseppe since I moved to Acton five years ago; if I'm not heading to the pub with Ozzy and Gary on a Friday night then chances are I'll be ordering from Papa Giuseppe to let my hair down and celebrate the end of the week.

WhatsApp, no messages. Email, nothing. Text messages, nope. Happy thirtieth, Jay, from yourself, your local pizza restaurant, and precisely nobody else.

I jumped off the Tube at Tottenham Court Road station, head still feeling slightly fuzzy and manoeuvred the crowds to make my way up the escalator, out onto the street and towards the Hungry Kats head office on Whitfield Street, which ran parallel to its more illustrious neighbour Charlotte Street. Anxiety levels were slightly above the norm having spent most of the walk to East Acton station and the subsequent Tube journey convincing myself that I'd left the iron on.

I entered the glass doors at the front of my office building which led to a large, grand open space reception area with an egg-like structure randomly placed in the middle of it. Art of some form I'd guessed when I'd originally arrived in the building for interview, and I'd wondered how much the company had spent on the enormous, complete waste of space. The familiar smell of marble polish filled my nostrils as I made my way across the reception floor, head turned towards reception ready to give the receptionists a good morning nod should they turn my way but their heads remained firmly on the screens on their side of the reception desk.

I nodded instead to the security guard and made my way through the barriers and towards the lifts which would take me downstairs to our basement office, an environment hidden from the general public by the elegance of the reception area. The basement was where the tele-servicing people and the sales team were based.

The basement office was completely open-plan with some meeting rooms bordering the floor to one side which were used for various training exercises and team catch-ups. The furniture was a monotonous uniform of metal and plastic and the desks were setup in banks of eight, four each side facing each other with a long walkway through the middle of the sets of desks which led from the elevator at the side of the room all the way to the other side of the room, splitting it in half, two signs hanging from the ceiling above the banks of desks indicating which department you were in. Being the sales and tele-servicing office, the noise in the basement could often make it difficult for you to actually think, with brash sales folk shouting possible deals down the phone to potential customers and tele-servicing people trying to politely deal with an irate customer complaining that our Hungry Kats 'Oh-so-special-beef-stew' cat food mix had given their beloved Felix the runs. Sometimes I wondered back to my days at university and the optimism with which I had viewed my future career and wondered what uni-me would think of actual-me now, on the phones every day dealing with pussy problems when I'd studied History and Economics at university in the hope of becoming an award-winning investigative journalist. Whenever those thoughts arose, I had to struggle to push them deep down inside, into that ever-expanding box of regret, frustration and sorrow – always the best way to deal with your troubles.

Upon graduation from university, I'd left for the world of work with a significant amount of optimism and hope; applying for various graduate schemes with newspapers and other media outlets, daydreaming of producing hard-hitting pieces bringing the socially unrighteous to justice. Each graduate application however seemed to be packed full of dissertation-length online application forms, followed by numerous interviews which, if successful, would lead to a full-day assessment with bucketloads of other hopeful applicants. And I dreaded them. Imaginary scenarios made up for groups of us applicants to sit round a table and work out how we can keep control of our costs when interest rates on our debt have increased and vandalism has caused damage to our premises for which we're uninsured. And I had ideas, honestly I did, but there were always a few loudmouths who sat there dominating conversation, rudely cutting in any time I attempted to open my mouth, saying and doing exactly what an article on graduate assessment days had told them to say and do, and each unsuccessful attempt to complete a recruitment process chipped away at my self-confidence. Until, one day, whilst job searching on my phone on my way back from another doomed assessment day, I came across an advert for 'call centre complaints workers, great salary, great team, great work environment', and I thought I can do that, surely I can do that. And so after a trip to the offices and an interview which lasted less than twenty minutes, I had a job, not the one I'd dreamed of, but it was a stepping stone, a means of earning income before I got my 'real job' and, eight years later, here I still was.

Anyway, I had my creative writing classes; at least I was actually doing something to work towards where I wanted to be, rather than moaning that I wanted to be a writer whilst doing absolutely nothing about it. I could do more, though. Maybe I should up the creative writing, probably been over a month since I actually did any. Mental note, get back into the writing routine. Then I was sure that at some point in the not-too-distant future I would read a passage to the class that I'd written and I'd be greeted by complete silence; a silence broken after a number of seconds by a solitary colleague standing and starting a clap which would get faster and more enthusiastic as the rest of the class joined in the standing ovation, culminating in the lecturer joining in what by now would be described as rapturous applause.

That morning I heard him coming before I saw him. Perhaps retelling the tale of him playing second row with Prince Harry at Eton and all the mad capers they used to get up to in the showers. Or maybe repeating his claim that he was actually fifty-seventh in line to the throne and that the crown refused to let him and his siblings travel together on airplanes in case a crash wiped out a number of potential successors to the throne all at one time, a story which I found as highly dubious as him being fifty-seventh in line to the throne. Or maybe telling the story of how he had trials for England's youth rugby team alongside Mike Tindall and that he's still friends with Mike and Zara ('well she's family, of course') to this day. It could have been any one of the far-fetched and factually impossible tales of privilege that he'd chosen to bore the ears of some poor unfortunate victim with today, but whatever it was, the buzz, or the frequency or the pitch of that voice seemed to actually pain my ears upon hearing it these days.

I'd found out quite by chance that he had in actual fact not been educated at Eton but at a private all-boys boarding school situated in a little village between Windsor and Ascot. I'd been speaking to a friend of a friend at one of my creative writing workshops and the subject, as it tends to do, moved onto where we worked and when I'd mentioned Hungry Kats he'd said he knew someone who worked there.

'Do you know Miles Bell?' he'd asked, instantly falling in my opinion as I associated him with Miles.

'Yes, I know Miles,' I'd responded through gritted teeth, 'loud, flash guy, went to Eton?'

This prompted a back and forth over the next few minutes to confirm we were talking about the same guy. He'd been in the same year at boarding school as a very quiet, skinny kid, without too many friends who spoke with a stammer and apparently spent most of his time playing Warhammer.

At that point I'd momentarily been overcome by a wave of compassion for a quiet, timid child who had clearly at some point decided to reinvent himself as someone new. But no, I'd quickly gotten over this compassion. I'm all for reinventing to become a better version of yourself, more confident, better at speaking to women; God knows I'd tried it myself so many times over the years, but the golden rule of this process surely must be don't decide to reinvent yourself as a massive bellend.

I'd tried to broach the subject of his background with him once. I guess in the hope that it would give us some sort of connection and, I'm ashamed to say, to benefit from the reflective popularity that might come from being closer friends with Miles. However, when I'd mentioned Miles' former schoolmate, I'd noticed him flinch and his face become noticeably paler.

'Never heard of him,' he'd spat before marching out of the kitchen without making his cup of tea.

Miles strutted along the walkway which separated the banks of desks. His mousey-coloured hair was thick and wild with an unruly quiff, head constantly glancing from side to side to check who was watching him strut. He wore a white Oxford button-down collar Ralph Lauren shirt, with the arms of a yellow jumper wrapped around his neck in a loosely tied knot. Garish bright-red chinos were paired with some brown boat shoes, brightly coloured yellow socks capping off what, in my opinion, was a truly hideous look.

I could hear him getting closer to my desk: please don't come over to me.

A hand ruffled through my neatly combed hair, the hand shaking my head just a little harder than I felt necessary for this to be considered a friendly gesture.

'Who cut this, the council?' Miles laughed.

The Chronicles of a Malfunctioning Male

'Hello, Miles,' I uttered, forcing a slight chuckle as if I'd found the whole offensive greeting and manhandling of my head a bit of gentle office banter rather than the attempt to remind me of my social status within the office environment that it very clearly was.

As it was I'm not even sure Miles heard my response as he was well past me by now, probably content in the knowledge that he had ruined the thirty seconds' of work I'd taken to do my hair this morning whilst also having gently reminded me of his opinion of my social class within the organisation.

I saw him now approaching behind her. He crouched down and I couldn't make out what he'd whispered in her ear but she threw her head back, extending her perfectly formed neckline, and roared with laughter.

What could he possibly have said that warranted that degree of laughter? He wasn't funny. OK, I suppose some people considered him funny but he was funny in a loud in-your-face 'Pay attention to me!' type way. The way where people laugh with you to get you to go away rather than being funny in a clever, carefully considered, logical sort of way. Yes, that's probably what she's doing; she's laughing heartily but inside she's crying in pain while he's around, sexually assaulting her with his eyes. Poor girl, I should save her really. But no, it's the twenty-first century and women these days are more than capable of batting off the odd pervert who gets in their way.

She placed her beautiful elbows on her desk, linked her lovely hands together and rested her perfect chin on them, her gaze fixed slightly upwards towards Miles' irritating... was it irritating? Yes, even impartially speaking, it was definitely an irritatingly smug face, as he rested his hands on her desk, triceps pumped so that his arms looked bigger than my legs, that lecherous smirk on his face glaring ominously down at her, almost like a predator, or like Tony Blair in those late 90s New Labour New Danger posters.

Yes, he's definitely got the look of a sexual predator. No jury in the land would be able to find that face not guilty when up on a sex charge. Please one day can he be up on a sex charge. I shook my head trying to force the thought out of my head. Get a grip, that's an awful thing to think about absolutely anybody. Even if he is clearly a humongous bellend.

The object of Miles' attention was Colette Willis. She'd been at the firm for about two months, two weeks and six days now. Approximately. When she'd first walked into the office I'd been on the phone to a customer. I was perched on the front of my chair, bent forward, my head resting on my fist with my elbow resting on my desk, my gaze fixed down at the walkway in between the banks of desks.

First came a pair of shiny black high heels into my eyeline, then came a pair of the most beautiful, slender, lightly tanned legs wrapped in a smart black pencil skirt, then a white blouse tucked neatly into the skirt. And then I saw her face; the most beautiful face I'd ever seen in my life, framed by long, bouncy, dark, loosely curled hair.

My mouth dropped open and I completely lost my train of thought and stopped talking to the customer mid-sentence. All I could do was stare at this angel walking towards me. Thinking back, it was probably just my imagination but I could've sworn there was a glow of white light around her as she walked. The bottom half of my jaw dropped open, a small bit of dribble beginning to edge its way onto my chin, then her eyes met mine and she smiled, her face scrunching slightly and her shoulders hunching up as she did so. And then she was past me. And that was my first introduction to Colette Willis.

Oh god, they'd both got up and seemed to be heading my way. I grabbed my pen, reached for my pad and started scribbling, 'Look for nutritional info on Hungry Kats Tuna…'

'I hear on the grapevine it's your birthday, old chap,' Miles said, slapping me ridiculously hard on the back as he did so.

'That's right, Miles,' I replied, mentally noting that he hadn't actually offered his best wishes for the occasion.

'Where's the treats, then, old boy?' he replied with what I could've sworn was a hint of aggression.

'They're in the kitchen, Miles, doughnuts for the team. Feel free to have one,' I said, praying that he'd wander off in search of some sugar and leave me alone with Colette who had perched herself on my desk, close enough that I could smell the sweet, floral scent of her perfume as she flicked nonchalantly through the pages of my call centre response manual.

'Oh, I saw that sorry sack of doughnuts but presumed there must be something else because there's only twelve doughnuts?'

I could sense others on the floor beginning to pay attention to our conversation; ears pricking up in the surrounding banks, heads swivelling and eyes beginning to peer over. I chuckled nervously.

'That's right, don't think anyone wants more than a doughnut each with summer creeping up on us, we'll all be in our bikinis soon!' I joked, trying to keep everything light-hearted.

'But there's at least twenty people down here, old chap?' Miles replied.

Oh will you just fuck off, you massive dick. I didn't respond.

'I think usually people just buy for their team, Miles, think that tends to be the done thing,' I chipped in, trying to keep my tone casual but noting the smirks on the faces of various people earwigging into the conversation.

As you well know, you big cock, I didn't add.

'Oh,' he responded with mock puzzled expression filling his irritating face.

'Leave him alone,' Colette giggled, giving him a playful push as he wandered away from my desk, pretending to count the people in the office as he went.

'Happy birthday,' Colette said, smiling at me, her gorgeous blue eyes fixed on mine for no more than two seconds, hand coming to rest briefly on my shoulder, before she stood up from her perch on my desk and made her way back to her seat.

'Thanks, Colette,' I shouted after her, possibly due to nerves slightly louder than I'd expected it to come out. Precisely no acknowledgement received from her, but a few grins and head shakes from colleagues in the vicinity.

Yes, you lot can fuck off too, I said in my head, giving them all my meanest stare to really show them who was the boss.

Chapter 4

Social responsibility has become a hot topic in the corporate world. It's no longer deemed enough for a company to set out just to make money, they need to be seen to be giving back to the community. How many of these companies actually want to give anything back to their community is hugely debatable, but Hungry Kats put on several events a year with the aim of raising money for the various charities that it supported and one of the most eagerly anticipated of these events was the charity auction ball.

The night of the charity auction arrived, and I was tingling with a mixture of nerves and excitement. I checked myself in the full-length mirror in the bathroom and it seemed like one of those rare occasions when I was pretty pleased with the man staring back at me. I'd taken a trip to Burtons during the week to buy a suit, even after Ozzy's protestation that getting one from there would make people think I was going to try and sell them a dingy studio with a mould problem in Deptford. But needs must and my budget could stretch only so far and Burtons had just announced a 50% off sale, so I arrived at the store slightly less optimistic after Ozzy's verbal bashing of the place.

I had, however, been pleasantly surprised at the range of suits available. I'd overheard Colette swooning over a picture of David Beckham in a navy suit during the week and I'd had to agree he looked particularly suave in it. I had my doubts as to whether it was a Burtons suit and had decided against bringing a picture to direct the shop attendant so, on arrival, I found a member of staff and asked for a navy suit. When I'd tried on the one they'd suggested I'd instantly been delighted. It was as if it had been tailor made for me the attendant said, and I had agreed enthusiastically. As I looked in the mirror thoughts swam around my head of replacing Daniel Craig as the next Bond, the first ginger James Bond; what a ground-breaking moment that would be for the gingers for justice movement.

Back at home, I checked the mirror one more time, adjusting my grey tie, and noticed that my hands felt clammy, I was beginning to feel the pressure. It felt like for Colette and I, everything had been building up to this night. I checked my hair, admiring the tidy cut Naz had given me a few hours earlier and very briefly imagined myself unholstering a Walther PPK from inside my blazer. 'For Queen and country' I said out loud, attempting to add a slight lisp and raising an eyebrow as I did so before I made my way out of the front door.

Anxiety levels had been raised on the Tube journey. It was the height of summer and the UK was gripped by an almost unprecedented heatwave (it had been hot for a week). It's a fact known by few outside of London, that the hottest place known to man is the Central line between Marble Arch and Liverpool Street stations when the temperature outside is over thirty degrees Celsius. Frodo had to trek all the way to Mordor to destroy the ring in a pit of infinite fire and rage, when, had he used his head, he probably would've jumped on a bus down to Shepherds Bush, taken a lovely stroll up to Holland Park, perhaps taken in the beautiful scenery of the Kyoto Garden first before hopping on the Central line and by the time he'd got to Oxford Circus it would've melted and evaporated into absolutely nothing before his very eyes. Then he could've gone for a couple of celebratory drinks in the pubs of Soho afterwards. That would've saved a hell of a lot of hassle and made for a really rather pleasant day out, although admittedly a rather less-interesting book.

I was unused to being dressed so smartly and felt slightly uncomfortable on my journey, as if all eyes were on me which was making me even sweatier than I normally would be on the underground, and I feared that by the time I arrived at the venue my shirt would be saturated.

Consequently, I spent a large amount of time trying to keep my mind on anything other than the intense heat, the waterfall emerging from my back and the fact that I was dressed in far smarter attire than the rest of the carriage. In practice this meant pretending to concentrate on my phone. I knew I'd be in the fresh(ish) air soon, but

I couldn't feel it and discomfort levels escalated almost exponentially until with significant relief I clambered up the stairs and out the barriers at the station.

On arrival I considered ordering a vodka martini but decided against it because a) I didn't like vodka b) I didn't like martini, and c) it seemed like the sort of thing a teenager would do at their post GCSE ball. I plumped for a bottle of pale ale and leant casually on the bar. I suddenly wished I had worn a hat as well. I was leaning casually on one elbow on the bar, a bottle of beer in the other hand, my weight rested on one leg the other one curled in behind the standing leg, the point of my toe just resting on the floor. If I had been wearing a hat, when anyone's legs came into view I could've casually used the bottle in my hand to tilt my hat upwards, make eye contact, raise my bottle in their direction whilst simultaneously giving a slight nod of the head and a raise of the eyebrow, all the while remaining almost nonchalantly rested on the bar, taking an occasional swig from my beer. I was glad I hadn't worn a hat though in actual fact, considering I was nowhere near cool enough to pull any of that off.

The firm had hired a golf club towards the outskirts of London for the occasion and the auction was to be held in the large function room which had a raised stage area as the focal point of the room, with a long bar along one side. Below the stage the hall was filled with round tables seating eight, each table adorned with floral decoration in the centre and plates and cutlery laid out for each seat. Surveying the room I was very impressed with how smart it looked, as a lady wandered over with a tray full of glasses of champagne offering me one as she went. Wow, I'd thought as I'd taken a glass, I wasn't sure I'd ever been to such a fancy event. Mustn't get too drunk tonight, I thought, I've got a job to do. I'd worked out I could afford to spend £150 bidding for the *Swan Lake* tickets; surely that would be enough, I thought, on top of having to pay for any extras on the date that added up to a lot of money. But there are some moments in life, some opportunities that you have to seize with both hands I'd thought, and this very much felt like one of those moments.

It had been a couple of weeks earlier that I'd walked into the kitchen at the office to make my afternoon cup of tea and had chanced upon Colette and Miles. Colette was leaning back against the kitchen worktop, Miles facing her, one arm on the worktop beside her, leaning in towards her in a horrifyingly threatening manner, Colette's laughter and hand brushing against his chest a clear cry for help and desperate attempt to push her oppressor away. As I was making my tea, whilst unintentionally eavesdropping on their conversation, I overheard Collette tell Miles that she was desperate to go and see *Swan Lake* and was really hoping someone would win the tickets at the charity auction and ask her along as their date. And so from that moment on I knew that I simply had to win the *Swan Lake* tickets and ask Collette to accompany me.

I'd actually arrived on time; i.e. when the invitation said the doors open, which meant the place was pretty empty. After a few minutes hovering at the bar, mailroom Jack had arrived. He spotted me and walked over, swaying and knocking into chairs as he went. The dress code had stated formal, of which I'd decided meant one below black tie, hence the suit and tie. Jack had evidently interpreted this differently and had opted for a stained pair of stonewash jeans, stains which I suspected were not part of the design, a pair of battered old Reebok trainers and a plain white t-shirt. Well, plain, but with the addition of various stains, this time definitely not part of the design. As he got up close, I noticed he stunk of aniseed and thought he must have spent a large part of today in the pub.

'I was gonnee go home and change but I couldnee be assed in the end. Sure not everybodees gonnee be dressed up to thee nines like yee,' he spat, quite literally, as I bobbed and weaved trying to avoid the shower flying from his mouth and hoping that the fumes seeping out of him wouldn't contaminate my aftershave.

'Yes I'm sure you're right, Jack, I'll probably look like a right dick dressed up in a tie when everyone else is in t-shirts,' I replied, praying that this wouldn't be the case. Jack had turned and wandered off and I'd noticed the back of his t-shirt was filled with the words 'Never mind the bollocks, we're the Sex Pistols' in bright-pink lettering. A nice touch.

Over the next half hour or so people filtered into the room and to my extreme relief everyone was dressed smartly; the men in suit and tie or tuxedo and the women in glamorous dresses and ballgowns, and with a few drinks in me I was feeling far more relaxed as I sat myself down at my designated table next to conspiracy Lorraine and Ben, a likeable younger guy from my team. The rest of the table was filled with others from my team and a couple from Finance and everyone seemed in good spirits as the food came and went and the wine flowed freely.

I'd been keeping my eye out for Colette and as I'd made my way to the loos I'd spotted her, chair turned sideways on her table facing in towards Miles, her hand on his shoulder as she laughed whilst he whispered in her ear, arm on the back of her chair, leaning into her, so close their bodies were almost touching. I have to win this auction, I thought with heightened determination as I turned my gaze away from the pair and marched resolutely towards the toilets.

As the desserts were taken away, the MC came out on stage. He was an overweight white man in his fifties, with an abnormally red face, pockmarked skin and badly thinning hair which had been swept from the front over towards the back of his head. Dressed in a black suit and loosely made tie with his shirt coming slightly untucked from his trousers as his stomach seemed to strain for freedom from the confines of his belt, he struggled, but eventually managed, to sit himself down on one of the two tall stools that had been set out on the stage, his belly becoming all the more prominent as he did so and clearly on display in the gaps between the buttons of his shirt below his tie.

'Ladies and gentlemen, my name is Terry and I am going to be your MC for the evening, so welcome to the Hungry Kats annual charity ball,' the MC started in a northern drawl which reminded me of Roy Chubby Brown after forty cigarettes. He continued, 'A clearly ostentatious occasion where we all pretend that the main reason we're here is for charity and not to get pissed and snog that bird from Marketing.'

And the audience chuckled, the alcohol having gotten everyone in the mood for a good time.

'To be honest though, ladies and gentlemen, I've had an interesting week. All this talk about charity and I've been thinking to myself, I wanna do something good for the world, so I decided to pop down to my local sperm bank and donate, you know, give something back to the world, help out the odd jaffa who's firing blanks. So I've gone in there and gone up to the desk and the lady on reception, cracking bird she was, lovely pair of tits, just the sort you want on reception at sperm bank, said to me, 'Would you like to masturbate in a cup, sir?' And I've given it some thought, and I've said, 'To be honest, love, I am very good but I'm not sure I'm quite ready to compete just yet!' The MC laughed deeply and croakily, a laugh that was surely the product of a million cigarettes over the years. I shot a look over to the directors' table where they all of a sudden seemed to have gone unnaturally pale, squirming uncomfortably in their seats.

'Anyway, ladies and gentlemen, we kick this evening's proceedings off with an absolute corker of a prize, but firstly I want to introduce my very, very glamorous assistant for the first part of the show. Come here, love, come sit on Daddy's knee.' The MC beckoned creepily to Rachel from the Hungry Kats admin team who was sporting a pink dress with pink hairbands and pink and white heels and whom I actually thought looked very fetching. Rachel timidly took to the seat beside him.

'No, love, jump up here,' the MC continued, patting his thigh as he did so. Rachel warily moved closer towards him before he grabbed hold of her when she was within reach and plonked her down on top of his lap.

'Let's forget the audience ay and maybe we just sit here and have a chat about the first thing that pops up?'

'Erm… OK,' Rachel responded hesitantly, seemingly unaware of the crude joke he was making.

'And what's your name, my lovely?'

'Erm. Rachel,' she replied, somewhat hesitantly.

'And, Rachel, you've worked at Hungry Kats for how long?'

'Erm…for just over a year now.'

'Just over a year, how fantastic, and a marvellous job I'm sure you do, Rachel, but anyway off you pop now, darling,' the MC said whilst lifting Rachel off his lap before standing up. 'Just a little bit of rearranging to do, ladies and gents,' he continued whilst fiddling with his trousers around the crotch area. 'Now then, ladies and gents, the first prize we have for auction is an absolute cracker; it's a night for two with dinner at the ultra-luxurious…' Terry paused and moved the card in his hand closer to his face, 'bloody 'ellfire,' he exclaimed, shaking his head before continuing, 'the ultra-luxurious, two-star Tired Heads hotel in London's glitzy Leicester Square. Gordon Bennett, what a prize, now shall we start the bidding at, say, fifty pounds, do I have fifty pounds anywhere in the room, will anybody bid fifty pounds for the chance to treat your wife or mistress to a night of passion surrounded by seventeen year olds from Essex trying to get pissed with fake ID and bemused tourists who have taken a wrong turn.'

The auction prizes came and went, the most notable moment being when Rothni from HR had taken the role of the MC's assistant and mailroom Jack stormed the stage, proceeding to sweep her up in his arms before attempting to run off with her. Unfortunately he got towards the edge of the stage and appeared to slip, dropping Rothni awkwardly on her back. At this point he abandoned the kidnap attempt and ran off towards the back of the room celebrating what he evidently appeared to think was a successful outcome to his storming of the stage. The unfortunate Rothni was subsequently carried off the stage and sat down on a chair at the side of the room as various concerned people tentatively checked that she was OK.

Swan Lake was the final prize to be auctioned and, as fate would have it, Colette was to be the MC's assistant for the prize. When she glided out onstage it seemed like a hush came over the audience as everyone forgot to breathe for a few brief moments. She looked absolutely breath-taking, more beautiful than I'd ever seen her look. Colette was wearing a floor-length black ballgown with a slit in the skirt which seemed to rise up almost to waist height revealing a beautifully toned and tanned leg going down to a sleek black, strappy stiletto. Strapless on top, the gown fully exposed her perfectly formed shoulders. She wore a pearl necklace hanging down just above her cleavage and her beautiful, dark hair was tied up in some sort of bun. Without hesitation, I could say that she looked the absolute image of perfection.

'Oh Jesus Christ,' the MC started, 'I am sweating like a fat lad in a spin class. Would you look at the state of that, you don't get too many of those to the pound, ladies and gentlemen. I tell ya what, forget about paying me for this evening, I'm just gonna take this young lady instead; that'll do me very fookin' nicely.' And I began to wonder if they actually got this guy from the Roy Chubby brown school of presenting.

'I'm only joking of course, ladies and gentlemen, I've 'ad my fingers burnt for kidnap before and it ain't something I fancy going through again. So, as mentioned, the final prize o' the evening is two tickets to the ever popular *Swan Lake*, best seats in the 'ouse, ladies and gents, at the world-renowned Royal Albert Hall. Now that is som'ing to get excited about, ladies and gents, I'm not wrong, am I? I'm going to be so bold as to start the bidding at fifty pounds for this fookin' incredible prize. And there's fifty pounds in the room, from me! Now my eyesight's beginning to go, ladies and gentlemen, so forgive me if I fail to see your bids now. Can I get sixty pounds in the room?' Hands shot up across the room.

'No advance on fifty pounds?' Shouts and panicked hands raised across the room and I began to get nervous that this borderline sex pest was actually going to rig the event in order that he won the tickets.

'My hearing's going too, by the way, ladies and gentlemen, going once at fifty.'

He couldn't possibly, could he? Where on earth did they find this guy from? Some Care in the Community programme?

'I'm only fookin' pulling your legs, ladies and gentlemen, I don't want to start a riot, and I can see some very panicky people in the audience, sweating more than a fat man at a buffet.'

The £190 Diane had paid for VIP family tickets to Thorpe Park had been the biggest spend so far of the evening so I was worried that my £150 wouldn't be enough for the *Swan Lake* tickets, given how popular they seemed to be, but I was determined to win. I just felt if I could take Colette on a nice date and we could spend a bit of time alone together that she'd get to know me, and at the very least then be able to make a more informed decision about whether she wanted to go out with me.

The bidding was up to ninety pounds already and rising fast. I was beginning to worry. Jamal from IT Support had just entered a bid of £160; there went my budget.

'Going once at £160, ladies and gentlemen, going twice at £160...'

Fuck it.

'One hundred and seventy.'

The crowd cheered, my table drunkenly crowded round me slapping me on the back and rubbing my carefully crafted hair. Colette beamed over at me and already it felt like money well spent. I couldn't be certain and I'm not sure if it was the drink giving me artificial confidence, but it seemed like Colette was pleased I'd beaten Jamal's bid. Maybe she does actually really like me and has been waiting for me to ask her out for ages. I think this is quite possibly the biggest pimping moment of my life, I feel like someone who has just invited MTV into my crib.

'Ahh, the ginger bastard at the back takes the lead,' the MC continued as I tried my best to act like I'd not heard him. 'Can I get an advance on £170, sir?' Jamal shook his head. He's out, I've done it; slightly over budget because of the earlier unplanned intervention, but all in all an excellent evening's work.

'Going once at £170… Going twice at £170… '

'£200,' came the cry. What. The. Actual. Fuck. I turned my head in the direction of the voice, but I needn't have bothered. Standing by his table waving a wad of cash in the air whilst minions crowded round attempting to touch/slap/hug/lick/fellate him was Miles. He performed a mock bow to the crowd.

'Do I have any advance on £200, sir?' Roy Chubby Brown was addressing me now.

'Go on! Outbid him!' my table urged. But I'd carefully worked out my budget; isn't the first rule of auctions to know your budget and not get carried away and exceed it? Once again, fuck it.

'£210.' Cue loud cheer from the crowd.

'Sir, any advance?'

'£250.'

You are an actual prick, Miles Bell.

'£260,' I shouted.

'Any advance on £260, sir?' Miles shook his head and drew a finger across his throat whilst looking at me and I briefly wondered whether that was an indication of his exit of the auction process or whether it was a thinly veiled threat; either way, I hoped he was out of the bidding.

'Are you sure, sir? Going once… Going twwwwwiiiiiiiiiiiiiicccccccceeeeee sirrrrrrr…' Just bring the fucking hammer down, for Christ's sake.

'And sold to the gentleman at the back of the room for £260. A great battle, gentlemen, with the weird-looking ginger kid coming out on top, well done, sir.'

Hmmm…not sure I like Roy Chubby Brown. I felt a hand on my shoulder and turned to see the infuriatingly smug face of Miles behind me. Who's smug now, Miles? Every penny I'd just spent suddenly seemed worthwhile. Annoyingly however, Miles' face still seemed to carry the usual smug smirk; why wasn't he nursing his wounds after his defeat?

'Well done, old boy.'

'Thank you, Miles, and a good amount raised for charity. Across the whole evening,' I added hastily, not wanting it to look like I was talking solely about my contribution whilst at the same time attempting to convince him that this was the important part.

'Yes, yes, of course, lovely for these little charities to get some pocket money. I mean I was thinking of buying the tickets and taking Colette along with me.'

'Oh really, Miles, sounds like it would've been a nice idea,' I replied, delighted inside that I'd foiled his plan.

'But seeing as she's coming round to my apartment tomorrow night for a candlelit dinner on my balcony overlooking Hyde Park anyway, I thought what's the point?'

I couldn't see the reaction on my face, but if I could have I imagine I'd have seen it drop approximately two feet from its previous position.

'Have a good one, old boy.' Miles ruffled my hair, patted me ridiculously hard on the back, grabbed my bottle of beer, spun and strutted off.

    Aaaaaaaand   checkmate.

Chapter 5

The Chronicles of a Malfunctioning Male

The following week I transferred the necessary money from my meagre savings to my current account, plus a little extra so that I could make the date as special as possible and paid the necessary sum to the 'Feeling 'Orny' charity, dedicated to the preservation and protection of the rhino. A charity chosen by Brenda from the reception team, an honour bestowed upon her due to having completed fifteen years' service for Hungry Kats. What a magnificent and distinguished reward for fifteen years' service.

After paying the money, I waited. Presumably someone would email to let me know the details of how I would receive my tickets. But nothing. By Wednesday I was beginning to get annoyed so I decided to email Calvin who had organised the auction.

Hello Calvin
Hope you're well. Just wondering what the arrangements are for sorting the tickets after the auction?
If you could let me know, that would be great.
Thanks
Jamie

Almost immediately my desk phone rang and I could see it was Calvin calling, I clicked the answer button on my headset.

'Hello, Calvin, how are you?'

'Great thanks, Jamie, and congrats on being the biggest winner of the night at the auction, did you have a good time?'

'Really good actually. Yeah, I thought it was a great night, really well organised.'

'Thanks, mate. I've had the management committee on my back though about my choice of MC; he didn't turn out quite as I'd expected, but what can you do, once he's booked he's booked!'

I searched my mind for the correct words to describe him with. 'Yeah, he was certainly a colourful character,' I replied, a pretty well-known phrase for describing an intolerable arsehole without the need to be quite so explicit.

'Yeah, you could put it like that. Anyway, the tickets, they're for this Saturday evening, so cancel any plans you had, who are you taking with you?'

I hadn't expected him to ask this, and I stumbled for an answer that didn't directly say Colette given that I hadn't asked her yet. I fiddled with the Biro in my hand as if this would somehow help me.

'Erm…well…'

'Spouse, partner?'

'Erm…well… I was thinking about asking Colette actually,' I mumbled, having completely failed to think of an appropriate response without mentioning her and then instantly wondering why I didn't just say I wasn't sure yet.

'Ah, Colette from Sales, yeah. Check you, ya sly old dog!' Calvin replied and chuckled down the line.

I chuckled back uneasily and tried to change the subject. 'So will you email me the tickets?'

'They'll be at the box office at the Royal Albert Hall for you, gate eight.'

'Great. Thanks, Calvin, really looking forward to it.'

'Superb. Make sure you let me know how you get on with Colette, you old smoothie.'

'Erm, yep. OK, bye, Calvin.' And I ended the call abruptly, Calvin beginning to make me vaguely uncomfortable.

I spent the best part of the rest of the day working out how and when to approach Colette to ask her if she might accompany me to the show. I wanted it to look casual, like an afterthought. Not like I'd been lying awake at night wondering whether it would be better to go for show and dinner or dinner and then show. On the one hand dinner and then show would be nice because it would mean we had time to chat casually over a drink and some food first before heading to the show, but I worried that maybe the show would be spoiled by the fact we both might have had a drink and eaten and feel slightly tired then sitting in a dark room on a full stomach. But then with show and then dinner, although it would be nice to talk about the show after having seen it, there was a perceived risk that after the show Colette might be tired and decide to shoot off. Yes, I think dinner and then the show was the way forward, and then maybe drinks after the show as well, now we're talking. But like I said, I hadn't been lying awake pondering these sorts of things, so I certainly didn't want it to look like I had.

I decided I'd go and get something from the printer, would be casually strolling back, studying my printout with extreme concentration etched on my face as I went, when I'd look up from my printout just for a split second, notice Colette out of the corner of my eye, and this would spark a reaction in my brain, triggering my memory into remembering that I had a spare ticket for *Swan Lake*, and, given she was the first person in my line of sight, I may as well casually ask her if she fancied coming along. A fool proof plan, I thought.

So later on that afternoon I was strolling casually back from the printers, sweat running freely down my back as I attempted to be the personification of nonchalance whilst simultaneously trying to look engrossed in my printout. Annnnnd…action.

'Ahh, Colette, how's it going?' A perfectly portrayed image of surprise etched onto my face.

'Hello, Jay, it's going very well, congrats on winning those tickets at the auction you big spender, was very generous of you.'

'Ahh, no worries, Colette, good bit of fun, wasn't it? The main thing is a few quid has gone to a good cause, expecting some sort of thank-you letter from those horny rhinos any day now.'

Definitely not the main thing, but I patted myself on the back for doing an excellent job of looking like I'd not given it a moment's thought since the auction.

'Oh, and Calvin said you wanted to take me with you?'

Calvin, you dick!

'Oh yeah, that's right.' Sweat on back, so much sweat on back. 'I was just wondering if you fancied joining me, but no biggie, whatever, cool, safe.' Safe, why did I say safe? Colette looked confused as I ran my fingers through my hair and rested my elbow on her desk, attempting to look casual but in actual fact looking instead incredibly awkward as I'd realised halfway into the lean that the desk was far too low for me to lean on it with my elbow but by that point I'd committed to the lean and so was now quite painfully leaning my full body weight on my elbow on the desk in not too far off a completely horizontal position, core muscles shaking at the strain, looking almost upwards at Colette.

'Ahh you're a sweetie. Yeah, why not. Calvin said it was this Saturday evening?'

'Yeah cool, this Saturday.'

'Great, well how about we sort out the finer details at lunchtime today? Nico's coffee shop at 12.15?' Colette asked.

'Coolio, yeah, I'll swing by your desk just before then and we'll grab some shit.' Grab some shit, why were these words coming out of my mouth? I didn't originate from south central LA. Colette gave me another confused look. For another inexplicable reason I gave her a peace sign with my hand and, with some considerable effort, returned myself to an upright standing position, turned and walked away, deep in concentration on the printout of a piece of paper with only the words 'Testing, testing' written on it whilst at the same time attempting to ignore the immense pain coming from my elbow.

Putting the embarrassment of my actions behind me, I began to meticulously plan what had now turned into a pre-date-date, gathering witty anecdotes in my mind that I might be able to drop into conversation mid coffee-slurp, carefully planning my walk for when I approach her desk to take her down to Nico's; cool, casual arms swinging freely to indicate the carefree nonchalance of a natural-born renegade, a relaxed pace clearly demonstrating that this is a man for whom the world waits, and not the other way round. Yep, this lunchtime date was going to be the start of something special, I was sure of it.

Now to an impartial observer, I'd asked Colette out on a date, and not only had she accepted my offer of a date, but she had already added another date. Now that's got to be a good sign, hasn't it? Surely that can't be viewed as anything but a really positive development?

Anyway, it will be an hour or so of time for us to get to know each other. But if I'd known it was today, I'd have worn better clothes. I had on an old white t-shirt which in all honesty was verging pretty close to grey these days, and an old pair of stonewash jeans I'd bought about a year ago which now had a hole in the left pocket causing me to repeatedly find my phone wriggling down my trouser leg when I forgot about it, and which were also getting very threadbare between the top of my legs on the crotch; a few more wears and there would definitely be a visible hole there and the jeans would need to be thrown out.

I was happy, however, as I'd had a haircut over the weekend and I always felt ten times better and fresher after a haircut. Anyway, she knows what you look like; she just doesn't know the real you, and that's what she'll get to discover on the date! I had a date! With Colette! I knew the chances of me answering any work-related calls with the necessary due care and attention required from this point up until lunchtime were pretty much non-existent, so I very slyly unplugged the cable from the back of my phone without anyone noticing, kept my headset on and pretended to be concentrating on emails, whilst every now and again just speaking into my headset to absolutely nobody.

As the time approached, I thought I'd drop Colette an email, just to make sure that she hadn't forgotten, and it always helps to get confirmation in writing.

A E Bem

Hey babes

No, that's awful, I can't start it like that, I sound like a prat, that's far too much.

Hey Colette!

Yep, that'll do, I like the inclusion of the exclamation mark; makes it sound like I'm saying it with a smile, jauntily, perhaps whilst wearing a fun novelty sailor's hat, jigging to some Scottish Highland music at a house party in Dalston, typing the email on my phone in one hand whilst the other hand holds my whisky sour, spilling slightly over the edges of the crystal tumbler as I jig. Yes, that's what the exclamation mark does. Only issue being that she is sitting across the office from me and can see that I'm sitting at my desk with a cup of tea and half a peeled satsuma in front of me. But still, I like the exclamation mark.

Will swing by your desk in five minutes, get ready to be coffee and sandwiched!

Yeah, that's it, show her 'fun-time-Jay'; wittiness combined with another exclamation mark, that would surely floor anyone. Now how do I sign off, kiss or no kiss? Go for the kiss surely, be bold, seize the day.

xxx

And send!

Within a minute my inbox flashed up with a response.

Cannot wait! Make sure you're not late picking me up!
xxxxx

Five kisses back! She was really upping the ante, the sexual tension bubbling in the sub-text of this email back and forth.

At ten minutes to midday I left my desk and headed to the gents, washed my hands, splashed some water on my face and stared hard at myself in the mirror.

'This is it, big Jay!' I said out loud, jabbing my forefinger out accusingly towards the reflection of my face in the mirror, 'now is your time, it's now or never, big man,' I continued, wondering simultaneously why I kept referring to myself as 'big'. I was about to continue when I heard one of the toilets in the cubicles flush, so I rushed to dry my hands and exit the gents.

My legs suddenly felt heavy with the burden of expectation and the knowledge that at this precise moment in time the possibilities were endless, but, in a couple of hours, all that could have changed. As I turned the corner of the corridor from the gents to the open-plan space of the office, I saw Colette sitting at her desk, elbows resting on top of it, a mirror in one hand, applying lipstick carefully with the other.

I concentrated hard on my stride, marching purposefully towards her, confidently, chin up, arms swinging high in front of me, like I owned the walkway.

'Hey, Colette, ready to be coffee and sandwiched?'

Colette checked her watch as I thought to myself I couldn't have been happier with how my opening line had gone.

'Am I ever!' Colette responded enthusiastically, which made my heart leap just a little bit.

'Great, then please could you step this way, madam.' Great second line, Jay, extremely smooth start.

Colette laughed and got up from her desk as I looped my arm outwards indicating for her to link arms with me, which she did immediately. All eyes in the office were now on Colette and I. There were several noticeably shaking heads, but, as I well knew, jealousy is a treacherous beast.

On the short walk to Nico's coffee shop, Colette talked a lot, mainly about the holidays she wanted to go on that year and the fact that she had now amassed over twenty thousand followers on Instagram and was considering trying to make a career out of Instagramming,

'People do that, y'know.'

'So I hear, Colette.'

'And they get all sorts of free designer goods just to post a picture of themselves with the product, and hashtagging it in the post.'

'Wow, that sounds great, and how do you actually make money?'

'Well when you become what's known in the industry as an "influencer" then the brands will actually pay you to advertise their products. You're basically free marketing for them.'

'Wow, except not free obviously because they'd be paying you?'

'Yeah, apart from that, it's free advertising for them, so just makes sense. I think I'll contact some brands soon and let them know I'm available to take payments and to take free stuff and that I'll happily do some posts for them.'

'Wow, that would be living the dream.' I replied, slightly unsure of the commercial viability of Colette's plan, but not wanting to dampen her enthusiasm or put a downer on our date.

Nico's was a small coffee and sandwich shop tucked away in a dead-end street a few minutes' walk from work. It was popular with local office workers at lunchtime and a sign in the window proudly declared that it served the best sandwiches anywhere in the world. Inside the narrow sandwich shop, to the left, was the counter with all the sandwich fillings on display behind a Perspex screen and presumably the eponymous Nico standing waiting to take orders. To the right was a small seating area with wooden tables and chairs tightly filling the rest of the room. As it was quite early for lunchtime, the tables were currently just half full.

'How about that table over there in the corner?' I asked, spotting a cosy-looking wooden table for two in the corner of the room, by the window looking out onto the street with no one seated on the surrounding tables. 'Looks pretty cosy!' I added.

'Hmm… how about this one here?'

'Right by the counter? Might be a bit busy with people queuing beside it but OK, happy with that!'

'Great!' Colette replied enthusiastically, eyeing her watch as she did so and settling her perfect backside down onto one of the wooden chairs nestled underneath the plain wooden table.

I handed a menu to Colette. 'Madam.'

'Thank you very much, sir!' Colette responded, playing along with the mock formality.

'If I may be so bold as to offer some advice, madam, this establishment has very recently been awarded its fifth Michelin star, a record throughout the world, and they pride themselves on their speciality which is the BLT, coming in at a very reasonable £4.50.'

Colette giggled and my heart soared just very slightly; this was going well, it was definitely going well.

'Well with that sort of acclaim, how can I resist! A BLT, a black coffee and a bottle of water, please!'

'An excellent choice, madam,' I responded, collecting the menus and heading up to the counter which, by luck, was completely free of any queue.

On ordering Colette's choices plus a BLT, latte and a bottle of water for myself, I settled back down onto our table.

'Your food, madam,' I said, sliding the tray of food towards Colette as I went to sit down. As I did so, my eyes fixed upon a large frame coming through the door. Our eyes met and the figure smirked and shook his head as he made his way towards the counter and consequently our table.

'Every day I come here for my lunch at 12.15, what an extraordinary coincidence it is to see you two in here,' Miles said casually as he approached behind Colette, her head spinning round instantly as she heard the sound of his voice.

'Oh, just bugger off, Miles,' she countered.

'I fully intend to. Enjoy your playdate, children.'

Miles and Nico enjoyed a warm greeting and it seemed like his lunch was ready and waiting for him as he picked it up and wandered out of the shop without giving a backward glance. That git had to put a dampener on things.

'How did your date with Miles go?' I asked as if casually enquiring, barely interested; just as a normal topic of everyday conversation.

'Date!' Colette responded sharply. 'Pah, if you could even call it that.'

Great, sounds like it didn't go very well at all!

'Anyway, I don't want to talk about him, he's a wanker,' she added.

'Great, well I've got no int—'

'Have you heard any rumours about him and Mia from Sales?' Colette barked, leaning closer to me, doing an excellent impersonation of a Nazi interrogator.

'Erm…no,' I replied, honestly.

'I'm sure there's something going on; she's always all over him whenever I see them together. She's such a slut,' Colette said harshly, staring somewhat manically at me and leaning even closer towards me over the table – this wasn't exactly how I'd envisaged the date going I thought as I leant back slightly in my chair, fearing that she was going to end up climbing over the table to demand to hear what I knew.

'I've always thought Mia seems quite nice, no?' I answered.

'No, she's a slut, definitely, I can tell, she's so blatant about it as well when she's around Miles, some girls just have no shame.'

'Oh,' I responded, slightly unsure what else to say. The rest of the date was something akin to a damp squib; Miles' appearance dampening the mood considerably and what had started out with so much promise fizzled to a depressingly uneventful end, but at least we'd finalised our plans for *Swan Lake* on Saturday, and on Saturday there would be alcohol, there would be the beauty and grandeur of the Royal Albert Hall, the romantic influence of the ballet and, most importantly of all, there would be no Miles bloody Bell.

Chapter 6

The Chronicles of a Malfunctioning Male

I sat at the restaurant, shuffling my feet below the table that I'd arrived at a half an hour before the 6pm Colette and I had agreed to meet, awaiting her arrival nervously. I'd picked the restaurant with the best Trip Advisor rating within a half-mile radius of the Royal Albert Hall, 4.83 stars over 793 reviews, and rated number one in *Time Out* magazine's 'most romantic restaurants in Kensington' article.

I had ordered a beer and I tapped my phone, glancing at the time. 17:48. Twelve minutes and she should be here. I'd worn my favourite roll-neck jumper and my smartest pair of dark-grey trousers, teamed with a pair of black suede boots. My hair still looked fresh from the haircut I'd had that week and I'd restyled it three times to try and get it just right.

The restaurant could seat about one hundred people at a guess, with the main part being in a glasshouse structure with pretty flora elaborately adorning the roof, hanging down and giving the impression that you were seated somewhere within the hanging gardens of Babylon.

As I looked around at the other guests dotted around the restaurant, mainly middle-aged couples, probably enjoying a night away from the kids, perhaps celebrating an anniversary or maybe a birthday, a message flashed up on my phone from Colette.

Hello babe, I'm really sorry but I'm not going to be able to make tonight, I've had such a busy day and I am just completely zonked out. Hope you enjoy the ballet anyway. C xxx

And that was it, just like that the dream evaporated, and a fog seemed to lift and my vision cleared and she seemed all of a sudden to be something of a twat.

And so I sat and ate alone, what was actually a really incredible meal, and watched *Swan Lake* which again was somewhat surprisingly enjoyable for someone who has never taken any interest whatsoever in the ballet. But what was evident was that no matter how much we enjoy something, sharing that enjoyment with someone magnifies it to a level I don't think you can achieve on your own. Part of the enjoyment is discussing that experience with someone, comparing opinions, and reliving it through discussion afterwards, bringing you and your companion closer together; things just aren't the same experienced alone. And so with the empty seat opposite me in the restaurant and beside me in the Royal Albert Hall, the artificial glean that I'd applied to my view of Colette dulled and her place on that pedestal I seemed to have placed her on slipped, and I vowed (with no crossed fingers) that I'd never ask her out again. And certainly not in the next week or so.

I realise now that as I came up the escalator that dreary Thursday morning at the beginning of August, where someone had clearly failed to let the weather gods know that we should have been entering the hazy days of summer, that I couldn't have known anything out of the ordinary was going to happen.

I reached the top of the escalator with my bag and umbrella in hand and made my way to the ticket barriers. Holding my bank card to the sensor, I walked through. The barriers closed on my umbrella and as I went to yank the umbrella free they opened again and I felt the bottom of my umbrella connect with something. Horrified, I turned round to see a lady who had clearly just come through the barriers after me, holding her face as others pushed to get round her, scowls of anger on their faces; the inconsiderate woman holding her face in pain costing them at least 1.5 seconds of their precious day.

'Oh my god, I am so sorry, are you OK?' The lady looked up, one hand still rubbing her chin.

'No problem, it's easily done. These bloody…'

'I know, but sorry again, I've got a history of spectacular acts of clumsiness but I really think I've excelled myself this time, are you sure you're OK?' She laughed at this point and it was impossible to fail to notice how her face lit up when she did so, creases forming around the edges of her eyes as they narrowed, the green in them sparkling with apparent joy and maybe a touch of mischief.

'Hmm… I'd have placed that in the careless rather than clumsy category, but don't worry, I think we're probably kindred spirits, I can't seem to go anywhere without tripping over my own feet, it actually makes for quite a refreshing change to have someone else inflict injury upon me rather than it being self-inflicted.' I smiled as it became apparent she was OK and there were no hard feelings.

'I actually give myself a pat on the back every day for not having fallen onto the Tube tracks or down the escalators. Well, everyday neither of those things happen that is,' I replied jokingly.

'I know, how do people go through their lives without injuring or maiming themselves on a semi-regular basis? Particularly people who have to navigate the London underground every day, it's genuinely mind-boggling.'

At which point, with perfect timing, a hurried, balding gentlemen in his fifties with cream mac and spectacles nudged into her as he made his way to the station exit, clearly aware that if he were to be at his desk at 9.01am rather that 9am, the world was likely to be doomed. Instinctively, I reached out and steadied her.

'Thanks,'

'No worries, I reckon he might be one of us.'

'Yes, or he could just be a prick,' she replied and I laughed.

'Very true and, on reflection, far more likely.'

'Anyway, I think we may actually be causing an obstruction plus I was late as I was and I don't think I'm getting any earlier. I'll blame it on a madman attacking me with an umbrella when I eventually get in.'

'Happy to be of service,' I replied. 'Are you sure you're OK?'

'I'll survive, I reckon, but you definitely do owe me one.'

'Agreed! It was very nice meeting you, even if not so nice bumping into you,' I said, quietly pleased with my wittiness and I held my hand out to shake.

'And lovely meeting you too…'

'Jamie.'

'Lovely meeting you, Jamie, I'm Claire.'

'Well you have a great day, Claire, and feel free to exaggerate the mad umbrella man story at work.'

'Oh I will. By the time I get to work your umbrella will have become a machete.'

I laughed and worried that she was funnier than me at the same time.

'You have a great day too, Jamie.' And we eventually let go of one another's hands and Claire turned to leave, but her eyes remained on me as she walked directly into the back of a large TFL worker. Apologising to the man she turned back to me and held her fingers to her head like a gun and pretended to pull the trigger before marching out of the station.

Chapter 8

'It just sort of felt like we clicked, y'know,' I said as Ozzy, Gary and I caught up that evening in the Prince Albert, Vijay lurking close beside us, clearly eavesdropping on our conversation whilst drying a solitary, already dry pint glass over and over again. 'When someone instantly makes you feel comfortable. She was funny, really funny actually, potentially too funny. I try to make sure what I lack in looks I make up for in dry wit, but if she's funnier than me, then that's not gonna work. She seemed like a genuine girl, and she was beautiful, definitely beautiful, unbelievably beautiful in fact and that's no exaggeration,' I continued, 'She had dark hair and almost sparkly green eyes and a smile which just seemed filled with real happiness and genuine goodwill, y'know? One of those smiles where you can't help but smile back. And as she was leaving we literally shook hands for about ten seconds I reckon, which was definitely longer than your average, standard handshake. And then when she walked off she kept her head turned and her eyes on me, like she wanted to keep on looking at me.'

'Sounds like she's almost definitely a complete weirdo, but did you get her number?' Ozzy replied.

'No, it literally didn't cross my mind to ask at the time.'

'You fucking idiot,' Ozzy said, shaking his head and taking a sip of his pint.

'Dick,' Gary contributed thoughtfully.

'Sounds like she was definitely interested, seems like she was blatantly giving you ample opportunity to ask and you just let her walk off into the distance like some sort of dick. D'you know how many people live in London?'

'About eight million or so?' I replied.

'I've got no fucking idea, actually, but what I do know is it's a fucking lot, so the chances of you ever bumping into her again are about zero.'

He was right as well. I'd never seen her before, knew nothing about her but her first name and the fact she was on her way to work. For fuck sake, why didn't I ask for her number? It wasn't even as if I was getting mixed signals; she laughed at my jokes which obviously made me instantly fall in love with her a little bit; she stopped for a chat for longer than your average stranger in London would, all after I'd attacked her with my umbrella; she'd practically held hands with me rather than go in for a standard handshake and then it appeared she didn't want to take her eyes off me as she was leaving. And she genuinely seemed smart and funny and nice and beautiful and she gave off a sort of warmth just by being there and her smile was filled with such kindness, she literally couldn't be a bad person, I'm absolutely positive of that. I am such a dick.

Over the next few weeks I tried to get to the station at exactly the same time as I'd bumped into her. Sometimes I'd even hang around for a bit, pretending I needed to queue for a ticket at the machine before getting to the machine and just pressing a destination and then cancelling any purchase. But no luck. So many people came and went through Tottenham Court Road station in the mornings that I may have lost her to the sea of bodies making their way to the daily grind, or it may well have been that she was just there on a one-off. She may not even live in London. Her accent had sounded Southern, but I'd never been great with accents; I was stumped.

I considered whether I might make a social media appeal to find her. I'd seen similar before: man seeks woman, met on Northern Line to Morden, we chatted about Australia and you said I'd have to take you some day, you wore a white blouse and ripped denim jeans. This was usually followed by a newspaper article showing the happy couple reunited and talking about how their love story had developed ever since that day and how they were getting married in a chapel in the Cotswolds that summer.

But I couldn't bring myself to do it. For one I wasn't sure I held sufficient social media influence to start something that would go viral. I had seventeen followers on Instagram and twenty-four on Twitter, which wasn't a great base to start from. And two, I wasn't sure I could take the humiliation of a newspaper article documenting how through the power of social media we were brought together and the inclusion of an interview with the bewildered lady in question:

'I'm a little shocked, to tell the truth. He smashed me round the face with his umbrella, apologised and then next thing I know, three million people in London are trying to find me. I think he's a bit strange, maybe a sandwich short of a picnic, and I've contacted the relevant authorities to alert them to the potential issue. He definitely has the eyes of a stalker.'

That last sentence hurt. There was absolutely nothing wrong with my eyes; they were not stalkery, pervy or leery. They were standard, good eyes for seeing with.

I tapped into Facebook and typed Claire and pressed search. As was inevitable, an endless list appeared. Why couldn't she have a really obscure name? Like Beelzebub. Beelzebub Jones. I'm sure even with a surname like Jones she'd be really easy to find then. But maybe she wasn't even on Facebook? Maybe she wasn't even from London? I had to face the fact that I was battling with the impossible.

I closed the app and cursed my lack of courage as I resigned myself to the fact that I'd let her slip through my fingers.

Chapter 9

The thing I'd very quickly realised about dating apps is that they become like a part-time job. So after finishing at my actual job where I was a paid employee, I'd arrive home from work and clock in for my shift on my side hustle; putting in the hours on the dating apps and trying my hardest to forget about the beautiful woman I'd attempted to attack just days prior. I'd initially signed up for Tinder one lazy Sunday afternoon; boredom combined with curiosity getting the better of me. I'd decided against being too fussy; my philosophy being to swipe right for anyone who I thought there could be potential with and would be worth getting to know. A sound starting board, I had thought. Three hours later, after what seemed like swiping left and right through a million faces, I didn't seem to have one match. Now I'm under no illusions that I'm some kind of Tom Hardy character, and upon asking a girl what their type of man is, not once in the entire history of the question being asked has somebody said 'just under average height, bright-red hair, lots of freckles, pale skin and generally bad dress sense', but at the same time I thought I was probably a comfortable middle ground between Hardy and Quasimodo. I worked out I'd probably swiped right of upwards of one hundred girls by this point and thought it was surely an impossibility for not one of them to have swiped right to me, even if it was by mistake. It seemed like a mathematical certainty. I messaged Ozzy, who had persuaded me to give it a go in the first place and asked how often he matched on the app.

All the time geez, bare girls on there

Hmm…not exactly the response I had hoped for.

Thus, in my predicament, I decided there was a pretty high likelihood that I was experiencing some kind of technical issue with the app and when it was resolved the matches would, with any luck, come flooding in and so I emailed the support function and waited patiently.

The Chronicles of a Malfunctioning Male

Thanks for your message, Jamie, we've checked the functionality and data on your app and can see all is working fine, happy swiping!
Tinder Support

For fuck's sake. I could just see all the Tinder support staff crowded round one PC. 'This fella has messaged to see if he's got a technical issue with his app because he hasn't matched with anyone!'

'Let's take a look at this profile then!'

Cue immediate hilarity and scenes of Tinder workers rolling on the floor with laughter, slapping each other on the back, pointing at my profile and laughing uncontrollably, one employee running and smashing through the office windows driven temporarily insane by an overload of activity in the part of the brain that controls laughter. I could see them printing out my picture and sticking it up on the office noticeboard, nobody being able to walk past without glancing up and bursting into fits of laughter. I'd be on the train home and random people would be coming up to me asking for selfies and I'd have no idea why, but the next day in the offices of Tinder a new photo of the clown himself with a Tinder employee would appear on the noticeboard, the worker in question going down as a 'ledge' for the rest of their days at the firm.

It's at times like this that you begin to question your whole view of yourself. I actually thought I was alright. I looked at myself and thought, could be better but could definitely be worse; got all the correct parts broadly in all the correct areas. And I actually thought I was a decent fella, and quite funny to go with it. I remember a girl at school once telling me I was funny. What was her name? Maybe I could get in touch with her and ask for some kind of reference? No, that would be weird, I think, contacting her fifteen years out of the blue asking for a reference for a dating profile. But maybe she's single now and it might prompt her to start flirting over WhatsApp and all of a sudden maybe we'd be out on a date? She did find me funny. Hmm…no, I'm pretty sure that if I contacted her out of the blue asking for a personal reference for a dating app, the weirdness of the situation would outweigh any desire she had to perhaps be taken on a date by me. The whole thing would reek of desperation. I think my main problem is that there are just too many other bloody blokes on these apps.

But choice is a funny thing, actually. You think of having a lot of good options available as clearly being a good thing, but, in my experience, often it's not. There are people swiping away on Tinder, and undoubtedly there are countless eligible and decent young bachelors on there for ladies to choose from and because of this, only the best of the bunch get the swipe right. And even then when a lady matches with one of the best of the bunch and starts a conversation, the inquisitive nature of the human being subconsciously tells her that there are literally thousands of other men on the app just waiting to be swiped and, the chances are, one of them is even better-looking and will be an even better personality fit, so why stick all your eggs in this particular basket? And so perfectly eligible men (and women obviously, the same happens the other way around) are being ditched because of the huge and easily accessible availability of choice.

And it's not just in online dating, these days it's everywhere; modern-day people never have a moment's opportunity to be bored, because they'll click onto Instagram and then Twitter and then Facebook and then check their WhatsApp groups. I came home from work the other evening and I had two hours to spare after dinner before I wanted to go to bed so I decided to watch a film. After a substantial amount of time scrolling through endless titles on Netflix, I picked a film about the life of Kurt Cobain, the Nirvana front man who ended up tragically killing himself. Ordinarily, I should have loved that film; I love Nirvana's music and I love those real-life, film-style documentaries. But I couldn't relax whilst watching it. For the first half of the film I was on edge, constantly asking myself if I was enjoying it, if it was any good, knowing that there were countless other options on Netflix that could potentially be better than this film, and knowing that the further I got into it, the less able I would be to turn back, switch it off and start something new before bed. And then the second half of the film I questioned whether I was enjoying it enough and berated myself for not picking something a bit more light-hearted and easy-going to watch before bed. That element of enormous choice played havoc with my mind and ruined what should have been a very enjoyable and relaxing couple of hours watching television.

I can just about remember the excitement when Channel 5 was launched; a new channel to watch on TV! There was so little choice back then, but I can remember loving Thursday evenings. I'd watch *EastEnders*, *The Apprentice* and then *Big Brother*. Some of these programmes may not have even been particularly good, but I sat there watching them safe in the knowledge that there was absolutely nothing else I'd rather be watching at that particular moment in time. Content in the moment. And I feel like that feeling of content, the peace inside that acknowledges you're happy with your decisions is infinitely harder to find these days because of the sheer volume of choice available in a whole world of different scenarios.

I scrolled over my Tinder photos which had been very carefully selected under the careful guidance of an experienced pro, Ozzy. He had suggested that I have one photo of me with a beer so that people know I'm sociable and game for a laugh, one of me with a fit girl so that girls would think I'd pulled fit girls in my time and he said that subconsciously this would elevate me a couple of leagues in the looks stakes. And finally, and he'd been very persistent on this, I needed to have a picture of me with a dog. He'd insisted that girls loved seeing pictures of guys with dogs; apparently it showed off a caring and sensitive side but whilst still enabling the man to retain his roguish masculinity.

I had argued that I should just show natural photos of myself so that someone could get a small insight into the real me, but Ozzy had argued that the real me had experienced very limited success up to this point and so it was time I tried a different tact. I had to concede that he had a point.

The picture with the pint we found without too much trouble, the one with the girl we'd had to delve back into the Facebook archives to one of me with Janine, an old university friend who was quite blatantly well out of my league and therefore fitted the bill perfectly. We couldn't, however, find one of me with a dog and so Ozzy had borrowed his uncle's pit bull terrier and we'd got a picture of me holding it back on its thick chain leash. Upon seeing the picture I'd argued with Ozzy that it looked like I was auditioning for an upcoming rap music video but he'd said it was our only option and I was forced to agree.

Looking back at the photos now, I looked at the one of me holding my beer and worried my eyes looked glazed, drunken and potentially lecherous, the one of me with Janine looked like I'd photobombed her and the one with the dog looked like I was working as an enforcer in the Yardie underworld. 'Snowflake', they'd have called me.

But in time I did manage to match with people and one particular evening after work I matched with a girl called Mel, a twenty-nine-year-old market research analyst from Swindon who now appeared to be 6.1 miles away from me, so I presumed she had taken leave from Swindon to come and live in the Big Smoke.

'Do not say "Hello, Mel," Ozzy instructed, forcefully.

'Why, isn't that what you would usually say upon meeting someone?'

'In real life, yes. Dating apps are not real life, that's the first rule of dating apps; until you meet someone, it's virtual reality and, in virtual reality, no one responds to a "Hello, Mel" message.'

'But what would I say in virtual reality world?' I asked.

'You've got to ask something about them, something which will pique their interest and make you stand out from the millions of other twats trying to get in their knickers. Do you have any idea how many blokes she will have matched with?'

'I don't know. She's very attractive, so I imagine a lot.'

'That's right Jay, a fuck load. Geezers will be taking one look at her tits and swiping right, they won't have even looked at her name, her face, what she does, what sappy bit of shit she's written down on her profile, anything, it will be tits, tick, and she will be an instant swipe right. And so every day she will be bombarded with, 'Hey, Mel, smiley face', and drips saying, 'How's your day going, Mel?' optional smiley face, and dick pic after dick pic after big, fat dick pic. Honestly, she's more likely to respond to a dick pic than the first two so if you're considering sending 'Hello, Mel' to her, do me a favour; slap yourself round the face, pull your pants down, take a picture of your tiny, shrivelled cock and send her that instead. It will give you a higher success rate.' I pondered briefly on the merits of sending a dick pic before, quite rightly, banishing the thought from my mind for the rest of time. Ozzy continued, getting more enthusiastic with his hand signals whilst speaking as he went.

'What you should be sending her is a question, but something a little bit outside the box, or something which might provoke a reaction. Something like "I guarantee I could make you wanna kiss me within five messages". Now that's a good one because instantly it's like you're challenging her and if she's got a competitive streak then she's likely to bristle at the thought of being challenged and losing and will likely respond, plus she'll like the arrogance of it all. This approach is for the professional however as your follow-up messages have to be top drawer because by message five you've got to have given something which is going to at least make her mind think she might wanna kiss you. Even if she doesn't admit it because her pride won't wanna let her admit that you won, she'll be interested enough for you to be able to say OK, you win this one but I guarantee that over a drink, face to face, mano e mano, you will not be able to spend the evening with me without wanting to kiss me, then bingo, you've scored yourself a date.

Or the second approach, the one for the less-seasoned pro, is a question which is a little left field, which will stand out in her head when she's scrolling through the millions of messages and dick pics. Something like 'So which member of Take That would you have been and why?' and then if you want to follow it up with a dick pic, you go for it.'

'I see,' I responded. 'Strangely, there's a weird sort of logic to what you're saying there. Not sure I should go for the seasoned pro approach just yet, so I should ask her what member of Take That she is?'

'Don't just go with that, you have to think of something within that kind of field and roll with it,' Ozzy responded.

'OK, hmmm... This is actually really difficult. I'm going to go with: which Spice Girl would you have been and why?'

'Great stuff,' Ozzy responded, shaking his head as he did so. 'Superbly original and imaginative. You prick. But go on then, do it.'

I typed the message, pressed send and waited.

'Hmm... No response as of yet,' I said wearily.

'Give her a fucking chance, she probably won't respond till tomorrow, if at all,' Ozzy countered.

And, just then, a ping on the phone, she'd responded.

'Looks like she's desperate, which is a good sign,' Ozzy said, bitterly.

'This is brilliant!' I cried excitedly. 'She said: *Ooh, a big Spice Girls fan, are we? Are you sure you're on the right app? Well just in case you are I'd say I'm Baby Spice, because I'm blonde, cute and innocent but with a bit of a mischievous streak. And which Spice Girl would you be, then?*'

I was completely and utterly sold already; she was cute and she was speaking to me, these apps are bloody brilliant!

'Shit, what should I write back?'

'Alright, don't panic, you big dick. Now you've got to respond wittily, something that'll make her laugh, whilst also being slightly flirty. Something like…' And Ozzy typed:

Baby Spice? Really? Innocent? I think someone might be bending the truth slightly, innocent is definitely not the word that springs to mind when I look at you, but OK I'll take your word for it. Well whenever me and my mates dress up as the Spice Girls, surprisingly enough, I'm always Ginger Spice, but I like to think it's because of my habit of wearing extremely revealing outfits, being slightly slutty and habitually having my mouth get me in trouble. If I had a big pair of tits I'd basically be Geri Halliwell.

'No don't say that!' I argued, 'she already thinks I'm on the wrong app, she'll begin to think I'm gay!'

'Course she won't, you dick'ead! She knows this is all just joking about, it's hashtag bantz.' Ozzy pressed send.

Two minutes passed of us sitting silently, staring at my phone. Ping!

How bloody dare you! Young man, if you were in reach I'd bend you over my knee! So do you and your mates regularly dress up as Spice Girls? Sounds like a fun bunch.

'Oh she is like putty, mate!' Ozzy exclaimed whilst jumping slightly out of his chair.

'She does seem keen, doesn't she!' I replied, gradually beginning to understand the flirty banter going on between the two of us. Or between her and Ozzy anyway.

'What shall we say back?' I asked excitedly.

'Give me a minute…' Ozzy began to type: *Suddenly very much wishing I was in reach! We're dressed up as Spice Girls more often than we're not, tbh. Just on sleepovers and things; dress up as Spice Girls, have pillow fights, do each other's make up, standard blokey sort of stuff. And who do you and your mates like to dress up as?*

I couldn't deny the back and forth of flirty conversation with an actual real-life girl (fingers crossed) was incredibly exciting. I slapped Ozzy on the back. 'This is brilliant, I'm SO in there!'

'Yeah, although it's sort of me who's more in, to be honest, mate,' Ozzy replied.

'No, look, they're all pictures of me she's looking at, and we're sort of jointly coming up with the responses so it's me really that's in.'

'OK, mate, if you say so,' said Ozzy as my phone pinged with another message.

Wow, you sound like a bunch not to be messed with, if you're regularly pillow-fighting in your panties you must have developed a ton of fight techniques. Well, I generally dress up as Beyoncé because I'm fiery, extremely curvy, and I have the voice of an angel.

'Wow, she is an absolute fucking saucepot!' shouted Ozzy, excitedly, 'we've come to the point now, we need to ask her out, any longer and it drags on and you end up being pen pals.'

'She really is a saucepot, and I like Beyoncé, maybe I could say something about being her Jay Z?'

'Yeah, erm… Jay, you could do. Not sure you really give off much of a Jay-Z vibe if I'm honest, you're sort of more, hmm…maybe Sinatra.'

'I see,' I responded, 'because I'm a timeless classic?'

'Yeah, whatever you say, Jay. Right, what do you want to go back with? She's not asked any questions which, in my mind, means she kind of wants to wrap this thing up. I reckon you say something funny and then ask her out?'

'Great idea, something about Jay-Z? What should I say?' I asked, my mind throwing up an absolute blank all of a sudden.

'Something funny, come on, I'm not gonna be with you on the actual date, you've gotta start thinking for yourself!'

'Hmm...think I'm a little tired after work, my brain isn't flowing like it normally would be, usually I'd have something witty to say,' I lied, but convincingly I thought.

'FFS, FFS! Right.' And Ozzy began to type. *Beyoncé, yeah, what a coincidence that is, because even though I'm white with red hair, I often get people coming up to me asking if I'm Jay-Z.*

'Brilliant!' I laughed. 'Knew I should put something about Jay-Z, and maybe say I too have the voice of an angel, like a young Aled Jones, something along those lines.'

'Erm...no, we'll leave that bit out, the fact that you're even aware of who Aled Jones is probably makes you a bit old and potentially too uncool for her,' Ozzy responded.

'Right, OK,' I replied, wondering why knowing the name of the singer of *The Snowman* could possibly mark me out as being uncool.

How about Jay-Z takes Beyoncé out for a drink this Saturday evening?
And send.

'Oh my god,' I exclaimed, barely able to contain my excitement and on the verge of wetting myself. 'We're going to have a date!'

'You're going to have a date, Jay. I'm not going to be there, and you'll have to speak for yourself. There won't be any phone-a-friend and you need to up your game because this one is a saucepot and she is bang up for it,' Ozzy said, wagging his finger whilst fixing me with his stern, serious look.

I agreed with his sentiment though; had to get the mojo going, get the creative juices flowing. I knew I could be funny and charming on occasion. I distinctly remember a night at university when I got chatting to a girl at the bar on a student fancy-dress night and whilst I felt like a prat because I was dressed as a ballerina at the time, after less than five minutes at the bar during which time the girl and I had done three sambucas each together, she had said that I was both funny and charming. That's not the sort of comment a guy forgets. Unfortunately we lost each other after that briefly and then she was sick on the bar a few minutes later and I never saw her again, but that doesn't change the fact that she said I was both funny and charming, a lethal combination if I do say so myself. The phone pinged.

Ha, you're funny!

Yes! I knew it!

Not sure I'm prepared to waste a Saturday evening with a Spice Girl dressing Jay-Z impersonator.

A little harsh,

But how about a drink Thursday evening?

'You've got a date, sunshine! You're free Thursday evening, aren't you?' Ozzy asked.

'I did get some mince out of the freezer which I'd earmarked for Thursday, but no, yes of course I'm free, let's do this!' I shouted, throwing my hand forwards for a high-five with Ozzy.

'Yes, my son!' Ozzy shouted, completely ignoring my proffered hand. 'It's game time! And if you don't get any action from this one, don't ever bother speaking to me again.'

I laughed, hoping Ozzy was joking.

Chapter 10

I sat at my desk simultaneously excited and nervous for my date that evening whilst also contemplating what I was doing wasting my life at a call centre for cat food, attempting to avoid as many customer service calls as I possibly could. I couldn't help but overhear 'Honest John' on the phone to a customer. Just 'John' to the rest of the staff at Hungry Kats, I'd labelled him 'Honest John' due to his excruciatingly painful habit of oversharing during water cooler small talk. Surely everyone is aware it's the unwritten rule of social acceptability that when you ask someone you know only in passing in the office how their weekend was, you have a limited number of acceptable answers which follow something along the lines of:

Yeah, was good thanks. Had a few drinks Friday, caught up with a few bits and pieces around the house; that was about it, really. How about yourself?

Yeah, was good thanks, pretty quiet really, nice to have a chilled-out weekend once in a while. How about yourself?

Yeah, was good thanks, helps when the weather's like this doesn't it! How about yourself?

Because you both know that this is just chit-chat to ensure you don't stand next to each other in a state of awkward silence when you are both vaguely familiar with each other. 'Honest John' has not picked up on this subtle social guideline and has regularly in the past overstepped the line. He once told me that he spent a large part of his weekend trying to sort his piles out with the help of his wife. Lucky girl. And on another occasion he told me he'd spent a large part of the weekend sitting on his sofa just crying because his wife had left him (I suspect the weekend of piles-related fun may have been the final straw). And when he told me this I felt really sorry for him, honestly I did, and I ended up giving him a hug. But I'm not a counsellor, and to be told this by to all extents a total stranger made me feel uncomfortable in the extreme. This level of discomfort was not helped when a few members of the finance team decided to come into the kitchen, catching the two of us in mid embrace, arms around each other, Honest John's face buried into my cest, tears flowing freely onto my shirt, me stroking his back in what I'd hoped was a calming and soothing manner. I was genuinely stumped with what to do as the finance team stood rooted to the spot, seemingly transfixed by what they'd witnessed, so for some reason I smiled softly at them to indicate all was well, and bizarrely and inexplicably followed that up by moving my right hand from stroking duties momentarily to give them the 'OK' sign.

Aside from all of this, I liked 'Honest John'. I really did. You always know where you are with someone like 'Honest John'. Someone for whom manipulation or intentional cruelty just doesn't enter their heads; they exist as they are and make no bones about it, being themselves to everyone who they may come across. Honest John was in the middle of dealing with a customer complaint when presumably the customer had made the fatal mistake of asking how he was.

'Well the athlete's foot's playing up, isn't it? Have you had athletes' foot before? No? Well, let me tell you it's no picnic. The in-between bit of a few of my toes actually went a bright-green colour the other week. No, straight up, I thought it was gangrene. Panicked I was going to have to have it taken off. Yeah, I know. It's calmed down now, though. Yeah. Yeah. Yeah. Anyway, Mr Bruce, enough about my feet, so you're telling me your cat's lost its appetite. You've lost *your* appetite? You've not been eating the Hungry Kats products, have you? They're not for human consumption you know? Says as much clear as day on the packaging. Because they're only the offcuts and rejects from food factories around the country, really. Yeah. Yeah. They'd never pass the health and safety regulations to enable them to be eaten by Joe public. Yeah. Yeah. No, I'm not sure about Whiskas, to be honest. Yeah, they are quite upmarket so maybe you're alright with your Whiskas, but definitely don't eat the Hungry Kats, yeah… I don't care how much you like the smell of the salmon in jelly, Mr Bruce, it's really not good for you…yeah…OK…OK…yeah…tada, Mr Bruce.'

Oh dear Lord, somebody shoot me now. I was more clever than the people in my team. I was, honestly. I'm not a particularly self-confident man, but that much was plainly obvious even to me. But whereas I was painfully conscious of my various weaknesses and this permeated itself into the face I showed to the world, generally a little unsure of myself, quieter than I probably ought to be and less willing to express views which generally 99% of the time would be far better than those which came out of anybody else's mouths, everyone else in the team seemed blissfully unaware of the flaws they exhibited day in and day out and seemed all the happier for it. I think it was Tom Cruise in *Vanilla Sky* who said, 'Ignorance is bliss' and he was right, it really is.

Whilst washing up my mug in the kitchen that afternoon, indulging in small-talk with Gavin, the office facilities manager, a man in his fifties who generally wore loose-fitting polo tops which he had a habit of hitching up to scratch his pale, bare, particularly hairy belly whilst talking to you, I noticed Colette sidling past the kitchen. Not wanting to let an opportunity pass, I interrupted Gavin mid belly scratch as he was telling me about the plan for the office to adopt two cats to live in the basement to deal with the growing rat problem we were encountering downstairs, and said in an overtly loud tone, 'That's right, Gavin, date tonight, just a Tinder thing y'know but see how it goes. She seems pretty hot so should be nice, off to a little wine bar in the West End and see where it goes from there?' Gavin looked at me with a puzzled expression on his face, completely baffled by what had just happened. I poked my head out of the kitchen, gazing in the direction Colette had wandered off in and noted that she hadn't seemed to have broken stride or noticed what I'd said as I watched her turn towards Miles' desk, now standing directly behind him, removing the wireless earphones from her ears and covering his eyes with her hands, giggling as she did so, at which point he grabbed her hands and pulled them downwards until she was effectively hugging him from behind. Fucking stupid wireless earphones, who the fuck invented the stupid easy-to-lose bastards anyway, what a fucking stupid idea that was. I turned back to Gavin, whose gaze still didn't appear to have left me.

'Good luck with the rats, Gav,' I said as I put my mug in the cupboard and exited the kitchen area as swiftly as possible.

Dragging my mind away from the downward spiral of personal character assassination and futile attempts to make a girl I was apparently no longer interested in jealous, I began to think about what to wear on my date that evening. I headed to the place where I do all my best thinking and sat there on the toilet. I decided that I wanted to look smart, but the sort of smart where someone hasn't given too much thought to their appearance. I wanted to come across calm, poised, perhaps giving off an air of almost aloof charm. So, in search of a minor miracle, I decided on the ground-breaking combo of brown shoes, jeans and white shirt and proceeded to let my anxiety levels run riot as I clock watched for the rest of the day, partly excited but mainly dreading the date that evening.

Chapter 11

That evening I was a nauseous mixture of nerves, excitement and a little diarrhoea which could have been due to the nerves or perhaps just a slightly unsettled stomach. Either way, I found it a nasty and unwelcome surprise.

In our latter discussions I had found out that Mel worked in Holborn and after three hours of research into the area, combined with discussions with Ozzy and Gary about the pros and cons of various drinking holes, I'd decided that we'd meet at The Perseverance on Lamb's Conduit Street. It seemed like a nice pub, not too fancy but not dingy by any stretch of the imagination and it was also on a quieter but also extremely nice back road in a lesser-known part of Holborn compared to the stretch between Holborn and Chancery Lane stations.

We'd arranged to meet at 7pm giving both of us ample time to finish work, mentally prepare ourselves (well perhaps that was just me), and get down to the pub. I arrived at 6:50pm, the palms of my hands already sweaty in anticipation of the meet. Adding to my nerves was the fact that she had basically been talking to Ozzy online and it was his wit and charm which had secured the date and not mine. This fact was weighing heavy on my mind. Come on Jay, 'Be more Ozzy'. But it was my pictures, I said to myself, and I can be just as witty and charming as Ozzy when I want to be; remember the girl at uni, Jay, so relax and enjoy the evening.

6:57pm – shit, should have run into the pub as soon as I'd arrived and downed a pint quickly before she got here, that would've settled the nerves a bit. But no, if she'd turned up and seen me inside necking a pint in one before she'd even arrived she'd be bound to think I had some sort of issue, and I didn't want to add an issue to the list of them which *actually* burdened me on a daily basis which she would no doubt discover in her own time anyway.

7:03pm, still not here. That's OK, it's a woman's prerogative to be slightly late for a date; sort of a prelude to the arrival at the chapel, I guess. I wondered if my nerves were magnified due to the lack of female figures in my life, not having known my mum and being an only child. I wondered whether Mum would have been able to give any advice in situations such as these, or whether dating wasn't the sort of thing someone would go to their mum for advice on.

Mel arrived at 7:18pm with no apology for her tardiness, but I instantly forced myself to overlook this in order that the date would not get off to a bad start. I spotted her coming down the road slightly earlier than was ideal. Not wanting to look rude and turn my gaze away from her, I therefore stared at her for the fifteen seconds in which she made her approach, a semi-demented smile forced onto my face, delighted when she reached close enough proximity for me to say hello.

'Hello, Mel, isn't it? Very nice to meet you,' I said whilst shaking her hand and pulling her towards me for a kiss on the cheek at which point she blindsided me by going for the double. Must have European ancestry, I guess.

'Jamie, isn't it? Has anyone ever mentioned you look just like Jay-Z?' she responded and I laughed.

'Funny you should mention that! Just the other day I was asked for an autograph. I signed Jay-Z, just to be polite and so as not to let down one of our fans,' I replied, to which Mel laughed somewhat hysterically and which relaxed me immeasurably. I knew I could be just as witty and funny as Ozzy!

Once inside, I ordered myself a pint of Camden Hells lager and Mel a large glass of Pinot Grigio and we found a spare table by one of the windows to sit at. Mel was wearing a tight leather skirt which came down to just above the knee, a burgundy t-shirt tucked tightly into it showing off her curvy figure and leather boots which came up to just below the knee. She had clearly spent a great deal of time doing her make-up which seemed to be caked on very thickly all over her face, resulting in her face and neck being two completely different colours. I thought she looked great, and she was here with me for a drink of her own free will.

'Cheers,' I said, and we clinked glasses. I took a sip of my drink, desperately seeking a conversation opener, but my mind had gone blank. Don't stop drinking until you've thought of something to say, I thought, as I stared at her increasingly confused-looking face. As I realised I'd basically finished my pint, I quickly put it down; worried that she may have noticed.

'Bloody hell, were you thirsty?' Mel asked, her forehead creased with concern.

She's noticed. 'Ha, yeah, I must've been, I guess! That's what happens when your date is eighteen minutes late.' Shit, why did I say that? It just sort of came out. But she was laughing.

'Oi, you cheeky git! I had train problems, OK!' she replied, smirking and holding up her middle finger. I think that was a playful middle finger, though.

'Weren't you working in Holborn? Why would you have been on the train?' I asked, channelling Colombo at his best.

'OK, OK, Inspector Fucking Gadget! I decided to have a quick drink with work people before coming down, is that OK with you? Are your back-up squad going to storm the pub and cuff me, because, trust me, I won't go without a fight.' I fully believed her. 'Besides, it's nerve-wracking meeting up with Ginger Spice and Jay-Z rolled into one.'

I grabbed the lapel of my jacket and pretended to speak into it: 'Roger rog, abort Operation Storm Pub, I repeat ABORT Operation Storm Pub,' I said, quietly relieved that I wasn't the only one who had been nervous at the prospect of the meet.

Mel laughed. 'You're such a cunt,'

Which I felt was a little harsh.

'Now, don't make me raise my middle finger at you again, there's much better things I can be doing to you with my middle finger.'

What could she do to me with her middle finger? Did she think I had a tiny knob and would just use her middle finger to wank me off? I didn't think I was large, but I certainly thought I warranted the use of a whole hand. Maybe she's just nervous and didn't really know what she meant; that's probably it.

The rest of the evening passed well, the conversation flowed between us, and at one point whilst laughing she rested her hand on my leg which caused me to jolt slightly at the shock, but her reaction didn't suggest this had put her off.

Most others had left, the bell had been called for last orders and the barmen were collecting up glasses and telling people it was time to leave when we clambered unsteadily to our feet from the tall stools and swayed noticeably, arms linked, towards the exit. The warm summer evening air hit me as we stepped outside and I suddenly realised that I was very pissed. I must have drunk about seven or eight pints, but what was more unbelievable was that Mel had been matching me with white wines yet she appeared more sober than me.

As we turned right towards Holborn station, outside the pub, Mel suddenly shoved me into the wall of one of the shops. For a second I thought perhaps I was being mugged again but, instead of making an attempt to steal my wallet, she pushed her face forcefully into mine and began kissing me aggressively. After about thirty seconds or so of me concentrating very hard on using my best kissing technique, Mel pulled away.

'Right, you're coming back to mine,' she asserted, turning around and raising her hand at a passing minicab with its light on which began to slow down and pull over.

'Erm...' I went to respond.

'You're coming back to mine!' she said, more forcefully this time, and she grabbed hold of my arm and began to drag me towards the minicab.

'Yes, yes, course,' I replied, 'a little nightcap.'

Mel turned, firmly grabbed hold of both of my arms and fixed me with a stern stare. Suddenly I felt a little intimidated by this cute, young, curvy, potential nutjob.

'No nightcap, Mr Z, just sex,' she said, looking directly into my eyes.

'Yes, yes, course,' I replied, consciously wary of upsetting Mel by now. 'A good old-fashioned bit of sex sounds splendid.' And I wondered why I was responding as if I were a character from the *Vicar of Dibley*.

Chapter 12

The Chronicles of a Malfunctioning Male

My eyes opened slowly to an unfamiliar ceiling and my brain scrambled to catch up with my body to identify what was going on and where I was. I felt pain in my head and a repeated thumping in my back and, very strangely, my bum was also sore.

My brain gradually began to focus and the events of the previous evening rushed back to me. My eyes focussed on Mel, standing on the bed above me, repeatedly kicking me in the back; the perfect way to awaken with my lover on a lovely English summer's morning.

'Oi, wakey-wakey, lover man, time to get dressed and get the fuck out, I need to get going,' Mel said, thankfully ceasing to kick me when she realised I was fully awake.

'Yes, course, I'll grab my bits.'

'Will make a change from me grabbing them. Let yourself out,' Mel replied as she closed her bathroom door, laughing hysterically, and somewhat manically I thought, to herself.

I gathered my clothes, which were strewn liberally throughout the bedroom and got changed into them. Before leaving, I shouted to Mel who was still in the bathroom with the taps running.

'Thanks for a lovely evening, Mel, I'll give you a shout soon.'

Mel's head and naked shoulders appeared around the bathroom door.

'Probably best we just leave it at one perfect evening, yeah. I'll never forget you. Have a nice life.' And with that she gave a somewhat exaggerated smile and pulled herself back into the bathroom, shutting the door behind her.

I spent the remainder of the day at work in a state of continuous semi-panic as I worried that my colleagues would notice that I had failed to shower that morning and would realise I was wearing the same clothes as I had been yesterday. The whispering would start, little groups forming in the corners of the office; sniggering to each other whilst glancing over at me. Then, without warning, they'd converge on my desk, just like they do when someone from the office is leaving and someone is going to give a leaving speech and a gift to the departing. They'd then start chanting, 'You had sex, you had sex' whilst individuals would step forward from the group at random to ruffle my already untidy hair and shout,

I'd try and argue with them,: 'I just went out and had a lot to drink and stayed at a mates house, you've got to believe me!'

After a good deal of time with my mind slipping into this spiral of non-existent events I would have to pull myself back from this preposterous storyline and say to myself that, realistically, the chances of people noticing that I was wearing the same clothes as the night before and hadn't showered was probably less than one in ten. That even if they noticed, the chances of them jumping to conclusions I'd been out having sex all night with a girl I'd just met were pretty close to zero. The chances that perhaps one or two people on the whole floor of the office would then decide to enlighten the rest of the people on the floor to the situation they believed to have occurred would be close to the chances of winning the lottery, and then the chance that the whole office would decide to descend on my desk and chant about my sexual conquest was basically the stuff only a pure idiot, such as myself clearly, would believe to be an actual possibility. Additionally, the chances that any of them actually cared about my love life, were very, very minimal, and also, and probably most importantly, above all this, why did I care?

This would give me some moments of calm before the sequence began again with an equally ludicrous scenario involving me cowering in the kitchen or being forced to hide in a toilet cubicle playing out in my mind, causing significant anxiety until my rational mind could take control of my subconscious once more. Needless to say, I was glad when the day was over.

Chapter 13

I don't know whether it's an only child thing in combination with having been brought up by a single father struggling to make ends meet, but I had a tendency to be far too serious about almost any given scenario. The memories of coming downstairs having had nightmares as a kid to see my dad sat at the kitchen table, elbows on the table, head held in his hands, concern etched in the frown on his face, bundle of papers covered in red writing in front of him stuck like superglue in my mind. Maybe that sort of upbringing, the anxiety that seemed to hang in the air at times, the worry, maybe it shaped me more than I cared to admit. I knew I should take a more light-hearted approach to certain situations, but it was as if it was hardwired into my DNA to be unable to.

'So you boned her, and then in the morning she said do one, and don't come back?' Ozzy asked.

'Well yes, I guess so. We had a reasonably nice evening. There were a couple of times I thought she was a bit odd during the evening, like when we were talking about something to do with leadership and she said she thought Pol Pot had some very interesting ideas on utilising the unemployed workforce. I simultaneously laughed at the notion of someone praising the leadership style of someone responsible for the death of twenty-five percent of the population they ruled over whilst also being impressed that she was educated enough to be aware of the leadership policies of Pol Pot, but then she met my laugh with a stony glare and took a slow and almost ominous sip from her drink. That threw me a bit, but I guessed maybe something had been lost in communication.'

'Whose Paul Pot?' Gary asked, unsurprisingly. 'That bloke from *X Factor*?'

'Look him up when you get home, Gary, homework for this evening. And it's Pol. P. O. L. Pot, not Paul. God knows who you'll find if you Google Paul Pot,' I replied.

Ozzy put a large hand on my shoulder.

'So what you gonna do?' he asked, gently squeezing my shoulder, apparently trying his best to appear as my chief counsellor, although having the choice of him or Gary I was pretty pleased he was stepping forward to claim the role.

'Nothing, I guess. The deed is done and she doesn't want to see me again. When I think back to the evening, I think we probably weren't brilliantly suited so will just put it down to experience,' I replied, shrugging my shoulders as I did, hoping Ozzy would stop grabbing my shoulder like I was some poor little child he was teaching a life lesson to.

'You do realise you've not done anything wrong, right? You are allowed to shag girls, y'know? The way you're speaking, you'd think you've just cost England the World Cup or something. Lighten up, man, you've got a shag, and it was about time. 'ave a beer, and let's try and continue this rich vein of form you're in tonight, ay!'

I knew he was right. I was taking this whole thing way too seriously. I looked at him staring at me, eyes wide, nodding slightly, begging for a positive reaction and I started laughing at the silly idiot.

He laughed back and slapped me on the back. 'My man, that's what I'm talking about, sambuca for the playa over here, please. Ladies, don't get too close because this man is on fire.' And we laughed some more before turning to look at Gary who was sat still, face completely expressionless. After a few seconds of us staring at him whilst laughing, he registered our stares.

'Hahahahahahah,' he laughed, his face turning instantly from glazed daydreaming to self-conscious fake-laughter, emanating from his mouth like an automatic machine gun.

'What you laughing at, Gary?' Ozzie asked.

'The joke, yeah, very funny, good one, Oz.'

'You're a fucking joke, Gary,' Ozzie responded, somewhat harshly I thought, but Gary seemed to like it and laughed again.

As I headed home that evening, my mind wandered. I couldn't help thinking about the girl I'd technically subjected to an unprovoked physical assault at the tube station. How would a date with her go? There was a connection there, I'm sure of it. Things just seemed to flow; we didn't seem to want to leave each other. God knows, I'd probably still be standing there now with her if she hadn't needed to leave. Plenty more fish in the sea, I guess. But I did really like that fish.

Chapter 14

It can sometimes be depressing spending your days working at something which holds no interest for you. A feeling of depression that only increases when you spend days training to be better at something that holds no interest to you.

Periodically, Hungry Kats liked to invite external trainers in to help motivate and develop their staff. Thankfully the feeling of depression which came over me every time I tried to learn how to deal better with difficult cat-related call customers was negated slightly by the knowledge that I was enjoying some time away from listening about the specifics of little Felix's diarrhoea or little Charlie's delicate palate, which was quite frankly a welcome relief. On this particular Thursday afternoon, an external consultant was coming in, apparently to help with increasing our productivity inside and outside of work.

Whilst the whole team of fifteen call respondents waited in the Attenborough meeting room, Jan the consultant walked in and started setting up her PowerPoint presentation. Jan was American and probably approaching her late fifties, with blonde hair and glasses, dressed in a power suit which seemed, if anything, slightly too tight for her. She spent a large portion of the training session name-dropping the various blue chip companies she had spent time working for before stating the high-powered role she had at the company: 'Of course, whilst at Google, I held the role of Chief Marketing Officer…'

Of course.

'And when I negotiated my six-figure salary at Cisco, I was just entering my thirties and they were entering a period of huge growth at that moment in time…'

'I was instantly promoted to the board after six months working at Microsoft as Head of Marketing…'

Not sure six months counts as being 'instant', Jan, I'd thought.

After each of these remarks in which she noted her remarkable achievements, she seemed to pause, tilt her head down and look out over the top of her glasses at all of us listening to her presentation. It made me a little uncomfortable and I tried to avoid eye contact with her, I was slightly worried she might chastise me for not giving a round of applause for her incredible achievements.

I spent most of the afternoon trying to avoid Jan's intimidating stare whilst simultaneously attempting to look sufficiently interested in what she had to say. For the last exercise of the day Jan flicked onto a slide which took us through 'A typical day in the life of Jan Straker'.

5:00am   Alarm goes, wake instantly and spend fifteen minutes going through emails received overnight from different time zones across the globe, responding to those that can be responded to sufficiently within one minute and setting reminders for later in the day for those that require further attention.

5:15am   Meditation

5:30am   Focus – what will I achieve today, how will I achieve it.

5:45am   Gym – mixture of cardiovascular activity and strength-based training incorporating HIIT workouts, weight-based training and combat-based training.

6:30am   Shower, lathering myself down generously with Shimmering Heaven shower gel before presenting myself meticulously to deliver to anybody who comes across me today the message that I want them to receive from my appearance – I MEAN BUSINESS. Apply Strong but Sensitive Facial Cream SPF 30 and Retinol Repair and Revitalise Daily Moisturiser – yes, that's why my skin looks so good.

6:50am   Caffeinate and drink a raw veggie juice combined with spirulina and essence of cacao.

7:00am   Stare at self in mirror and repeat:

'I mean BUSINESS' five times

8:00am   Arrive at desk and field any requests which have been marked for urgent attention from previous day.

9:00am   Meetings – making sure to get up and leave any meeting I feel is not utilising my time in the most effective way possible, taking note of the meeting chairperson and emailing them the reasons for my departure from the meeting and making detailed suggestions as to how they can increase the efficiency of their meetings in future.

12:00pm   Salad – no sauce, no seasoning. Focus on this afternoon with every chew.

12:15pm   Stare at self in mirror and repeat:

'You are killing today, you are destroying today, today is your BITCH!'

12:30pm   Meet with rest of the board and detail all improvements to process which you have implemented and let them know of the quantitative and qualitative impact these process improvements have had on the company.

1:30pm   Meet with direct reports and go through progress on their action plans. Set out detailed disciplinary procedures for those failing to achieve the objectives of their plans.

3:30pm   Respond to emails from this morning which had been parked for attention later in the day. Respond to emails received during the day. Respond to emails which are not relevant with the following:

Not relevant. Please come to my desk to discuss further if you believe this assertion to be inaccurate. Otherwise ensure to email me in future with only important information. (Ensure the rest of the board is cc'ed on response so that they are aware and can keep a log of repeat offenders with respect to time-wasters)

6:00pm   Make list of items for urgent attention tomorrow morning. Take note of direct reports who are no longer in the office.

7:00pm   Attend networking event remembering always the six essential rules of introduction:

Power shake

Power stare

Power intro (always speak first, speak over them if you have to; you are the dominator of this relationship) 'Straker, Jan Straker Chief Executive Officer, EasyBrands, Non-Executive Director, Slick Lines, and SoftCell. And you?'

Power card presentation – remove card from sterling silver holder, present it to them showing the wording clearly.

Power close – close at the point where you feel you're getting nothing from the relationship, 'You have my details.'

Power departure – turn, walk minimum of ten metres away from new member of network (head up, eyes front, surveying room).

And repeat.

9:00pm Evening meal – protein, vegetables, small portion of wholegrain carbohydrates.

10:00pm Reflection on day – make detailed notes on what parts you will do better tomorrow.

11:00pm Bath

11:30pm Bed

'Do you know what that looks like to me,' Jan asked, her American accent seemingly increasing in strength as she looked directly at me. I squirmed down in my chair, the words 'narcissistic evil global dictator' filling my mind, but prayed desperately that this was a rhetorical question, her gaze burning holes into my forehead as I tilted my head downwards to avoid her glare.

'That looks to me like the type of day a winner has. You, Gingey?' Oh god. 'Would you agree?'

'Erm… ye, yes, I, I, I'd…say so, seems highly productive,' I stammered, a thought briefly flashing across my mind as to whether Jan Straker had the authority to dismember me if I gave an answer she wasn't looking for; she certainly seemed to exude the confidence of someone who had such authority.

'That's right, Gingey,' she replied as I exhaled with massive relief, delighted in the knowledge that all my limbs appeared safe for now. 'Highly productive is what that day is.' Jan went on putting a huge amount of emphasis on the second part of the sentence, 'Get. Shit. Done. Get shit that doesn't needa be done outta your way, and get outta there.' I glanced briefly around the room and was relieved to see that most of the team appeared to be petrified of Jan Straker. 'What we are going to do is run an exercise whereby you are going to write down the schedule for your typical day. Is that clear to ev'rybody? Do I have any questions?' Jan surveyed the room as fifteen bodies shrunk as low down in their chairs as they possibly could. 'Good, let's get started then, you have thirty minutes, starting from, now.'

Hmm…my daily schedule, OK here goes:

7:00am   Alarm goes. Snooze.
7:09am   Snooze.
7:18am   Snooze.
7:27am   Snooze.
7:36am   Consider getting up so have time to have breakfast, decide against it. Snooze.
7:45am   Snooze.
7:54am   Hit stop button on phone alarm. Turn on lamp so don't fall back to sleep. Lie in bed trying to keep eyes open so don't fall back to sleep, trying to build up the motivation to pull back covers and actually get out of bed.
7:59am   Pull back covers. Lie in bed thinking it's very cold, really wish it was the weekend.
8:02am   Slide out of bed and walk to the bathroom. Put contact lenses in, brush teeth and jump in the shower, consider masturbation, dry self and do hair.

The Chronicles of a Malfunctioning Male

8:15am   Put on pants and socks (preferably a matching pair). Open wardrobe and perform sniff test on clothes. Put on shirt that smells less than five wears since wash. Put on jeans and shoes.

8:25am   Walk to East Acton train station repeatedly wondering whether have left the oven or iron on, even though have used neither this morning.

8:35am   Hop on central line to Tottenham Court Road.

8:54am   Get off at Tottenham Court Road and walk to office.

9:04am   Arrive at office. Get cup of coffee. Work, answer phone to cat food related queries, issues and complaints.

10:15am   Poo break

10:30am   Work

11:15am   Tea break

11:30am   Work

12:30pm   Lunch break – walk to Tesco and buy sandwich, crisps and drink, £3.99 meal deal.

1:30pm   Work

2:15pm   Poo break

2:30pm   Work

3:30pm   Tea break

4:00pm   Work

5:00pm   Remove headset, tidy desk and leave office

6:00pm   Meet Ozzy and Gary in the Talbot for two pints before heading home for healthy home cooked dinner.

7:30pm   Decide to have a couple more pints and eat a little later on in the evening, in true continental style. Tell Ozzie his dating advise is debatable at best and argue that he needs a more successful track record to be dishing out advice, willy-nilly.

9:00pm   Order burger and chips in the Talbot, might as well stay for a couple more pints. Get deep about how we may not have the love of any actual girls, but as long as we have the love of each other that's all we need and is more than we can ask for. Agree we're lucky to have each other, tell each other we love each other, hug each other, agree that the ladies of London don't know what they're missing by leaving us three eligible bachelors on the shelf. Tell Gary that his ex-wife is a cunt and never deserved him. Apologise for calling Gary's ex-wife a cunt.

11:00pm   Leave the Talbot and walk home, singing *Born to be Wild* and *Lust for Life*.

11.15pm   Brush teeth and fall into bed, potentially fully clothed.

Hmm…am slightly worried that Jan Straker might attempt to strike me if she reads this version of my typical day. I may need to touch it up a little around the edges. I decided to re-write the typical day and instead went with this:

700am   Alarm goes, jump out of bed, perform series of stretches.

7:05am   Perform 50 star jumps, 50 press-ups, 50 sit-ups and 30 seconds sprinting on the spot. Repeat x 3.

7:30am   Shower and ready myself for work, focussing on the day in front of me whilst in the shower and visualising what I'm going to achieve. Repeat out loud, 'I will achieve my goals today.'

8:00am   Breakfast of muesli (no-added sugar) and blueberries.

8:15am   Straighten my tie in mirror by front door and march out into the world, ready to smash the day.

8:25am   Hop on Central line at East Acton for Tottenham Court Road. Spend tube journey staring at fellow commuters and repeating out loud in my head, 'I am better than you, loser, if you cross me today I will crush you like a fly, or possibly even like an ant.' If fellow commuter catches my eye, never be first to break eye contact. Never.

8:44am   Arrive at TCR and walk to office.

8:52am   Arrive in office, check emails and ensure am logged in, ready to receive calls at least a minute before lines open at 9am.

The Chronicles of a Malfunctioning Male

8:59am   Repeat in head, 'Hungry Kats is my life, and you're a tiger among pussies, Jay.'

9:00am   Work – showtime.

10:30am   Check emails, respond to urgent ones that can be done so quickly – park others with reminder for end of day.

10:45am   Back to the phones.

12:30pm   Lunchtime – brisk walk to get fresh air into my lungs and assess my morning performance. Lunch of chicken breast and fresh avocado.

1:00pm   Return to phones, repeat to self, 'You thought I was bad-ass this morning, just wait till you see what I've got in store for you this afternoon, motherfuckers, you thought I was bad-ass this morning, just wait till you see what I've got in store for you this afternoon, motherfuckers.'

3:00pm   Check emails, respond to urgent ones that can be done so quickly – park others with reminder for end of day.

3:15pm   Back to the phones

5:00pm   Lines close, remove headset and tidy desk. Take a moment to assess performance and self-evaluate which calls I handled excellently, and which could have been brought up to the requisite level of excellence and how.

5.15pm   Respond to emails which had been parked earlier in the day.

6:00pm   Leave office, shake hands with fellow colleagues, depart with catchphrase, 'You're only as good as your last game, people. Tomorrow. WE GO. AGAIN!' Exit office to chorus of cheers, whooping and general exhilaration from team members.

7:00pm   Arrive at racket club, play tennis/squash/badminton.

9:00pm   Home for healthy homecooked meal including protein and complex carbohydrates to keep energy levels up at a steady rate so as not to cause spike in blood sugar levels which will result in an inevitable crash in energy levels.

11:00pm   Hit the hay, repeating before sleep, 'You thought I was good today, just wait till you see me tomorrow, you thought I was good today, just wait till you see me tomorrow.'

Although it wasn't entirely accurate, there were definitely elements of truth in it. I did get out of bed and get ready for work and get on the Central line and come to the office, answer the phones and take lunch and go home at the end of the day and have a homecooked meal sometimes. And me and Ozzy did once go to the racquet club and play squash because he really fancied one of the girls who worked on reception there. The extra detail was just fluff really, just the padding out of the story, I guess; everybody does it.

'Now if you can hand your daily schedules to the front of the room, we'll take a quick peek at just a few of them, see if we can spot any areas for improvement, see if there is anything from others' routines that you think you can incorporate into your own.'

Oh shit, I took my routine and slowly pulled it below the desk I was sitting at.

'Hey, Gingey. Get your routine up to the front of the room,' Jan demanded, nearly causing me to jump out of my skin.

'It, it, it's probably more of a personal thing, not sure anyone would find it too interesting, really,' I stammered desperately.

'Schedule. Here. Now. Gingey,' Jan replied, walking up to my seat, right hand held out in front of her to collect my schedule, left hand on hip. I handed the schedule over. Jan started looking over a few at the front of the room as we chatted quietly amongst ourselves.

'Gingey,' Jan called out, making me visibly shudder, 'I like your schedule, Gingey, this shows exactly the sort of thing I'm looking for. It's not perfect by a long shot, but I'm impressed. Looking at you, I did not for one second think you had this in you. You look more like a louse than a lion, but I want you to read it out. I'm sure the rest of your team learns a lot from you as it is, but I'm sure they could learn more still from hearing how you break out your day.'

'Erm…probably not entirely necessary, bit of a private thing really,' I said mentally seeing myself clinging onto the edge of an icy and slippery cliff, dangerously close to falling into the abyss.

'Gingey, we're all here to learn, and this is a sharing, collaborative and non-judgmental environment; I think your colleagues would be really intrigued to hear how you break out your day and the motivational methods you use. Hit it,' Jan replied, pointing her index finger at me in the manner of a gun before pulling a mock trigger.

The abyss, the abyss, so close to the abyss.

'Erm…w—'

'Now, Gingey!' Jan almost roared.

'OK, Jan…if you think it will help then I'll—'

'I do think it will help, now hit it,' Jan cut in impatiently.

I began the sequence of my day. Each time I looked up from my schedule I noticed the faces of my colleagues getting either more and more annoyed, irritated or angry, most seemingly verging on irritated, I thought.

I got towards the 6:00pm part. 'I think that's probably enough from me, Jan, don't want to hog the limelight,' I said, feeling the desperation in my voice as it emerged from my mouth.

'Gingey, 6pm. I. LIKE. 6PM. A LOT. Now shoot.' Jan pulled the trigger at me again.

'Leave office, shake hands with fellow colleagues, depart with catchphrase, 'You're only as good as your last game, people. Tomorrow. WE GO. AGAIN!' Exit office to chorus of cheers, whooping and general exhilaration from team members.' I dared not look up at my colleagues, but even without looking up I could feel the majority of those previously experiencing feelings predominantly of irritation slowly turning to anger. Maybe no one will remember this in a day or two, I thought, or maybe people will find it funny, I could make out it was some big joke I was playing on Jan Straker? I made the mistake of glancing up at my colleagues and noted that Anita, an ambitious, young, pretty girl who was general extremely pleasant and very good at her job appeared to actually have steam coming out of her ears. Oh god, I'd never been Mr Popular at work but I think this stunt might actually find me struggling to find anyone to sit with at lunch. It'll be like Borstal; I'll be walking along in the canteen with my tray and people will trip me up and pour spaghetti hoops in my hair and force me to tell the canteen staff/wardens that I tripped up and accidentally threw the spaghetti hoops over my own head, and they'd knowingly shake their heads and tell me to be more careful.

'Now THAT is what I'm talking about, Gingey, that sort of enthusiasm and zest for success that's gonna get you EVERYWHERE, Gingey. And I mean EVERYWHERE. Now, Gingey, I want you to leave first and lead us to the pub with your war cry.'

Oh god. 'Erm, it's not really the usual setting, probably better to save it for the real deal, after a day on the field, at battle,' I replied, clutching at straws where there were none.

'Gingey, this ain't no dress rehearsal. Now, DO IT.' Jan Straker fixed me in her glare, hands on hips and the rest of the room also directed their gaze at me, bemused expressions on their face, waiting patiently for my next move. Oh bollocks.

I wandered round the room shaking hands with everyone, bewildered expressions filling faces everywhere I went, occasional shakes of head and occasional glares filled with what seemed to me to be the threat of violent intent. Apart from Jan, of course, who nearly broke my knuckles while shaking my hand, simultaneously beaming at me from ear to ear.

'Y-you're only as good as your last game, people,' I muttered, head down, in almost a whisper.

'Louder, Gingey, as you would do on a regular day, picture the normal scene.' Hmm, the normal scene. Oh fuck it, damage is done now.

'You're only as good as your last game, people!' I roared, noticing heads turning from outside the meeting room in the office space to where the noise was coming from. 'Tomorrow. WE. GO. AGAIN!' I roared and was met with stony silence.

'Come ON, people! As if this was the real deal, a normal day, I want the whoops and the cheers,' Jan urged the room. 'Gingey, again.'

Oh FFS. 'You're only as good as your last game, people. Tomorrow. WE. GO. AGAIN!' I repeated in the same roar, this time to be met with lacklustre and sarcastic woops and cheers, accompanied by looks which if couldn't kill, could almost certainly maim or seriously debilitate.

'Gingey, that's dynamite, dude, the rest of you need to work on your enthusiasm. I think you could all do with taking a leaf out of Gingey's book, and you know it. Right, pub, there's several bottles of white wine with my name written all over them. Gingey, you're our leader, take it away, dude.'

I walked out of the office praying that she'd stop the focus on me whilst also hoping that I'd be taken out by a pack of hungry wolves as I left the office to succumb to the sweet release of being eaten alive to relieve me from the agony of this day.

The Marquis of Granby was thankfully busy so I was able to manoeuvre myself into the outside area, away from any colleagues and place a sufficient number of randoms between myself and any one of them who wished to do me actual bodily harm. One pint I was going to have, and then I was out of there sharpish, I'd deal with the repercussions of today, tomorrow. Always the most effective way of dealing with your problems.

Jan Straker was making her way towards me, barging through people in the crowd as she went, bottle of white wine in one hand, large glass filled to the brim so that it was spilling over most people she barged into as she went.

'Hey, Gingey, whatcha doing over here all on your own?' she asked, taking a gulp which got rid of about half of her glass of wine after doing so and strangely walking her forefinger and middle finger up from my chest to my chin.

'Erm…well. I—'

'I know the reason, Gingey,' Jan cut in.

'You do? Right. OK, well I—'

'It's natural, Gingey, don't sweat it. They see you as a leadership figure, an authority figure, and therefore find it more difficult to interact with you in a social capacity.'

'Erm…yes, I expect it's that,' I replied, trying to appear as if I knew that was the reason by raising an eyebrow and nodding knowingly.

'It's a compliment, Gingey, a mark of respect. Hell, it happened to me my whole damn career. Everywhere I went, it was the same; they're intimidated by your power, Gingey, your authority, your charisma and persona,' Jan said, stroking my shoulder as she spoke. I frowned slightly and nodded my head.

'Ain't nothin' you can do, Gingey, that's life, we're winners, leaders, they're also-rans. The price you pay, Gingey,' Jan said, this time stroking my cheek with the back of her hand.

'I knew the minute I saw you, Gingey, that you were a power person; it's written all over you. I knew you could handle yourself with aplomb in the office environment, and in my experience a man that can handle himself in the office can handle himself in the bedroom as well.'

I coughed and spluttered, beer shooting out of my mouth and down my chin. Oh god, what was happening here? She had now run a hand in-between the buttons on my white shirt, was grabbing onto it and pulling me closer towards her. I was not particularly attracted to Jan Straker, but I'm not sure what it was; the situation, my lack of success with women, the fact that this sort of thing literally never happens to me, I don't know, but all of a sudden, right on cue, exactly when I didn't want him, I got a boner.

I arched my back to try and move my waist as far away from Jan as possible, but this only had the impact of it seeming like I was leaning my head in closer to hers at which point she wrapped one of her hands round the back of my neck. I gently pulled my head backwards from Jan but this moved my waist forwards,

'Ooh, well hello, Gingey, so nice of your friend to come and say hello,' Jan exclaimed, eyebrow raised as she did so.

'So how old do you think I am, Gingey?' Jan asked, pulling me closer to her as she did so that our bodies were pressed up against each other by now within the crowd of people around us, my erection digging into her midriff, one hand still on my neck, the other having made its way onto my bum. Shit, how do I answer that being nice, but without looking like I'm taking the piss?

I actually thought she was in her late fifties, even though her skin appeared pretty devoid of wrinkles; her complexion reeked of years and years of industrial-grade Botox. Her hair was straw-like, as if it had been bleached too many times and had finally given up on her and her figure was good for a lady of her age, but I suspected that the tight power suit was carefully selected to hold her in at all the right places.

'Hmm…' I responded, buying myself some more time to think and taking the opportunity to pull back from her slightly as if taking the chance to survey her in more detail. Jan, turned her face slightly to the side, maintaining eye contact and flashing a half smile.

'Hit me, Gingey, don't be shy.'

'I would say… Early forties, although it's certainly hard to believe you've reached forty.' I lied horrendously, but hoped she was arrogant enough that she'd buy it without question.

'I'm fifty-two, Gingey, fifty-fucking-two. But do you know why I look so good? Because I'm a winner, Gingey, in everything I do.'

I adopted a facial expression which I desperately hoped displayed shock and awe.

'Well, I am shocked and slightly in awe, Jan. You look incredible for your age, you really do.'

'I look incredible full stop, Gingey. But thanks, you ain't too bad yourself, kid. Now when are we heading back to my hotel room? Get away from the loser crowd.' Again I choked slightly on my pint, this time spitting some of it back into my glass.

'Erm…well given our professional relationship, I'm not sure it would be wise to complicate things, beside which I have a prior engagement this evening which I need to head to now,' I replied praying that I wouldn't anger the beast.

'Girlfriend?' Jan asked.

'No, just friends and family I've planned to meet,' I replied, instantly kicking myself that I hadn't just said, yes, girlfriend.

'Well that's OK, Gingey. You run along and play with your little friends. But, Gingey, I'm going to be back and, just so you know,' Jan said, as she grabbed my head with both hands and squeezed it hard, 'We. Are. Going. To. FUCK.'

I swallowed hard, and whimpered, 'OK, Jan,' backing away from her to the edge of the crowd.

Her beady, invasive eyes tracked me every step of the way until I was out of sight.

Chapter 15

That Thursday, straying from the usual routine of sinking pints down the pub, Ozzy, Gary and I had decided to head out for a meal, and a healthy meal no less. As we made our way to a trendy new vegan restaurant in Ladbroke Grove, I became painfully aware that we were nowhere near cool enough to eat there. We asked for a table for three and I half expected to be met with a simple shake of the head and a wag of the forefinger from the short, dark-haired, liberally tattooed waitress we were greeted by, casually dressed in loose-cut faded denim jeans with t-shirt tucked tightly into them, fringe falling floppily over her forehead, dimples pierced with a single silver stud on each side of her cheeks and large round spectacles adorning her face.

Thankfully she merely expressed her disdain through the faintly disguised scowl on her face, clearly distraught that the three of us had decided to darken her door, and we were led over through the small restaurant. The furniture a mish mash of different styles, presumably picked up from the local dump or from various car boot sales, we were seated on a table for four people by the window looking out onto the main road. It was 7pm and the restaurant was already buzzing with people, all seemingly enjoying the supposedly healthy foods being served up to them.

'I'm telling ya, this is the place to get birds, they're all over this vegan shit these days, and I mean fit birds, too,' Ozzy spat, literally, part of the falafel he'd just stuffed into his mouth coming back the way it had gone in and landing precariously close to my hand on the table.

'I see your point, Ozzy,' I responded, moving my hand slightly further away from the offending offcut of falafel, 'and looking around there are certainly a lot of attractive girls in here, but how the hell do we get talking to them in a restaurant? It's not really appropriate to sidle up and say, hey, do you mind if I grab a bite of your falafel. That's not really socially acceptable.'

'Oh for fuck's sake, I've led the donkey to the water and now the donkey wants me to drink it for him,' Ozzy replied, sitting back and folding his arms as he did so, looking to the ceiling as if in disbelief.

'Sorry, Ozzy, but unless I'm very much mistaken, you're also single, which makes us both thirsty donkeys in this scenario.'

'We should order some water,' Gary chipped in.

'We should, Gary, you're right.'

'Maybe we can write a note and just screw it up and throw it at the table of girls we like the look of?' Gary continued.

I shook my head in exasperation. 'a) I don't think they will appreciate it when our ball of paper lands in their stir-fried veg and b) we all left primary school a long time ago which I think was the last time a tactic like that actually worked. Unless the girls around us are discussing snaring us by approaching our table and showing us their knickers, then I think it's fair to assume they've probably outgrown those primitive methods.'

'They might be planning on doing that, you never know,' Ozzy added.

'If they are,' I responded, 'I will right here and right now sign over the deeds to all of my worldly possessions.'

'Oh no, you're not signing over your debts to me, you can keep them, pal.'

'I don't even have a credit card, never mind any other debts!' I rebuked.

'Anyway, good week?' Ozzy continued, changing the subject.

'I followed Hayley to her office on Wednesday morning,' Gary mentioned, as if it were a lovely way to spend a summer's morning.

'Gary, seriously, mate, you really need to stop doing weird stuff like that. Not only is it creepy, and I know deep down you're not a creepy guy,' at which point Ozzy tilted his head and screwed up his face, 'but actually, Gary, I think you're bordering into the illegal doing this. Did she notice?'

'No, I don't think she noticed. I just miss her, it's just nice to see her,' Gary continued.

'But this is how it starts, Gaz,' cut in Ozzy, 'one minute you're saying it's just nice to see her, but she doesn't want to be within a country mile of ya, the next minute the police are bursting into your house and you're sat there combing the hair on her decapitated head.'

'Ozzy, for fuck's sake,' I said angrily, placing a hand on Gary's shoulder hoping to indicate that I totally rejected this notion, even if deep down I had to quietly admit he did have all the hallmarks of a tragic and disturbing murder culprit. But no, Gary was a decent human being, he would never head down that route.

'I'd never hurt her!' Gary protested.

'Pretty much what every stalker turned killer says before killing their stalking victim and claiming it was just so they could be together forever,' Ozzy hit back.

'Look, guys. Seriously, this isn't helping, but, Gary, on a serious note, mate, you need to stop this following. Why do you follow her, anyway? Why do you have any feelings for her? She's an absolute dick and has been a complete cock to you, you should hate her,' I asked, pleading with him to see some sense because she truly was a massive dick.

'I know, I will stop following her, that was the last time, I promise.' And Ozzy went to respond, but I held my finger up and gave him my sternest of stares – a stare that has cut many a man in two in my time – and he thought better of it.

'Well my week was shit, my team all hate me,' I continued, changing the subject again.

'I thought your team already hated you?' Ozzy responded, I had to admit semi-accurately, 'and no offence, mate, but I see you as quite a hateable character,' he continued harshly.

'What! How am I a hateable character?'

'What, I said no offence!' Ozzy responded as if this was the acceptable precursor to giving any insult imaginable to someone and for them being physically unable to take offence.

'OK, thanks, mate, no offence taken,' I replied, ensuring that my tone clearly indicated that offence was very much taken.

'What happened?' Gary asked.

'We had a training day, and I ended up lying about my daily routine, and didn't expect anyone would know but then the training coordinator made me read it out to the team and it makes me cringe to think of it now. I did look like a complete prat.'

'People will have forgotten in a week or two,' Ozzy responded, in a display of uncharacteristic sympathy. 'Anyway, so as much as we've found a place filled with fit birds, it looks like you two sad saps aren't gonna take advantage of it so I've found this for us to do,' Ozzy continued whilst scrolling through his phone and showing us an advert headlined 'Boxing Speed Dating' with a picture of a muscular topless man and a girl kitted out in Lycra, all sweaty, with boxing gloves leaning into each other and laughing.

'Hmm…not sure how much of a boxer I am, really?' I responded, simultaneously attracted by the thought of the sweaty girls in Lycra and put off by the thought of a sweaty me in gym gear.

'That's what it's for, numbnuts, to learn boxing, whilst meeting girls,' Ozzy responded.

'Will that many girls actually want to do boxing, though?' I pondered.

'Yes, loads! It's the big thing now; they all want to learn boxing to keep fit, it's blown up on the female scene,' Ozzy replied.

Gary was nodding along, I could only presume to something completely unrelated.

'And how do you know what has "blown up on the female scene" Mr Finger-on-the-pulse,' I said sarcastically.

'Because I'm down with the girls, aren't I? I speak to them, I know them, their minds.'

'I never see you speaking to any girls, Ozzy?'

'And their bodies,' Ozzy continued, winking as he did so. 'What have we got to lose?'

'Yes, fair point, let's go for it,' I finally conceded.

'My man,' Ozzy replied enthusiastically, slapping me on the back as he did so, 'Gary?'

'Yep, girls and fighting, I'm in,' Gary replied, worryingly aggressively.

Chapter 16

It may surprise you to know, but Gary, Ozzy and I weren't quite regulars on the gym scene, mainly on account of none of us being particularly good at sport and the fact that none of us were bothered enough about the fact that we didn't have six packs to give up our free time to lift an object up and down for absolutely no reason at all when we could have been enjoying ourselves.

So it was that the following Thursday evening, hearts heavy with trepidation, the three of us trudged towards a gym tucked down a side street by Liverpool Street station, nervous at the thought of being in an environment surrounded by Lycra-clad, eligible bachelorettes, instantly judging our uncoordinated, un-gym-friendly, unworthy bodies.

The girl on the desk eyed us suspiciously, as if we'd walked through the wrong door, then smiled falsely, 'How can I help you, gentlemen?'

'Erm…' I replied hesitantly, the other two having shuffled me forward to the front of the desk, 'we're here for the boxing speed-dating,' I said hesitantly, half expecting to be told that for some reason guys like us weren't allowed to partake and only massive steroid hungry beefcakes like the one on the flyer for the event were permitted.

'Brilliant, the male changing rooms are just over there,' the girl replied, pointing towards a door in the corner of the reception area 'and the room to the class you can access directly from the changing rooms, it's just next to the shower area. Most of the others are already through and warming up, I believe, it's going to be a fab event. Now, do you guys need wraps, gloves and a towel?'

Not quite understanding what we were agreeing to, we all replied yes in unison, collected our equipment and headed to the surprisingly luxurious changing rooms, words of encouragement from the girl on reception telling us to 'smash it' ringing in our ears as we went.

The changing rooms struck me as surprisingly lavish for those of a boxing gym. I had been expecting spit and sawdust, but there were oversized lockers coated in chrome, hangers waiting inside to be used and large mirrors everywhere presumably for gym-users to admire their progress after emerging from the showers. The whole gym had been given an 'industrial-luxe' feel by means of exposed ductwork and piping above our heads towards the ceiling and with the faint sounds of rap music emerging from the direction of the doors to the class the atmosphere was almost intimidating. Across from us in the changing rooms, also getting ready for the class, seemingly oblivious to our entrance was the competition. One man stood topless facing the oversized mirrors, flexing an enormous set of pecs before proceeding to shadow box in what seemed to me to be an alarmingly professional manner before heading out the door by the showers which led to where the class was.

'That guy didn't put a top on,' I whispered to the others, Ozzy still gawping at the doors through which the man had walked, mouth wide open, seemingly incapable of tearing his face away.

'I know,' Gary responded, worry etched on his face.

Ozzy had managed to regain control of his gaze but looked equally worried. 'Course, it's boxing, isn't it, you don't wear tops for boxing,' he replied, sounding as unsure of himself as I was of him.

'We have to do this with no tops on!' I responded in exasperation, desperately wishing that we'd not signed up for the event and that we'd find a small hole in the wall from the changing room which we could tunnel through and escape to the freedom of the outside world.

'Yeah, hope the same rules apply for the girls,' Ozzy replied with a smile, holding his hand up for a high-five with Gary, who failed to respond before Ozzy instead clipped him around the head.

'I knew this was at best a bad idea, but now it's looking like it's going to be an absolute nightmare. I don't want to go out there topless, did you see the size of that bloke then? Who's going to want me when he's there doing all his stuff with his fists etc.'

'Don't think things will go that far in there,' Ozzy replied seemingly deciding against holding his hand up to Gary for a high-five this time.

'You know what I mean, you saw him shadow boxing in the mirror; he looked like a trained fighter. We're useless at boxing and we're useless at dating, so why did we think it would be a good idea to come to a speed boxing dating event!' I said, the nervous energy within my body building by the second.

'Look, let's just get our shorts on, get out there, punch some shit, chirps some shit and see what happens. Your negative attitude isn't going to get us anywhere,' Ozzy responded, his words sounding far more confident than the expression on his face.

'I guess you're right' I responded reluctantly, still eyeing the walls for any sign of a tunnel.

I wasn't overweight, I've never been overweight, I guess body wise I was just a nothing. I guess that's how you'd describe someone with absolutely zero definition of any kind; the only thing to distinguish between my chest and my stomach were a belly button, two nipples and the positioning of my arms, legs and head.

I took one last look in the mirror before we headed to the door, the three of us stood there, my body making Casper the ghost look positively Mediterranean, Gary looking like an overweight, overly hairy yeti and Ozzy breathing in so much he looked like at any moment he was going to exhale and fly away like a deflating balloon. Legs sticking out of our shorts like cocktail sticks out of a pair of cheese cubes, Gary not even having managed to get a pair of matching socks to wear. I shook my head, struggling to envisage the girl in the event poster taking a second glance at the three of us except to screw up her face to express her discontent with us being in the same place as her.

'Right, let's get this over with then,' I finally uttered disconsolately and the three of us trudged over to the door by the showers leading towards where the class was to be held.

As we emerged on the other side of the double doors our mistake was instantly evident and was compounded by the stares our semi-naked presence commanded from all eyes in the room, expressing a mixture of surprise, amusement and confusion, a sickly cocktail of general distaste as if a skunk had scurried into the room and sprayed its odious gas liberally from its anus. The door had led into a small corridor, a few metres wide and about ten metres or so long, double doors at the other end of the corridor presumably leading to where the class would actually take place. There were about thirty or so men and women, the ladies to the left of us against the left wall of the corridor, the men on the right. At the front, by the double doors was the large unit of a man we had seen in the changing rooms, topless but with a t-shirt in his hand. What was not difficult to recognise instantly was that every other man in the corridor was wearing a top of some form, either a t-shirt or one of those Lycra type tops that men often wear to workout. Obviously none of the females were topless.

The three of us stood frozen to the spot as the eyes of the rest of the class remained on our bizarrely topless bodies. The unit at the front of the corridor pulled his t-shirt over his head and looked us up and down, confusion written all over his face.

'You guys gonna put some tops on?'

None of us spoke, frozen with fear mixed with acute embarrassment, the three of us were rendered completely incapable of speech. A number of seconds passed and the awkward tension was unbearable, the whole corridor of people staring at us waiting for us to respond. Finally, realising that Gary and Ozzy were more likely to melt into puddles like the terminator and retreat underneath the gap between the door and floor back to the changing rooms, I spoke up.

'U-usually when we box we don't wear tops,' I stammered quietly and unconfidently.

'You box a lot, then?'

'No, first time.'

'You said usually when we box we don't wear tops?'

'Yeah, I guess I meant if we had boxed before, we would usually have worn no tops.'

I was already acutely aware as to how strange my response had been, but the befuddled expressions of the rest of the class as well as the unit who was quite clearly the class instructor served as useful confirmation of just how bizarre it was.

'OK, well we usually wear tops in the class, to be honest, so feel free to grab some or if you're more comfortable topless then go for it,' The instructor responded, rather kindly I thought. 'We'll grab some tops,' I responded as the three of us retreated back to the relative safety of the changing rooms, an audible laugh following us as we closed the changing room door behind us.

'You idiot, Ozzy, I thought you said because it was boxing people would be topless!'

'Don't blame me, you prat, you're the one who clocked the instructor and started going on about this topless business.'

'My god, that was so embarrassing!'

'Why did you say that we usually didn't wear tops when we boxed and then said we'd never boxed before? That sounded pretty stupid, if I'm honest.'

'Oh you've found your tongue now, have you, Ozzy? Because out there I didn't hear a peep out of either of you so it was come up with something to say quickly or have us look like a bunch of violence-craving mutes.'

'I think we should've taken the mutes option,' chipped in Gary, apparently in all seriousness.

'Well, Gary, the two of you have said nothing so far, so you both still have the option to be the violent mutes when you head back out there, just don't expect it to get you very far with the ladies!' I snapped, now completely exasperated with the whole situation.

Why and how had we got ourselves into this situation? This would never happen to other groups of lads. Other groups of lads would see the flyer, decide to give it a go for a laugh, come down, do a bit of boxing, a bit of flirting and probably end up with a date or two by the end of it. Yet I could have put money on the fact that when we came down to give it a go we'd end up feeling awkward, embarrassed and dateless. I hadn't expected that we'd have exceeded ourselves and managed to come across as actual dunces to the rest of the class, but we were clearly having an exceptional day of being us.

'Right, are we heading back out there then?' I asked after we'd all got our tops on.

'I guess so,' Ozzy responded, even his at times overly confident persona seemingly flagging by this point.

'Gary?'

Gary held his fists up to his face in what I'd presumed was his best boxer stance and I took that for him meaning he was ready.

As we trudged back through the double doors to what was if not the corridor of death was certainly the corridor of uncertainty, the others had already headed through into the gym classroom. The instructor held the door open for us and we entered into a large circular room with punchbags hanging from the ceiling throughout with a little bit of space in the centre of the room where just one bag hung where the instructor took his position. The room was almost pitch black save for some low-level lights enabling you to see what you were doing, and a spotlight shining down on the middle of the room to illuminate the instructor as he barked out instructions. Bizarrely, he seemed to have adopted what seemed like an American accent now when he spoke and as he barked warm-up instructions he seemed to be attempting to almost rap what he was saying which surprisingly made me feel slightly better as the embarrassment I had felt just minutes earlier subsided and transferred into embarrassment for him. Uplifting music blared out of speakers throughout the class giving the whole studio the feel of a particularly sweaty nightclub; the faint stench of BO replacing the typical smell of old beer-stained carpet.

To the rhythm of the music and sounding like a karaoke version of Jay-Z, the instructor barked enthusiastically, 'Left jab, left jab, left jab, left jab, right jab, right jab, right jab, right jab, how you all feeling, people, can I hear a whoop-whoop?'

The rest of the class whoop whooped enthusiastically as Ozzy, Gary and I exchanged puzzled looks from the safety of our bags towards the outside of the circular room.

'So, peeps, here's how this shit is gonna rolllllllaaaaa. I want all the sexy ladies in the house tonight, can I get a whoop from the sexy ladiesaaaaa.'

'Whoop' echoed around the room in a high-pitched chorus, the silhouettes of various ladies throughout the room high-fiving each other.

'Yes yes, my ladies, innnnnnnsideaaaaa. Now you sexy ladies are going to take a bag, where's my gents innnnnside can I get an arrrroooooooo!'

'Arrroooooo' swept through the bags in a deeper, angrier tone. Trying to get involved, I whispered 'Arrroooo' very quietly, easing my way into the atmosphere, just gently dipping a toe in as it were.

'Yes yes my brothers out thereaaaaaa. My bredrin out there are gonna rotate from bag to bagaaaa from lady to ladyaaaa, you will have two minutes with each lady so I want you to work hard, smash that bag, do your best to impress because within two minutes you'll be ouddathere, no hanging about on those bags, two minutes is all you've got, ladies and gentsaaaaaaa.'

My warm-up had been distracted by the instructor's bizarre change in accent and interesting choice of vocabulary, but, in the words of PJ and Duncan, I felt ready to rumble.

'Ladies, start your engines pleaseaaaa,' the instructor barked to a titter of laughter amongst the female contingent in the room.

'My bredrin I want you all to find a bag with a lady on it now, there should be one for everyone and then we are going to rotate clockwise on my order.'

I walked towards a bag and stood by it, a girl behind it on the other side. Should I go around? Shake her hand? Say hello at least?

'Two minutes start now and let's jab, and jab, and jab…'

Too late, the jabbing had started and to the backdrop of what I can only presume was some sort of drum 'n' bass I was jabbing in time to the music.

Two minutes was getting closer and closer and I hadn't said hello or made any eye contact whatsoever with my female partner. I was actually slightly uncertain she even knew I was there, it wasn't like I was hitting the bag particularly hard. Maybe I should try and get around to talk to her, but how could I talk to her with the music so loud, with us meant to be punching a punchbag and with that weird instructor rapping instructions in our ears. The whole thing was a logistical nightmare.

'And that's your two minutes, ladies and gentlemenaaaaa, CHANGE!'

I emerged from the shadow of my punchbag and saw on the other side an extremely attractive blonde-haired girl, petite but with very toned arms and ripped abs exposed between her leggings and crop top. We made eye contact and I smiled and lifted my hand in greeting at the precise moment that she bent down to do her shoelace. I stretched my arm out to the ceiling from the wave and pretended to stretch my shoulder as I rotated clockwise to the next bag.

'And hook and hook and hook, come on, people, I wanna see dose bags moving from the forceaaaa, this is a knockout shot, peopleaaa, picture your boss and smash this out like you smash out every dayaaaa!'

I hadn't had a chance to say hello again, but this time I positioned myself at a slight angle so that I could see the long, slender arms of my opposing female hooking surprisingly viciously into the bag. I shuffled slightly to the left around the bag to the point where I could see the beautiful, concentrated and apparently angry face of the tall and lean dark-haired female on the other side. She looked up briefly from her flurry of hooks and I took my chance, smiled widely and raised my eyebrows and followed this up by pretending to throw a punch at her rather than the bag in what I thought was a reasonably clever yet appropriate manoeuvre from my repertoire of humour given our setting.

The girl frowned and gave me a distinctly puzzled look and I withdrew my punch, nodded in time to the music whilst still smiling manically at the girl before very slowly but surely shuffling back around the bag so that her disapproving eyes could burn into my face no longer.

'AND CHANGEAAAAA'

OK, Jay, two practice rounds, this time get there quick. I near sprinted to the next bag where a short and powerful-looking red-haired girl, hair tied back in ponytail, was waiting, skipping gently from one foot to the other in time to the music.

'How's it going, I'm Jamie,' I shouted in her ear above the sound of the music.

'Fay,' the girl replied and smiled as we failed in an attempt to shake hands with our gloves on, both laughing slightly over-exaggeratedly at the fact.

'And cross and cross and cross and cross,' the instructor interrupted at precisely the wrong moment and Fay turned her attention from me to apparently trying to knock the bag from the metallic fastenings attaching it to the ceiling and I retreated to my side of the bag.

Right, need to make a lasting impression as I leave this bag, Fay seemed lovely and she smiled at me, although having a girlfriend who could quite clearly beat me up would be intimidating. I glanced around the room and noticed other guys talking to their partners whilst punching, one guy was breakdancing between punch combos, another had taken his top off. For fuck's sake, it's OK now, I guess, nobody is looking at him like he's a weirdo; they're distracted by his chiselled abs and massive pecs.

I noticed a figure doubled over as if in severe pain, seemingly attempting to be sick, and realised it was Gary. To be fair, his partner was giving him a lot of care, rubbing his back as he crawled painfully along the floor. Maybe it was a genius ploy to garner the sympathy/comedy vote? No, with some that might be plausible but not for Gary; his mind is incapable of thinking in such a deceptive fashion. He's genuinely in pain and trying to be sick, in the middle of the gym floor, good work, Gary. I also saw Ozzy between the bags a couple of girls in front of me bobbing and weaving and jerking around as if he were Mike Tyson in his pomp, the girl on the other side seemingly taking absolutely no notice of his bizarre display of what I'm sure he thinks is boxing prowess but actually made him look more like a demented cowboy riding a bucking bronco.

'And change, gentlemenaaaaa.'

I walked round the bag and on the spur of the moment put my hands together and bowed in the manner of a martial arts master, cringing only slightly as I did so, and I rose to see a confused look on Fay's face matched only by the equally baffled and quite frankly slightly disgusted look on the face of the man following me onto the bag with Fay. Maybe I should just karate chop him right in the side of the neck. No, no, have to remember you've done the bow that's all; you've never actually done any martial arts training so getting flattened by someone you've karate chopped in an unprovoked attack is not going to make this humiliation any easier to take.

Increasingly, as we swapped from bag to bag, my levels of discomfort grew as I noticed guys and girls on other bags becoming increasingly flirty and increasingly touchy-feely whilst boxing, almost as if this were a night out and the alcohol was slowly taking effect and loosening inhibitions in the room. With this increased level of discomfort, I retreated to arriving at the bag, saying hello, punching the bag for two minutes before feigning exhaustion at the end of the two minutes to the girl, laughing idiotically for no apparent reason whatsoever and waving a gloved hand at the opposing girl before moving onto the next bag which signalled one more step closer to the sweet sound of the final bell. I wished someone would throw in the towel because I was done!

Gary, however, was evidently not done, as I glanced to my side, two bags away I noticed that he'd seemingly managed to recover from his earlier ailment and was back up on his feet, which was good. What was less good however was that he seemed to be nursing a girl who was doubled over, an un-gloved hand holding her nose, what appeared to be blood seeping through her fingers. Clearly we weren't satisfied with leaving the dating event with only unmitigated humiliation, we'd decided to add criminal assault to our rap sheet before we snuck quietly out of the gym at the end of the event, the sound of the rest of the attendees mingling, chatting and laughing mocking us as we sloped dejectedly away from the source of our shame.

Chapter 17

'I mean, are we just flawed as people?' I asked as we sat in the health food café a few doors down from the gym gulping our protein shakes, 'is that what it is? Because I feel like a decent human being inside but every other man seems to make it look so easy when we make it look like we're aliens from another planet? It's like we're those aliens from that *Third Rock From The Sun* show, come down to earth and trying to be human but not quite getting it right.'

'No, I got on alright in there, not too bad, think a couple of the girls were up for it but the problem with me is when I get into the boxing I'm kind of in the zone and so I'm in fight mode as opposed to loving mode, and believe me those two do not mix,' replied Ozzy, apparently in all seriousness.

'I was sick,' Gary responded with more honesty.

'I know, Gary, could you not have made it to the toilets, or at least to outside the class?'

'Felt it coming for a while but thought it probably wouldn't actually come, and then it did and it was too late.'

'What did you do,' I asked, amazingly not having noticed the stench whilst in the class.

'Just left it there and carried on.'

'Perfect, so some poor cleaner would've had that unexpected surprise to look forward to when they came in to mop after we'd finished.'

'I guess so. Then I punched a girl in the face.'

'Yeah saw that as well, Gary,' I replied.

'By accident,' Gary added urgently.

'Yeah I guessed that, Gary, I didn't think you'd decided the best way to snare a date on a boxing speed-dating class was to show off your strength to the lady in your crosshairs by breaking her nose.'

'No, I was feeling sick again so I closed my eyes and just kept swinging and she moved her face in the way.'

'Fair dos,' I replied, 'Could've happened to anyone, I guess, except obviously it was only ever going to happen to one of us rather than anyone else in the room. I mean why are we so bloody useless?'

'I think what it is is that we're just real, you know, we came from the school of hard knocks…'

'We went to St Raphael's school in Uxbridge, it wasn't exactly downtown Compton,' I cut in on Ozzy.

'No but it was real, we didn't get given nothing, we're self-made ya know, most of this lot were born with a silver spoon in their mouths, they're just used to getting what they want, we're used to having to fight for it.'

'Well we literally did just try and fight for it and lost to those "silver spoon" guys who apparently fought for it a lot better than we did.'

'You're deliberately mixing up what I'm saying here, Gary, you're with me right?'

'I know what you mean, yeah,' Gary responded

'No you fucking don't, Gary!' I responded, exasperated with the pair of them. 'Maybe you're right in some way, maybe it's a confidence thing, maybe these guys have been brought up having everything and that has brought with it some sort of ingrained feeling of entitlement and therefore they expect to get what they want and this mindset means that more often than not they do get what they want. But surely that's just a mindset, surely we can adopt that, no?'

'It's more difficult than that, mate, you can't just adopt what you don't have in you?'

'But why not? We walked into that class and not one girl would've known whether we or any of the other guys in there were schooled at Eton or schooled at St Raphael's…'

'Oh *schooled*, darling,' Ozzy mocked in a posh accent.

'Shut up, I'm trying to make a point here. They would've been none the wiser, so why on earth would they have any form of hidden advantage over us, bar their mental mindset?'

'You've lost me,' Ozzy replied.

'Oh forget it,' I said and pushed my chair back forcefully, causing it to screech on the floor as I got up to pay the bill.

But it was true, I thought, as I travelled home that evening. What is it that differs between two guys in terms of their success in love and in life in general? Why did those guys in the gym today have so much success whilst we, almost inevitably, fell flat on our faces, and, kind of as expected, completely humiliated ourselves in the process? Is it something you're just born with, is it in your genes? And if it is in your genes is it something you can work on? Or do you get what you're given at birth?

These thoughts bugged me long after I'd jumped into bed and I twisted and turned all night not able to get the fear out of my head that I could lead my whole life not realising my potential because I wasn't able to be the boss of my mind and control my outlook on life and the confidence I projected.

Chapter 18

The debacle and embarrassment of boxing speed-dating was gradually beginning to fade from my mind as I left work and headed towards Clerkenwell for the start of my new creative writing course. I tried to do one course a year although lately I'd been finding it difficult to find spare time to dedicate to writing. So I was excited to be starting my new course as I knew for ten weeks I'd have two hours every Wednesday evening dedicated to learning to become a better writer. I'd always enjoyed creative writing, all the way back to my days at school when my interest had been sparked by receiving an award for a short story I wrote about a school trip which took a turn for the worse and saw the coach attacked by a disturbed monster. Ever since then I'd had a dream of becoming a published writer. Over the years I'd written various short stories and entered various competitions but had yet to build on the short story success that I'd had at school. Even with that being the case, however, it hadn't dampened my enthusiasm.

After registering with reception at the university, I was directed to a small lecture room within which the course would take place. I took my seat and introduced myself to the man next to me, a portly older man with a deep-red face, a large moustache and a thick mop of unruly, greying hair on top of his head called Nigel. You don't get many Nigels any more. A dying breed. Very rarely you go to meet a newborn and the parents say, 'And I'd like to introduce little baby Nigel! We'll all call him Nige.'

The room had about thirty seats in it and there were about twenty people seated when a youngish fair-haired man, probably in his mid to late-twenties, with round spectacles, entered and introduced himself as the tutor. We were a few minutes into his introduction to the course when the door at the back of the room opened. In my memory the next part happened in slow motion. I know it definitely didn't happen in slow motion because at the time, I had no idea of the significance that this opening door might have, plus, in real life, slow motion doesn't actually happen. I'd turned my head briefly to the direction of the door and was turning back to the front of the room when I sharply returned my gaze. Into the classroom walked a lady with long, wavy dark hair, and a smile that seemed to fill her face and bounce around the room as she flashed it at the tutor and mouthed the word sorry before she quietly shuffled into one of the spare seats at the back.

It was her, it was definitely her from the station! My heart began to beat at double speed and adrenaline began to fill my veins so much so that I suddenly felt the need to get up and sprint on the spot to get rid of the excess energy coursing through me. Wisely, I didn't do that, it would definitely have marked me out to my fellow students and, most importantly, to Claire, as an oddball. And I didn't want them finding out I was an oddball this early on, generally people tended to find that out gradually.

I struggled to focus for the rest of the session as I worried about saying hello to her at the end. How hard could it be; casually walk up to her and say hello, how are you doing? Go in for a hug and a kiss on the cheek? Or handshake? Don't think I know her well enough for a hug and a kiss on the cheek, but is a handshake a little dismissive? Will she definitely remember me? One of the good things about having bright-red hair is that I generally tend to think that if I remember someone then they should really remember me. But this was different; I had a reason to remember this girl, being that I'd thought about her non-stop since meeting her. Surely this was fate, I thought. Surely this was god sending a sign, looking down on me with a little sympathy and saying, go on give him another chance then. Should I ask her for a coffee, or does that make me sound a bit boring, how about a drink? Or should I just wait for a while, play it cool; she must be signed up to the course so would be back next week. But what if she decides it's not for her and doesn't return. No, I couldn't risk it, I would definitely ask for her number or her name, or something that would ensure that there was no possible way that I could lose contact with her, short of my untimely death. Perhaps her national insurance number, address, birth date, registered address of employment, parents' names, their parents' names and maybe a copy of her birth certificate, just to be on the safe side.

The tutor wrapped up a session which had been a complete waste of money for me seeing as I'd not paid attention to one word since Claire had walked through the door and people began to gather up their things before leaving. I grabbed up my pad and pens quickly and made my way towards her at the back of the room. She had her head down, busy collecting her things and putting them in her bag. I stood and waited. She then began checking her phone. I continued to wait. I was just beginning to wonder at what stage did waiting turn into lurking when she looked up at me, an expression of recognition instantly registering on her face, accompanied by a wide, beautiful smile. She pointed at me. 'Oh my god! You're not here to attack me again, are you?'

I laughed. 'No, no plans to attack you on this occasion, I noticed you come in late and thought I'd come over and say hello.'

'I know, slap on the wrist for me, for my tardiness, and I didn't even have the excuse that I was clocked round the face with a stray umbrella this time. The tutor has probably already marked me down as the problem student!'

I couldn't help notice how witty she appeared to be. 'Well just in case he hasn't, I delivered a note to him just letting him know to keep an eye on you.' She laughed, and it felt so good to have made her laugh that the hairs on the back of my neck stood up.

'Well thanks for that. I'll have to send him a note next week to let him know to keep an eye on you just in case there's another violent outburst.'

'You wouldn't dare if you don't want another whack round the face.' Instantly I was worried I'd taken the joke too far and gone into the territory of being a threatening relative stranger. 'Sorry,' I quickly added, 'obviously I'm joking! My mouth runs away from me sometimes!' And she laughed again, and I felt good again with the slight addition of relief this time.

'I think I get that you're joking. So what are you doing here?'

'The same as you, I presume. I've always liked writing and I like to do a writing course at least once a year. I heard good reviews about this course. How about yourself?' I asked.

'I've made a bit of a resolution recently, I suppose, to make a conscious effort to try new things that I've always fancied doing. And I've always really fancied turning my hand to some creative writing and seeing how I get on with it. It sounds like you're a pro though, so maybe I'll have to copy your homework!' I laughed.

'Far from a pro! And copying homework will only add to your growing reputation as the course problem student!' And I decided to go for it. 'Listen, would you fancy grabbing a drink or a coffee or something?' I asked, trying to sound as casual as possible in doing so.

'Well it is "Wet Wednesday", isn't it, so why not? Let's grab a drink, shall we!'

'Great, "Wet Wednesday" it is!'

We left the campus and walked round the corner to The Red Lion, a quirky old pub decorated extravagantly with a moose's head protruding from one of the walls and a mish-mash of newspaper cuttings, photographs and posters adorning every space on the walls and the ceiling.

'What do you fancy?' I asked. 'It was Claire, wasn't it?'

'That's correct, bonus points for excellent memory skills, Jamie, was it?' she asked, unaware that I'd had her name in my head every day since the day I'd attacked her with my umbrella two months prior.

'That's right, kudos to yourself for equally impressive recall skills.' I was pleased that she had remembered my name.

'Hmm… I will have…a glass of dry white wine, please,' she said, rubbing her hands together as she did so. Just very fleetingly, a small voice inside of me thought; she seems particularly excited to have a drink, maybe she's an alcoholic. Instantly I pushed that little voice way out of sight; why do you have to try and sabotage something almost instantly, looking for a reason to dislike her, what is wrong with you?

'An excellent choice, madam,' I responded. 'A glass of dry white wine and a pint of lager please, mate,' I asked of the barman. 'Large or small wine,' he responded, directing the question towards Claire.

'Pint, please,' Claire answered and a look of shock momentarily appeared on the faces of both the barman and I.

'Joke, joke,' Claire said, smiling as she did so, 'but I will have a large, please.' She turned to me. '"Wet Wednesday", isn't it?'

'Very true,' I answered as Claire accepted the glass proffered by the barman. We made our way to a small wooden table with two seats over towards the entrance. The last of the evening sun was pouring in through the window beside the table and Claire actually looked radiant under its glow.

'Cheers,' I said, raising my glass towards Claire.

'Cheers,' Claire responded. We clinked glasses, retaining eye contact as we did; Claire leaving her gaze on me for slightly longer than I thought was usual, and if I didn't know better I could have sworn she was flirting, very subtly, with me.

'The eye contact is important,' she continued, 'don't want to end up with seven years bad sex.'

Just hearing Claire say the word sex sent a shockwave of electricity through my body.

'Is that what happens if you don't retain eye contact, is it?' I asked.

'Well that's what they say,' she replied. 'I'm sure it's not actually true, but I figure why risk it so always make sure I keep the eye contact, just in case.'

'Well bad sex is better than no sex at all,' I responded and instantly regretted saying it, fearing I sounded like a loser.

'You say that,' said Claire, 'but I'm not actually sure it is. I think if it's bad why bother, you might as well spend the night having a warm bath and reading a good book.'

And I instantly made a mental note that if I was ever lucky enough that things did get that far with Claire, I simply HAD to be good at the sex. I'd always thought I was probably OK at the sex, I didn't imagine I was blowing any minds but I'd worked out a routine over the years which, on the rare occasions it had been called into action, seemed to work reasonably well. But OK would not do if Claire and I were to hit it off, I simply HAD to be much better than OK, and I made a mental note to Google sex tips when I got home to reinforce my boudoir repertoire.

'Well a hot bath and a book are pretty hard to beat, so I'd say even average sex might struggle to beat that!' Then I wondered why I was saying things which seemed to heap even more pressure on me. I quickly changed the subject. 'So I don't think I've ever seen you at Tottenham Court Road station, bar that one time?' I asked.

'Why, have you been looking out for me?'

Oh shit, could she know somehow that I had been?

'No! Of course not,' I lied mid-chuckle, trying to hide my instant discomfort. 'But I tend to recognise faces from round the station when I'm coming in and out at similar times every morning and evening,' I recovered, secure in the knowledge that there was surely no way it was possible that she knew that I'd been heading to the station at the same time every day in the hope that I'd bump into her again.

'No, I'm very rarely at that station actually. I work as an audit manager for a large accountancy firm and one of my clients is out that way, but they're a very small client so generally I'm only out there two or three times a year so no wonder you've not seen me around there.'

We continued back and forth for the next couple of hours. Claire was engaging, articulate and passionate. She spoke enthusiastically about her love of travel and the various frustrations she found within her career of doing something for such a large chunk of her life which didn't fill her heart with passion and pride. She said she would love to be a charity worker and help those less fortunate, but felt scared to make the jump.

'And now you're starting your journey towards your first novel?' I asked.

'Hardly!' she replied, taking a sip of wine as she did so, 'I just thought it seemed like a fun thing to do, and I think it's important to do things that you find fun, that don't necessarily have a "goal" at the end of the journey, that you just do solely because you enjoy doing them.'

'You're right,' I said, in genuine agreement with her rhetoric. 'I enjoy having my feet tickled, so I'm going to make sure I allow time for myself to employ a designated foot tickler at least once a week going forwards.'

Claire laughed. 'Well if the audit doesn't work out I'll let you know my tickling rates, but I don't come cheap,' she responded, clutching her wine glass tightly, smiling broadly, head tilted slightly downwards, eyes locked on mine.

We were halfway through our third drink; conversation had flowed so easily we just seemed to be on the same wavelength, I thought, when the bell rang out.

'Do you want one for the road?' I asked.

'No, the road does not need one,' Claire replied. 'Got work tomorrow and any more than three glasses of wine and I'll wake up wishing I hadn't!'

'Good point,' I replied, 'I get carried away sometimes'

'Well it's good to get carried away from time to time, just maybe not on a Wednesday evening with work in the morning, even if it is a designated wet Wednesday.'

I grinned in response and realised that I really didn't want the evening to end and really didn't want her to leave.

We left the pub. Claire said she needed to head to Angel station to get back to Balham, so I said I'd walk her back to the station. She protested there was no need, but I argued it was a nice evening and would be a nice walk. As we walked, my mind went into overdrive on what I'd do when we got to the station. The issue was we weren't on a date, we'd bumped into each other by chance, and decided that we'd 'grab a drink'. That isn't a date. On a date you're assured that the two of you are on the same page about there being a potential romantic theme to the evening, but in this scenario it was hard to know where you stand. She had certainly seemed flirty at times and I was pretty certain that we'd both enjoyed each other's company. But maybe she was just one of these really friendly girls, maybe she had a boyfriend? No, I thought, surely if she had a boyfriend, she wouldn't go for a drink with, to all intents and purposes, a random stranger? But maybe she would? Was there really any harm in it, though? She certainly hadn't behaved inappropriately for someone with a partner; surely a man and a woman can get to know each other and become friends without there needing to be a romantic element to it. It wouldn't be questioned if it was a man I'd met at the writing course and decided to grab a drink with, so why should the fact that Claire is a woman change that?

'Right, well this is me,' Claire said as we arrived at the entrance to Angel.

'So it is,' I replied. 'Listen, would I be able to get your number? Would be useful in case I have any questions about the course.'

'Sure, you can take my number. If I start getting late-night calls filled with heavy breathing I'll know who to tip the police off about,' Claire replied, 'and message me questions solely related to the course, yeah', Claire continued, raising her right eyebrow ever so slightly and I was sure I detected a hint of sarcasm in her voice as she tapped her number into my phone. 'That's Claire Barrett, double R, double T.'

'Great, I'll give you a missed call and you'll have mine. Jamie Green, one G, one R, two Es, one N.' Claire smirked and hit me over the top of the head with her handbag.

'Oh you're a card, aren't you!' she laughed.

'Now who has issues with violence?' I responded, the alcohol in my system helping to loosen me up.

'Right,' Claire went on. 'I shall see you next week then, I guess, don't forget to do your homework.'

'Yes, next week, homework will be completed in good time, don't you worry about that.' And both of us paused momentarily, waiting for the other to make a move. I brought my hand up for a friendly handshake. Unfortunately, at precisely the same time, Claire moved her body in towards mine for a hug. My outstretched fingers jabbed sharply into Claire's left boob, 'Oh god, I'm so sorry, that was a complete accident,' I gasped, flustered and panicked.

'So, GBH followed by sexual assault. They say murderers tend to build up to it, should I be worried for my life? Is that where this is leading?' Claire asked with a cheeky grin on her face.

'God no, I would never murder you,' I gasped, still in a fluster. A couple linked arm in arm walking past as I said it gave me a horrified look and turned to look at Claire, who gave them a smile, seemingly reassuring them that everything was OK and they carried on their way.

'Well that's good to know,' Claire responded, holding her hand out for a handshake. 'Slowly with the hand, Green, carefully does it. This is an invitation to a handshake and nothing more, Mr Gropey Groperson.'

Still feeling exasperated at the whole situation, I responded, 'Yes, yes a handshake, excellent.' I shook her hand and with a smile she turned on her heel and walked into the station entrance. With a swipe of a card she was through the ticket barriers and down the escalators.

And, strangely and unequivocally, I knew that I had fallen in love with the lady descending slowly on the escalator down into the depths of Angel station.

Chapter 19

'Get the fuck out of here,' had been Ozzy's exact response when I'd explained I'd bumped into Claire from the station at my writing class, sounding like a young but ambitious Italian/American in 1920s New York City trying to muscle his way into the upper echelons of the US Mafia.

'She was definitely leaning in for a kiss, mate,' said Ozzy whilst clutching his bottle of Peroni as we settled in for a drink at the Prince Albert and I'd explained the full story of my chance encounter with Claire.

'It did sort of seem that way,' I replied, 'and I did think she was quite flirty all evening, but above everything else we just seemed to get on so well; we just clicked. We chatted about all sorts of things; work, hobbies, what we hoped to do in the future, everything just seemed to flow so well and, since leaving her, I sort of can't wait to see her again. And she's genuinely funny, extremely witty, she's clearly extremely clever.'

'Well that all sounds good then,' Ozzy responded, 'when are you seeing her again?'

'Well I guess on Wednesday at the writing course.'

'But you've got her number, surely you'll send her a cheeky little text?' asked Ozzy.

'But what do I say, "hello, see you Wednesday"?'

'I don't know, maybe ramp it up a notch, maybe ask her if she fancies getting a bite to eat after the class on Wednesday. But I think you've got to let her know that you see this as a date, so when you ask, make sure you say: would it be OK to take you for something to eat? That way it's implying that you're going to take her out for something to eat and it definitely gives it more of a date vibe rather than two pals on the same writing course grabbing a bite to eat after their class. Whatever you do you've got to make sure that you kiss her, because the longer these things go on without a kiss the harder it becomes and you get to the stage where both of you think we must just be friends. And you don't want that, do you?'

'Well no, she seems absolutely lovely, and she's definitely beautiful, so yes I think I'd love to have something extra come of it,' I responded, being extra careful not to blurt out that I loved her.

'I don't think you should take dating advice from Ozzy,' Gary chipped in.

'What the fuck is wrong with my advice, you dick,' Ozzy responded, seemingly offended.

'I'm just thinking about the time I was going on a date with the girl from South Harrow and I was going to meet her mates and I'd told you that she had said she was a feminist so you said you'd put a screensaver on my phone of a famous feminist.'

Ozzy and I looked at each other and laughed, recalling the incident.

'I turned up and when all of her friends were in close vicinity, made a point of pulling out my phone and pressing the home button within eyeshot of all of them, and they gasped and said, *Oh my god why have you got a picture of her on your phone?* And I said, *Because I'm a big supporter of feminism*, beaming proudly and placing my arm around Katie whilst she squirmed and tried to get out of my grasp.'

Ozzy and I were laughing out loud now.

'It's not funny, they said. *What about the children she killed, she's definitely not a feminist.* Little did I realise you'd put that Myra Hindley's picture on my phone who apparently isn't famous for feminism, rather is more famous for killing small children!'

Ozzy and I grabbed onto each other for support as we fell about laughing.

'It's not funny! I liked her and she would never see me again, told me pretty much instantly it wasn't working and asked me to leave!'

Cue further laughter, slightly harsh but picturing the scene was too much.

'I waited outside the pub for half an hour and then sneaked back in to see if she'd calmed down, but she just seemed even more angry. Told me I was becoming really creepy and wanted me to leave and not contact her again. I tried to protest that I didn't know who it was and was only trying to show support for feminism but I just don't think she got it and one of her male friends pinned my arm up behind my back really roughly and marched me to the door of the pub and literally threw me through it. I tripped as he shoved me and fell face first into a muddy puddle. I looked up and there she was at the pub window with her mates, all laughing uncontrollably at me. I think sometimes because I might be a little bit different people think I don't have any feelings at all, but that hurt.'

Seeing that Gary genuinely seemed quite upset by the outcome of the whole incident, I tried reasonably unsuccessfully to control my laughter while Ozzy was at the stage of laughing silently, unable to breathe, with tears streaming down his face.

'I know, mate, that doesn't sound nice,' I replied, having stifled the laughter completely by this point. 'The moral of the story, though, is don't trust this idiot,' I said, pointing at Ozzy, still incapacitated through laughter.

'It's not funny,' Gary spat sulkily. 'And that's exactly the point I was making. Don't listen to that idiot's advice.'

'Come on, Gary, admit it, it is a bit,' I replied, putting an arm round his large frame and giving him a gentle, friendly squeeze.

Gary shrugged me off, smirked and let out his trademark machine gun laugh.

Finally having recovered from his fit of laughter, Ozzy changed the subject. 'But what about that sort at your work that you're obsessed with?'

'Colette, yeah, that's an issue, I guess. I think there's almost been a slight infatuation with Colette—'

'Slight?' Ozzy cut in.

'Yes, slight!' I continued, momentarily agitated by the implication that it had been anything more. 'As I was saying, a slight infatuation for some time now and I guess that doesn't just instantly disappear. But the more I think about it, the more I'm unsure of how nice a person Colette actually is. I'm not saying she's a bad person or is evil or anything like that. I guess maybe she's perhaps just a little bit selfish,' I said with a sigh.

'Well personally I think you need to fuck this Colette off, you've been working with her for fucking ages and you've got absolutely nowhere with her. This Claire bird sounds like she's genuinely interested and you say she's beautiful and there's a connection between the two of you, so if you don't forget about that Colette bird sharpish you're a fucking mug, mate,' Ozzy said, very kindly.

'I think you're right, to be honest, mate, but feelings aren't things you can just switch on and off. When I see Colette I feel these things and I think these things and sometimes you can't just put a block on them,' I argued.

'You sound just like a fucking bird,' Ozzy responded angrily, downing the rest of his Peroni as he did so in an overt display of machismo.

'Oh sorry, I'd forgotten what a massive geezer you are!' I spat back, mockingly downing the rest of my pint, burping and slamming the pint glass down on the table as I did so before apologising to the girls on the next table as they looked over in disgust. 'See how you bring me down!' I said, smirking as I did so.

'Don't blame me for your poor table etiquette!' Ozzy responded, laughing as he did so.

As I wandered home that evening I thought to myself about my next step. I had to grab the bull by the horns, I thought, what if Claire had been moving in for a kiss the other evening? I'd have looked incredibly dismissive by holding out my hand for a handshake. Admittedly groping her boob whilst doing so was more friendly but obviously that was an accident so maybe she thinks I'm not interested? What if she likes me but runs off to Morocco forever with some other fella because she thinks I'm not interested? She was the one doing all the flirting and the moving in for, at a minimum, a hug and possibly even a kiss, and I probably flirted very little in comparison and went for a formal handshake to end the evening. No, Ozzy was right, I had to send her a message and make sure that I offered to take her out for something to eat after the tutorial on Wednesday. That would be a clear statement of intent that I would like to take her on a date surely. I would insist on paying for the evening, not in a cocky, arrogant way, but I'd say I've invited you out for a meal so it's only fair I don't expect you to pay, and then surely she would see that I was interested in her.

And for the first time in what seemed like an eternity, I went to bed that evening filled with a sense of genuine excitement.

Chapter 20

The Chronicles of a Malfunctioning Male

I think Sundays are my favourite day. I know things still go on, almost pretty much as normal these days; shops are open, transport runs pretty much as it does in the week, but there's still a definite atmosphere of relaxation, one where it's seen as socially acceptable to spend the whole day lounging and recuperating.

And this Sunday was special, as this Sunday I was going to message Claire and ask her out on a date. Sunday seemed the perfect time to message Claire about Wednesday evening. A few days in advance so hopefully won't be too late notice, at the end of the weekend when after all the fun (I'd spent the weekend tidying my flat and rearranging my furniture in a desperate, and ultimately failed, attempt to give myself more room and watching the whole of series two to four of *Minder*) has been had and people are enjoying a bit of downtime before getting back into the rat race.

Yo, Claire, how's it hanging? I typed into WhatsApp. No, that's a stupid thing to say to a girl, to anyone actually – sounds like I'm a bit part in *The Fresh Prince of Bel Air*.

Wassup, Claire, how's tricks? No, too Budweiser advert.

Easy, Claire... No. Just no.

Hey Claire, hope you've had a great weekend. I was wondering if I could take you for dinner after class on Wednesday? X

Hmm…kiss or no kiss? Yes, kiss definitely. To not put one is lacklustre, and I'm asking her on a date, for fuck sake, definitely kiss. And send. And wait. It's 19.17, she was last online at 19:15. Two blue ticks! She's read it. That does mean she's read it, doesn't it? Yes, pretty sure it does, one tick means it's delivered, two blue ticks means the message has been read. Hmm…last seen at 19:19, she's gone offline after reading it, why hasn't she responded? Give her a chance, for fuck's sake, she's probably in the middle of doing something and has just had a quick glance at her phone. You've not sent her a message filled with abuse, you've asked her to dinner, she'll respond either saying that she would like to take you up on the offer or that she can't make it/doesn't want to come to dinner with you. Oh god, I hope she doesn't say she doesn't want to, or words to that effect. I think she's too nice to just say, 'I don't want to have dinner with you, you weasely little scrotum.' She'd say something like, 'Ahh, thanks for the invite but I've got to shoot off after class, maybe some other time.' Which would get the message across in a kind way without being so direct as to look like she's turned me down completely, yet we'd both know that there would be no other time.

My phone buzzed and I grabbed it from the sofa so quickly it nearly shot out of my hand and onto the floor.

Hey, Jay, my weekend has been perfect, thank you. Relaxing – lie-ins, no work, me-time, bliss! Dinner sounds splendid, I look forward to it! X

And I've no idea why I did it, but I got up from the sofa, moonwalked over to the mirror on the wall in my living room, smiled at myself and winked. Right, enough of the looking in the mirror 'I'm Tom Cruise from *Top Gun*' shit, I've got three days to plan the perfect date! Better respond first, try not to sound too excited though.

Sounds like a brilliant weekend! Great, I'll book us a table then, let me know if there's any food you don't like. X

Claire responded quickly. *I'm open to anything, looking forward to a surprise, thanks for booking! X*

I Googled 'restaurants in Clerkenwell'. Dans Le Noir.

Dining in absolute darkness, being hosted and served by a visually impaired person, will change your perspective of the world by inverting your point of view. It is a sensory experience that awakens your senses and enables you to completely re-evaluate your perception. Unusually, you will discover a sensory journey, a human exchange and a social conviviality…

Wow, sounds like a very unusual concept, but not a first date place surely, I want us to be able to see each other and talk to each other.

Maybe I'll make a list and put the pros and cons of each and then make a decision.

Morito: pros – intimate restaurant, great reviews, tapas, seems datey but not too formal datey. Cons – can't book for dinner, may end up in a queue.

Quality Chop House: pros – excellent reviews, nice decor, everyone likes a steak. Cons – vegetarians don't like steaks. More pros – Claire mentioned nothing about being vegetarian which surely she would have mentioned if that is the case.

Shawarma: pros – Middle Eastern food, apparently relaxed atmosphere, authentic decor. Cons – decor perhaps too relaxed for a date, maybe doesn't scream romance, more mid-week catch-up with friend.

Zetter Townhouse: pros – impressive building and decor, excellent reviews, cocktail lounge in the building which would be lovely to retire to after food. Cons – just looked at the prices on the menu, ouch.

I weighed everything up and decided to push the boat out. As Ozzy always said when trying to get me to spend money on something I didn't particularly want to do, 'You can't take it with ya!': the type of cavalier attitude that sees people bankrupted and turfed out of their homes at the age of thirty-three. But sod it, something about this girl seemed special. I didn't want to look like I was trying too hard, but, at the same time, I wanted to show that I'd put some effort in and that I liked to go to nice establishments.

Chapter 21

The Chronicles of a Malfunctioning Male

That Wednesday in class I couldn't concentrate at all, rendering yet another week's tuition fees absolutely worthless, and was made to look a fool when to the question of 'Jamie, can you tell us any of the methods the author uses to build tension in the atmosphere in this scene?' I replied, 'It helps to have a dedicated space that you use for writing.' A response which garnered puzzled looks all round, although when I spotted Claire out of the corner of my eye I did notice that she appeared to have burst into a fit of giggles.

Class finished and I walked up to Claire noticing how she looked particularly stunning today, wearing a floral dress which fitted her perfectly and her long dark hair bounced off her shoulders as it sat in large waves and when she smiled at me her eyes sparkled seemingly with happiness and mischief in equal measure.

'So are you hungry?' I asked.

'I sure am, where are we heading?'

'There's a place nearby called the Zetter Townhouse, I thought we could head over there for a meal, I've not been before but a mate from work recommended it,' I replied, trying to seem casual and also trying to make it look like I had mates at work.

'Ooh lovely, I've never been either but know of it, it looks super fancy!'

Great, this was a good response, I thought, and we made our way from class towards the restaurant. One thing I absolutely loved about Claire was that she always appeared to have interesting things to say, things to talk about. I always thought I talked a reasonable amount but I think I'm more of a listener than a talker, so when I connect with someone who interests me in what they have to say, it's a rare but refreshing change.

Today, as we walked towards the restaurant, Claire was talking about a holiday she had taken last summer to Greece. She was very interested in Greek mythology and had wanted to go to Rhodes to see where the Colossus of Rhodes had straddled the port area many years ago and visit the ruins and see the whitewashed buildings sitting on the cliffs looking out to the sea in Lindos.

'It was absolutely stunning,' she went on, 'sitting on top of these white buildings having walked through a maze of passageways and alleyways to get there and then looking out onto the clear blue Mediterranean Sea and eating the most amazing Greek food I've ever tasted. I think Greece is hard to beat. I mean, how do they make their Greek salads taste so nice?' Claire asked, eyeing me quizzically, hands held palms facing up to emphasise the question.

'I'm kind of hoping that's a rhetorical question, Claire,' I replied and she laughed.

'I just don't know, it's only a few ingredients thrown together, no cooking, no nothing, but I've tried to recreate it back home and it never tastes the same.'

'Maybe it's the mixture of the ingredients and the sea air,' I answered semi-seriously, 'maybe you should knock up the salad and then quickly jump in a cab down to Brighton to enjoy it.' Claire laughed again and pushed me away playfully.

'I'm not sure Brighton would have the same effect somehow.'

'Yeah you're right, you're probably more likely to have a seagull shit in it,' I replied, 'maybe that's the secret ingredient you've been missing.'

Not being particularly accustomed to eating in fancy restaurants, as we arrived at the restaurant, I was instantly overwhelmingly impressed and mentally patted myself on the back for my selection. The restaurant was set within a terraced mansion on a row of near identical townhouses. They had clearly been maintained particularly well as they retained the charm and character of period buildings of the Victorian era but had clearly been given a modern-day dab of polish. We ascended the few steps up towards the oversized, solid wooden door which had been painted pristine black and led to the restaurant entrance.

And if the exterior had impressed me, the interior positively wowed me. Inside the entrance and throughout the restaurant, the walls and the ceilings were decked in elaborate and intricately designed flora which gave the impression of entering an extremely colourful and tasteful indoor English country garden, or walking into a scene from *Alice in Wonderland*.

'Wow, this restaurant is amazing!' Claire exclaimed as I casually asked the smartly dressed woman at the entrance for the table for two that I had booked earlier that week, momentarily panicking as she took slightly longer than expected to locate the booking before directing a nearby waiter to show us to table 22 which was tucked in a nicely secluded spot in the corner of the main restaurant, a few feet away from a grand piano which stood elegantly beside an open fireplace.

'Well yeah, it's OK,' I responded nonchalantly after the waiter had left us to our menus, 'for London, of course. Normally I'd prefer to jet to Paris for dinner which I tend to find infinitely better, but for London this is fine,' I continued intentionally pretentiously.

'OK, Mr Foodie, well if you charm me enough this evening I'll allow you to jet me off to Paris next time then,' Claire responded cheekily, squeezing my forearm as she did so, the sensation of her hand on my arm feeling warm and relaxing.

'Sorry did I say Paris? No, I meant Acton. I usually jet off, on my bicycle, to Acton, and I find the food in the plethora of fried chicken establishments there far better than in these unauthentic central London dives.'

We eyed the starters intensely for a while, swapping ideas on what we might choose. Claire had a wonderful way with words and as I sat there gazing at her beautiful face lit up with enthusiasm as she discussed the merits of choosing the pâté for a starter due to her love of caramelised red onion over the possibility of choosing the whitebait, because, in her words, 'who doesn't like whitebait?', I felt like I could watch her face and listen to her voice all night, falling almost into a distant and perfect dream.

'What do you fancy, Mr Starey Starerson?' Claire asked as she looked up, jolting me out of my dream and back into reality.

'Sorry,' I replied in a mild panic at having been caught out staring at her, 'I wasn't staring, I was just thinking intently about what I'm going to order.'

'It's OK if you can't tear your eyes away from the beautiful face that God cursed me with,' Claire continued winding me up, the smirk on her face growing as she did so. 'So what will you have for a starter then, seeing as you've given it such deep consideration.'

'Oh, er…' I responded, even more panicked this time as I realised I didn't know what was on the menu, 'erm…the…'

'Your thinking time didn't go quite as planned, did it? Or have you forgotten what starter you were so intently focussed on, just then?'

'Erm…well…just shut up, you, before I reach for my umbrella again!' I continued jokingly as I saw the smirk on Claire's face develop into a full-blown laugh.

'Is this how this relationship is going to be, ay, based on the threat of violence executed through the use of your dreaded umbrella?'

And both of us suddenly became slightly more conscious of ourselves as we realised the term 'relationship' had been used. Claire, who was lent forward into the table on her elbows, looked down at the plate in front of her, avoiding my gaze, and brushed her hair behind her ear as she did so. I leant forward into the table on my elbows also and took her hands which were clasped together in one of mine and with the other hand gently lifted her chin up with my forefinger so that her eyes met mine once more.

'Yes,' I said, 'to a relationship based on the threat of violence.' We parted hands and I picked up my glass and raised it to Claire's and we clinked together and drank before both descending into a fit of giggles.

Eventually we settled on the whitebait and the pâté to start and shared them before both ordering fillet steaks for our mains. During our mains the conversation turned to previous loves.

'I think it just took me a little while to realise that actually she wasn't a particularly nice person,' I said honestly before I stuffed some of my steak into my mouth untidily, then, realising I had to wait a few seconds before finishing my story, rolling my hand in circles to indicate there was more to come and frantically chowing down on my mouthful of food so that I could finish what I'd started. 'She could be extremely charming but, actually, I think she was…she is, quite a selfish person. And weirdly it isn't easy to say that because I spent a significant period of time with her and I don't want to feel like that time was wasted on someone. I think sometimes you can like the idea of something better than the actual reality of a situation,' I finished, suddenly wondering if I'd said too much, and worrying that it sounded like I still cared for her, which I did I suppose, but certainly not in that way, certainly not in a way that would ever make me get back together with her.

'I know exactly what you mean, but I don't think time is ever wasted,' Claire replied, 'as long as you learn from your past.' We were once again both sat on our chairs leaning forward into the table on our elbows and this time Claire reached forward and took one of my hands in hers. 'I was with my ex-boyfriend, fiancé I should say, for a long time. I thought he was the man of my dreams,' Claire continued and instantly I pictured myself with a faceless man in a headlock, 'until it turned out that he really wasn't. I was on my lunch break whilst working on a client up near St Paul's, just browsing the shops, and I saw him; he used to work up the road in Bank. And I was just about to call out his name when I noticed him walk into Agent Provocateur, you know the lingerie shop?'

'Yes, I know of it,' I replied.

'So I thought oh wow, what's he thinking of getting me so I decided to follow him in. And friends often ask me, were you spying on him at this point? And I always say I genuinely wasn't spying on him, I was actually excited to find out what he was going to buy me! And so I saw him pick up a lingerie set and I remember thinking it was a nice choice; stockings, suspenders, classy, but with just a hint of sluttiness to it, tasteful sluttiness.' And I laughed.

'Ahh, tasteful sluttiness, the best kind of sluttiness I find; highbrow sluttiness.'

'Exactly that,' Claire continued, 'except when he called the assistant over she asked him what size he'd like it in, and he responded a size 8. And I'm a size 16 so size 8 would definitely be no good to me whatsoever. I was confused and backed out of the store quietly. It was like I'd pressed rewind on myself; on CCTV I must have looked like some kind of nutter.'

'Which wouldn't have been wholly inaccurate,' I said, almost instantly worrying that this wasn't the time for jokes.

'Oi!' Claire replied, pulling her hands back from mine before I grabbed them back. 'By the end of the day I'd convinced myself it was nothing to worry about. He could have got my size mixed up, maybe it was a joke present from the whole work team or something, a little odd but I could see it happening at some workplaces, so when I got home I said to him that I'd seen him out at lunch that day and I'd noticed him buying lingerie. And he blew up, 'Why were you spying on me? What's wrong with you?' And I felt awful for a minute and tried to explain I wasn't spying, and then he just came out with it: 'I don't love you anymore. Look at the state of you,' which I felt was a little harsh. 'I've been seeing someone else for over six months now and I love her. I think you and I are over.'

'Wow, what an arsehole,' I responded almost instinctively.

'And do you know what I thought?' Claire asked.

'I can't possibly imagine?' I responded, dearth of any ideas for what would be going through someone's head after such a revelation.

'I thought: I'm glad he was grammatically correct in using "you and I" rather than "me and you" and I laughed.'

'You're joking, right?'

'No I'm not, actually, that was the first thing that came into my head. Why am I such an oddball?' Claire asked, tapping her temple with her forefinger.

'You're not an oddball,' I said. 'If it's any consolation, I think you're lovely,' I continued, the alcohol clearly freeing my tongue and releasing me temporarily from my inhibitions. 'Granted, on this occasion, the response was quite odd. But to confirm, I don't think you're an actual oddball.' Claire laughed and squeezed my hands. 'Just some things you do sit firmly within the odd category.'

'Well thank you for not thinking I'm an oddball. The tears came later though, believe me, but looking back, I'm a far stronger person now than I ever was in those days, far less insecure, far more confident in myself, and I think that's something that's important to take out of all of that.'

I agreed wholeheartedly.

'And when I look back, I almost pity him. I now genuinely believe he wanted to get caught and do you know why?'

I shrugged and shook my head, unable to fathom why someone would possibly do something so awful to anyone, not least the beautiful and lovely girl sat in front of me, never mind why they would actually want to get caught.

'Some people think it's the thrill but it's not. I think that probably for a year or so he realised he didn't want to be with me, but I think he was too weak to actually do anything about it, to actually sit me down, look me in the eye and say "sorry but I don't love you anymore".'

I nodded along, weighing up the thought in my mind, and I could see a logic behind the reasoning.

'So instead of being strong and telling the truth and letting me go my own way and not wasting more of my time, he just carried on, probably getting less and less careful with his deceit until he was caught and then he had a ready-made excuse for his actions by saying it's because I don't love you any more, I love someone else, basically justifying his cheating as a crime of love, like he was auditioning for a role in a Shakespearean play or something.'

'I see what you mean, actually.' I nodded, everything she had said making complete sense to me.

'Anyway, that's enough about the past. Learn from the past but never dwell on it, turn around and look forward with hope and excitement.'

'I'll raise a toast to that.' And we toasted to looking to the future with hope and excitement, surely two of the most wonderful emotions known to mankind.

Conversation flowed back and forth, the food we both agreed was first class, and the cocktails were the icing on the cake. Admittedly I felt I may have set the bar fairly low in the past, but as we left the restaurant and Claire linked her arm in with mine, my chest swelled with pride and I felt like this had been the best evening I'd ever had.

'You must let me get the food next time,' Claire scolded after I'd picked up the bill and we'd left the restaurant to wait for the taxi Claire had ordered.

'Who says there's going to be a next time,' I replied, the booze clearly making me far braver than normal.

'Oi!!' Claire responded, 'meanie.' And I laughed and she joined in, and I got the distinct and unmistakeable feeling that I wanted to be with this girl, the one I was linked arm in arm with, for the rest of my life.

We waited for Claire's cab with her cuddled into me, head leaning against the top of my chest and my arms round her, rubbing her back to keep her warm. As Claire's white Toyota Prius arrived, she tilted her head upwards towards mine.

'Well I guess this is me,' she said.

I moved my hands from her back and placed them each side of her head, cradling her face as I did so, lent forward, closed my eyes and kissed her.

Our lips must have been together for about five seconds, and as I gently pulled my head away from hers, Claire's eyes remained closed for a second or two longer.

'That was nice,' Claire said, scrunching her face up as she did so and hunching her shoulders up towards her head.

'It was,' I replied as I pulled her head gently towards me and kissed her again for just a second.

'Right,' Claire responded after a couple of seconds of staring in a drunken and dreamy haze at each other, 'I guess I'd better jump in this taxi before he gets bored of watching us snogging and buggers off.'

'Unfortunately, I guess you're right,' I replied.

'I've had a great evening, thanks again for getting dinner.'

'It really was my pleasure. I've had a lovely evening too.'

I pulled away from Claire, and we walked the few yards to the cab. I opened the door for her and she shuffled into the back seat, holding onto my hand as she did.

'I'll speak to you very soon,' I said.

'Looking forward to it,' Claire replied and with that I smiled, closed Claire's cab door and watched as she headed off into the twinkling red and white lights of the London traffic.

Chapter 22

I don't believe in love at first sight and I don't really believe in there being 'the one', I mean what if my 'one' lived in Outer Mongolia, or suddenly got run over by a bus, or, as would be pretty likely, decided that I definitely wasn't their 'one'? Would that mean there was just no way I could ever find love; the whole concept just doesn't make sense to me and my practical mind.

What I do believe is that there are certain moments in your life which are pivotal to the direction in which it will head and I believe the decision to choose a partner, the decision to devote yourself to one special person is one of these. Partners have such a huge effect on a person. They can build you up and they can break you down, they can make you feel as strong as an ox or they can make you feel a shell and shadow of your true self. And I don't think you can ever be totally sure when you choose a partner. How can you be? No one can read the future. So it's a huge decision, but at some point you have to make that leap of faith, jump in with both feet, no hands clinging onto anything behind you. Sink or swim.

Chapter 23

'So how did it go with the bird?' Ozzy enquired that weekend in the Prince Albert.

'It went really well!' I answered enthusiastically, 'you know when conversation just flows, and it felt like we could have stayed there talking for hours. She is actually really interesting to listen to and her sense of humour is gre—'

'Fucking hell, you don't have to go on, so did you bang it then?'

'Ozzy, for fuck's sake,' I answered angrily.

'Come on, man, we just want to know if you did the rumpy-pumpy, innit, the old 'orizontal okey-kokey,' Vijay intercepted, having glided over from the bar; a habit he seemed to have developed for involving himself in any bit of gossip he overheard.

'Vijay, this conversation doesn't even include you so I don't know why you're getting your big mouth into it,' I responded as Vijay and Ozzy looked at each other, laughing now, and I got increasingly pissed off that they seemed unable to see that I didn't find it a laughing matter.

'Touchy about the new bird, innit.' Vijay laughed as he glided back the way he came.

'So you fucked it then?' Gary added, predictably slow on the uptake.

'Gary, did you not just witness the interchange between us and garner that I don't want to talk about it, and I don't want Claire talked about in that way!' I countered, hoping this would bring an end to this conversation.

'Couldn't get it up?' Gary responded, clearly not getting the hint.

'No, you took your pants off and she burst into fits of giggles, pointed at your pathetic little wotsit, got dressed and left,' Ozzy chipped in.

'Yes, yes, your powers of perception are truly wondrous, you are both spot on as usual. I took my pants down, she laughed at my penis, I made a vain attempt to try and get it up anyway, failed, and watched as she walked out of my door, laughing still as she went.'

'Knew it,' Gary said deadpan as I gave him a puzzled look, wondering whether he had read any sarcasm in my voice or believed what I'd said to be a very candid confession of events.

'Right,' I said. 'Glad we've sorted that out then, who wants another drink?'

'Yeah, lager, please,' they both replied in unison.

'Yeah, well, you can both go fuck yourselves,' I replied, smiling as I did so, getting up and heading to the bar to buy a solitary pint as Ozzy started laughing and Gary stared into the distance, apparently wondering what could have prompted such an angry outburst.

Chapter 24

The funny thing about happiness (or, conversely, the lack of it) is that it filters into every part of your life. When you're happy you find yourself getting ill less, you find yourself bouncing out of bed in the mornings and you find yourself taking little setbacks in your stride rather than crying into your morning cup of tea.

That Monday morning I headed into work with a mixture of nerves, excitement and fear. I'd been selected by senior management to accompany a sales team to a new client on account of my length of service with the company and the product knowledge I had built up along the way. This was potentially a big opportunity for me. The world of sales seemed very glamorous. Dressing in sharp suits, indulging in a lot of meals out and drinks with clients and the potential to earn lucrative sums of commission. Looking at the sales people in our office I wasn't sure I met, nor wanted to meet the flash, brash persona that most of them exhibited. But I genuinely happened to feel that as long as I believed in the product I was selling, and every time I watched a cat eating a Hungry Kat product, I couldn't deny, they genuinely seemed to enjoy those meaty chunks, that through honesty and flexibility I would be able to develop a relationship with a client which would prove to be mutually beneficial.

The major, and it really was a major, downside to the opportunity was that it would mean working in much closer proximity to Miles.

'Mutually beneficial?' came Miles' response after I'd been asked by the sales team what I'd thought the basis of sales was. 'Mutually beneficial?' he continued, presumably to emphasise how ridiculous he found my idea. Three junior sales staff and I were sat round the table in the Forsyth meeting room, Miles having perched himself with one bum cheek on the table.

'Yes,' I responded, slightly unsure of what error I clearly appeared to have made. 'I think if the client sees that we genuinely want to provide a service and a product which will impact favourably upon their business, we will gain their trust and I think this is the best way to develop long-term and stable relationships with clients.'

'Long-term and stable relationships. Christ almighty, let me give you a bit of wisdom one of my incredible masters at Eton taught me. There is no such thing as a good business relationship; it's all a pretence, because each party will bugger the other one senseless given a sniff of a chance. And do you know why I'm the best? Because I like buggering,' Miles said, bizarrely, face too close to mine, our eyes locked for far too long for me to feel any level of comfort.

'Today you guys will bring the lube, and I will do the buggering, because if we don't, then it will be us bent over that table with our pants down, do you hear me?' Miles gestured to the rest of the room where the other sales staff all appeared slightly uneasy, but where they all nodded their heads in unison and consequently I felt vaguely humiliated.

'Right, Jamie, you can jump in with me and I'll drive us to their offices, are you guys OK getting the Tube? It's only up by Euston,' Miles shouted, his bad mood seemingly having evaporated.

'No problem,' the scared sales juniors chorused, presumedly glad to escape the awkwardness before hurriedly shuffling out of the meeting room.

Miles drove a Porsche. I'd known this before getting into his car because he had a habit of taking his keys out of his pocket and putting them down in front of him whenever he sat down and therefore it had been hard not to notice the Porsche key and keyring. It was a black Porsche Boxster, I noticed when we got to it. 'Genuine leather interior,' Miles remarked when we got in. 'Six-speed gearbox, 0–60 in 8.4 seconds, maxes out at about 150mph. I took it up to 138mph once on a stretch of the M1 on my way to a dirty weekend with some filly but had to take it down again pretty sharpish; the police are always on your case when they see a young guy in a motor like this.'

'It's very nice,' I said, trying to make it sound like I cared and was actually interested in the car, but, due to my poor lying skills, no doubt failing.

'And not that I need the help, but it is an absolute babe magnet,' Miles continued, turning his head towards me, winking and smiling.

'I bet,' I responded, refusing to return the smile and realising that I didn't actually care if he could tell I didn't care.

As we set off to the client offices, I was surprised at how excited I felt to be meeting our customers and to be involved in a sales meeting for the first time. Miles decided to give me a pep talk as we went.

'This is your first sales meeting, isn't it, so just get a feel for it, how these things work, obviously everyone will introduce themselves and then we'll get down to business. I'll be leading the pitch; we won't expect you to contribute anything today, just observe, see how these things work and then we'll wrap things up, maybe go for a quick scotch and then get back to the office.'

'Thanks, Miles, that sounds great.' Sounds like a sensible plan, I thought, nice introduction to the sales scene, just dipping my toe in the water.

We arrived at the offices just around the corner from Euston Square station and saw that the rest of the pitch team were waiting for us in reception. The reception was a large space with three ladies sitting behind a long desk at the end of it. Identical box-shaped lilac sofas were interspersed throughout the floor with a wide pathway in-between them for visitors to get to the desk and the security barriers beyond the desk, which were manned by several men dressed in suits who looked like they could comfortably also man the local Wetherspoons at the weekend. On the wall to the right was a huge screen playing promotional videos.

We collected our temporary passes from reception and within a few minutes a man in his early forties, tall, lean and dressed casually in untucked shirt, jeans and boots came and collected us. He introduced himself to all of us and I could feel that my hand had gone a little clammy as I shook hands with him and introduced myself as Jamie. We were led into a glass lift which looked out over the offices as we were taken up to the seventh floor. The Miles schmooze machine appeared to be in full flow as we went as he playfully recalled an anecdote of how he couldn't go nearby Euston Square station without recalling the time he'd had to sleep on the park bench for three hours after missing his train home when he lived north of London. Our host appeared unsure how to react to this story, however, laughing awkwardly before being saved by the ding of the lift as we arrived at our floor.

We arrived in a large meeting room with one large rectangular table in the middle of it, the windows looking out towards central London providing a beautiful view of the London landmarks towards the city and the many buildings along the Thames. London still had the ability to take my breath away. Four additional client personnel were sat on one side of the table, all dressed casually whereas we were all dressed in suits and ties. I wondered whether we had overdressed but then I thought that if I were on the other side of the table I'd be happy to see people touting for my custom to come smartly dressed, thinking it indicated a professional approach and sent a message of respect for the client.

'Thanks for coming into see us,' said Chris once everyone was seated, the man who had collected us from reception, 'we're very interested to hear what you have to say so if you'd like to kick off then we'll let you get straight to it.'

'Thank you very much, Chris, and thanks to all of you for taking the time out of your day to see us,' Miles began, standing as he did so before launching into a well-worded and I suspected oft-used introduction to the Hungry Kats product range. I had to admit Miles came across very eloquent in his pitch, making expressive use of his hands and with a relaxed, unforced smile on his face throughout. Miles continued for about five minutes, during which time the others from the pitch team chipped in to provide specific information on the current customer demographic, sales trends and market data, '…and so if there are any questions then please feel free to direct them to us now.'

'Thanks a lot for that, Miles,' said Chris. 'Obviously extremely important to us, what price would we be paying per unit?' Miles was obviously well used to this question, as you would expect, and produced a printout which he slid across the table to each of the client staff. 'As you can see, price per unit is on a sliding scale whereby we offer incentives dependent on the number of units ordered. And also, between you and me, I think I can be a little bit flexible with the standard rates we have on the sheet there. I'll just have to say you threatened me at knife point!' Everyone in the room chuckled at this and I sensed Miles was closing in on a deal.

'And what are the health benefits for the cat of eating the Hungry Kat product?' asked an attractive blonde lady wearing a floral dress, hands clasped in front of her, resting on the desk, a necklace of beads hanging from her neck. 'I'm going to allow our product specialist Jamie answer you on that one,' said Miles smiling broadly, and funnily enough he seemed to be gesturing to me. Even funnier, he'd said my name as the person who would respond to this question. And funniest of all, the gaze of everyone in the room appeared to be on me now. What the actual fuck? Just observe he'd said, first client meeting, get a feel for it. I didn't know the answer to that question. I had no idea I'd need to know the answer to any questions like that. But as I sat there, people continued to stare. What if I just slowly slide down my chair until I'm under the table and out of view of everyone? Maybe they'd forget who they were looking at? No. The pause was getting too long now, people were still staring, 'Erm…yes…multiple health benefits for the cat from using the Hungry Kats product.' Come on, think, you idiot! I racked my brain, my mind searching frantically throughout the deepest recesses of the millions of neural endings running through my brain, 'But we find the major benefit…' Come on! '…and the one we find resonates most with our client demographic…' Going to have to say something. '…is the benefits to the cats'….stool…extraction…mechanism.'

'Stool extraction mechanism?' asked the attractive lady, a puzzled expression on her face.

'That's right…' As I scrambled around my mind again in vain to remember the attractive lady's name, 'lady…' Oh god. 'The stool extraction mechanism.' Think of a way out, for the love of God, think of a way out. 'The anus.' Good job, you absolute dick.

'The anus?' asked the attractive lady, a puzzled expression forming on her face. It seemed like the table had shrunk in size and everyone in the room was suddenly two yards closer to me. I felt the sweat forming on my forehead and beads of sweat were running freely down my back by this point. I had no doubt I was as red as a beetroot and the familiar dizzy feeling of awkward embarrassment swarmed over me, infiltrating every inch of my being.

'That's right. We find cat anus health is increasingly important to our clients, which is why we are very happy the Hungry Kat product range addresses this need. If you want your cat to have a nice anus, this is the product for you.' Seven floors, about four metres from my current position to the window, if I sprint, I think I could build up enough speed to smash through the window and then I'd be free from this room and this meeting. With any luck I wouldn't die, maybe a car would break my fall and I'd just face a lifetime of horrific life- changing injuries. By the time I was out of hospital I'm sure people would have forgotten all about this little meeting. Maybe I'd get a bit of compensation; windows should have been strong enough to resist a sprinting male's weight. Maybe window companies would use me as the benchmark, and I'd get a new career sprinting at double-glazed windows to see if I could shatter them or not.

'OK… Interesting. Thank you very much,' said the attractive lady as she turned her head and raised her eyebrows to Chris, who wore a deep and concerned frown.

'No problem at all,' I replied, momentarily wondering if maybe my response hadn't sounded quite as strange as I thought it had in my head. A quick glance to my left to the rest of the pitch team confirmed that this was not the case; their faces filled with a mixture of shock, anger and horror glaring back at me. Although I could have sworn I noticed a hint of a smirk on the face of Miles. For some reason I smiled, raised my eyebrows and nodded back at them. A job well done. 'Right then, guys, off to the pub to celebrate one in the bag, me thinks,' I envisioned myself saying to the rest of the team as we left the meeting.

I was left to get the Tube back to the office afterwards; Miles zoomed off in his Porsche and the rest of the team got on a different carriage to me. I guess there was room for improvement in the sales pitch space at the moment. Yes, that would be my mark for today, C-: room for improvement.

Chapter 25

Although work was proving to be as depressing and unfulfilling as ever, outside of work my love life seemed (to the complete surprise of myself) to be blossoming.

Claire and I spoke every day. The feeling of excitement when I felt my phone buzz and saw that I'd received a message from Claire was matched only by the disappointment when I'd look down to see that O2 had messaged to let me know my bill was ready or that I'd used up all of my inclusive data, and our little chats in the evening over WhatsApp fast became the highlight of my day.

It wouldn't have been unfair to say that I was completely smitten by Claire, and, me being me, was simultaneously terrified that she would break things off. The problem was that although we had by this point been out a number of times and were gradually getting to know each other better and better, there had been no clarification as to what it was we were actually doing, how each of us actually viewed the situation and whether we were both on the same page with regards to moving forward.

So I decided to bite the bullet and invite Claire over to my place for a three-course meal cooked by yours truly at which I determined that I'd ask Claire if she would like to be my girlfriend.

I'd never cooked a three-course meal before, but how hard could it be? I wanted my meal to be both tasty, well presented and to exude a sophistication that I hoped would in turn reflect positively upon me, the chef. I could see it now; Claire marvelling at the texture of the scallops and me modestly suggesting that the key to the exquisite taste was in the freshness of the organic ingredients which I'd obviously sourced from a local food market, all the while fully aware that we'd both know the real key to the delicate intricacy of the menu was the culinary skills of the widely travelled, experienced and cultured chef. I could see the smugness of my raised eyebrow now; graciously accepting the acclaim, the bottle of vintage wine we're sharing only adding to the atmosphere of general exotic indulgence and elegance.

The Chronicles of a Malfunctioning Male

When I asked Claire over for a meal she seemed genuinely very excited which was great and she said there was nothing food wise which she wouldn't try with the exception of anything containing nuts as she had a slight nut allergy.

I settled on a menu of asparagus wrapped in Parma ham with a drizzle of balsamic vinegar for starters, spag bol with a twist, a remake of an old classic, and nobody of sane mind dislikes Bolognese, and, for dessert, my pièce de résistance, baked banana with brandy, brown sugar and vanilla ice cream. Ben & Jerry would take care of the ice cream, and I would take care of the rest.

The theory was that I would pop down to Portobello Market and source the freshest of ingredients. I could see myself checking the veg for firmness, gently wafting the scent of the balsamic testers towards my nose before tasting and critiquing the blends of flavour and selecting the pick of the bunch.

In the end, however, in the interests of time, I headed down to my local Lidl and picked up the ingredients there. This meal will succeed or fail on the skills of the chef, I told myself as I manoeuvred through the hordes picking up some absolute bargains.

The Bolognese I decided to cook in advance, the rest would be pretty quick and generally quite easy, I'd thought.

The front door to my place opened straight into my living room with a narrow kitchen adjoined on the end through a door-less doorway. The sofa which typically sat in the middle of the room, dominating the space, I pushed back against the wall to the right of the room. This left a large space in the middle of the room into which I placed the small wooden and, if I'm honest by this stage in its life, rather battered, foldup dining table. A red and white check tablecloth hid the tattiness of the table however and onto the tablecloth I placed an empty, old bottle of wine with a single white candle in it.

Taking a step back to assess the ambience, I was pleasantly surprised at how quaint and romantic the setting looked. If for a second you could ignore the incessant sound of the traffic outside, you could be forgiven for thinking you were in a very old and exclusive restaurant, perhaps tucked away in a remote corner of the Outer Hebrides, where the owners cook for one cover every night, more as a hobby rather than a business and customers have to trek for miles through blustery conditions, over treacherous, mountainous terrain to get there. Or something like that, anyway.

    I decided to dress formally for the occasion. I decided that would be another detail to this remote restaurant in the Outer Hebrides. Every evening, for the arrival of the two customers for that night, the proprietors of the restaurant would adorn their most formal wear for the evening, the elderly man dressing in black tie with white silk scarf and matching gloves, and the ageing lady with the sparkle in her eye wearing a full-length ballgown, silk gloves coming up to her elbows, smoking her cigarette from one of those holder things that they used to use many years back at high-society events. So I decided to put on the suit which I'd worn to the charity auction and styled my hair as neatly as I possibly could.

    Claire was arriving at seven thirty, so I took the pre-prepared Bolognese out of the fridge at 7.15pm and started gently simmering it so that by the time we had done our starters it would be nice and hot, ready to eat.

    I got all the ingredients for all the courses out and ready, wrapped the asparagus in the Parma ham and waited for Claire's arrival. I'd managed to find an old tin bucket rummaging through my old storage stuff and had washed it up, filled it with ice and stuck a bottle of Lidl's finest sparkling wine in it, from Romania I believe, an underrated country making great strides in the sparkling wine game. I laid a white tea towel across the bucket to finish off the look. I cracked open a bottle of Heineken, lit the candle, put Magic FM on the Sonos just quietly for some background music and waited for Claire's arrival, content in the knowledge that everything was prepared as far as it could be and that, thus far, all was in hand.

At 7.30pm on the dot the doorbell went, I opened the door and, before Claire could come in, bowed slightly,

'Welcome, madam,' I said, proffering my arm to Claire to take and guiding her in through the door. Claire wore a long beige coat with a big fur collar and a pair of nude heels. She grinned widely as she stepped through the door, 'May I take your coat, madam?'

'You certainly may,' Claire responded, removing her coat to reveal a beautiful black dress which came down to just below the knee and had dots of white scattered around it, the dress coming down low to reveal a hint of cleavage; tasteful, yet extremely sexy at the same time. She looked amazing.

I hung up Claire's coat and led her over towards the table.

'Oh wow, this looks wonderful!' Claire exclaimed as she approached the table I'd laid out. 'And a candle in a wine bottle, you old romantic!'

'Less of the old, please!' I replied as I pulled Claire's chair from beneath the table and tucked her into it.

'Will Romania's finest sparkling alcoholic grape based juice suffice for madam?' I continued, wondering at what point I was going to stop the pretence of being a *Fawlty Towers* style waiter before it got tiresome, unfunny and annoying.

'Ooh yes, please,' Claire replied, elbows on the table by this point, the fingers of each of her hands intertwined and her chin resting on top of them.

I popped the cork and poured a glass for each of us, carefully making sure to thumb the bottom of the bottle as I'd seen waiters do in the past, the white tea towel hanging over my forearm, gently wiping the bottle on it once glasses were poured and returning the bottle to the ice bucket.

'So, what's the first course?' Claire asked.

'The first course is a veritable treat for all the senses.'

'Wow, where's this culinary confidence come from? I didn't have you down as a whizz in the kitchen.'

'I don't know, actually. I don't really know why I said that.'

But after all that the first course was potentially the finest starter I'd ever tasted, in my more than humble opinion. The Parma ham crisped perfectly around the asparagus which was neither too firm nor too soft, and the balsamic vinegar added a delicate tang which almost sizzled on the tongue. All of a sudden my mind was filled with visions of me running the kitchen of a Michelin-starred restaurant in Mayfair, chastising my staff when the balsamic drizzle was smudged slightly on the plate as it came out to be served, throwing it away and ordering them to start again and this time to bloody well get it right.

'I actually can't recall a time when I've enjoyed a starter more,' Claire exclaimed as I collected her empty plate.

'Well, Claire, I'm a man of many hidden talents,' I responded far too cockily for a man who had just put some Parma ham and asparagus in a pan and poured some balsamic on it. 'You'll come to realise this in good time.'

'OK, Charlie big potatoes,' Claire answered, seemingly unimpressed by my added swagger since the success of my starter.

'Charlie, who?' I responded before dumping the plates in the kitchen sink and getting back to the business of building on the success of the starter with my main course.

As I tucked into the spag bol with a twist I was again pleasantly surprised with the taste. Granted, I'd not made the Bolognese nor the pesto, opting for the timesaving method of buying a couple of jars, but still, it took skill to blend the correct amounts of each and the pasta was boiled by me, nothing on the table had touched a microwave, something of which I was particularly proud.

'Mmm…this is delicious spaghetti Bolognese,' Claire exclaimed as she munched her way hungrily through the dish, 'did you make the sauce yourself?'

'Of course,' I replied. 'I mean, I didn't mix all the ingredients together or anything, I mean surely nobody bothers doing that when they do jars of it down at the supermarket, but I did make it all myself.'

'I see,' Claire responded with a puzzled expression on her face. 'So you heated it up, basically? I'm not sure you have quite grasped the concept of *actually making the sauce*.'

'Hey! It's a little more complicated than just heating it up, I'll have you know! And anyway, it comes with a special twist!'

'Ooh, what's the twist?' Claire asked eagerly.

'Well I looked up some recipes on the internet because I wanted to make something a bit more special than standard spag Bol, given it's a special night – the first time I'm cooking for you – and there was a menu which combined Bolognese with a pesto, to give it some extra flavour,' I said proudly, awaiting the acclaim my genius most clearly deserved.

'Oh good god,' Claire replied, the expression on her face seemingly almost startled by my creativity.

'I know, not seen it done before – I mean obviously it has been done bu---'

'Jamie, pesto has nuts in it!' Claire cut in, an air of rising panic clearly audible by now.

'What! N-no, just pesto, the sauce, the green stuff—'

'Yes, Jamie! It's a nut-based dressing! Oh my god, I'm feeling hot, my face is tingling, I've not got my fucking EpiPen! Jamie, call an ambulance now!'

'What?'

'An ambulance now, Jamie!!'

'Oh shit, OK.' I dialled 999, returning to the living room and standing by Claire as I did so, stroking her hair as I spoke.

'Ambulance please, my emergency is that we have a lady with a nut allergy and I've given her nuts. By accident!'

I looked at Claire's face and it had turned bright red and swollen significantly.

'Oh shit, her face has swollen up, everything, lips, eyes, cheeks, her head is enormous… Yes an ambulance now please, immediately! Enormous!'

I hung up, the operator saying a paramedic rapid response unit was on its way right now from Charing Cross Hospital and would be with us in a matter of minutes with an ambulance following shortly.

'Are you OK, Claire? Oh my god I'm so sorry, just breathe, Claire, don't panic, the ambulance is minutes away and then they're going to get you sorted. You look absolutely fine, no problems at all here.'

'Moo muwwy imiot,' Claire managed to get out of her swollen mouth, tears coming out of her red and puffy eyes by this point.

'Just breathe, Claire, just breathe' I added, not knowing what else to advise, rubbing her back and trying to comfort her as best I could.

'Can you breathe OK, Claire, don't try to speak, just nod if you can.'

Claire nodded, but I was too panicked to feel any smidgeon of relief. I heard the sirens not too far away and then the blue lights flashing outside and I rushed to open the door,

'She's in here,' I shouted to the two paramedics rushing into the room.

'Hello, can you hear me? Just nod if you can,' the middle-aged male paramedic, kitted out in the green uniform, asked Claire who was sitting still, tears streaming down her face, but concentrating on breathing. Claire nodded.

'I'm going to give you a shot of adrenaline. You're alright, you're going to be absolutely fine,' the paramedic said and I breathed a huge sigh of relief at his confidence and professionalism, and it was not an exaggeration to say I could have kissed him right there and then. Repeatedly. But I decided to let him do his job and treat Claire instead.

The female paramedic handed him a ready-made syringe and he took Claire's arm and injected into a vein on the inside of Claire's arm at the elbow fold. Claire instantly sat upright, her eyes widened significantly and her arms shot out rigidly. Within a minute, however, as the paramedic went through checks on Claire's wrist and her breathing, checked her eyes and opened her mouth to check her tongue and airways, the swelling was beginning to subside and again I considered kissing the paramedic, who coincidentally turned to me at the precise point the thought was going through my mind.

'We should take her in and monitor her for the next few hours as a precaution,' he said coolly. 'She has had a reasonably severe reaction to the nuts she's digested but all her vital signs are good. She's going to be right as rain within a few hours. You did well to ring the ambulance so quickly – in these situations acting quickly is absolutely vital, and you're lucky you're just around the corner from the hospital.'

'Oh my god, thank you so much, you guys are actual heroes,' I said addressing both of the paramedics who seemed to be taking the whole experience remarkably within their stride, the relief flushing slowly out of my system and causing me to go light-headed.

'You're going to be OK, beautiful, just keep calm, you're in good hands now,' I said, crouching down to her level as she remained seated, a reasonable degree of facial swelling remaining and the tracks of her tears still evident although her breathing seemed to have returned to normal levels and she was able at this point to take nice deep breaths.

'Just rest, Claire, don't try to speak for a bit,' the paramedic cut in and Claire closed her eyes as the paramedics manoeuvred Claire onto the stretcher.

As we travelled on the ambulance towards the hospital, I sat beside the paramedic alongside Claire who remained prostrate on the stretcher, my hands holding almost desperately onto hers as we went.

'I'm so sorry,' I repeated to Claire, absolutely horrified that I could potentially have killed her. 'I'm so sorry, I wanted everything to be perfect tonight, I wanted to ask you to be my girlfriend,' I said and immediately regretted that having slipped out at the most ill-advised of moments whilst being simultaneously relieved that Claire was asleep by this point.

Out of the corner of my eye I caught sight of the paramedic turning his head away from the pair of us. He proceeded to rest his elbows on his thighs and divert his gaze downwards between his open legs, seemingly shaking his head very slightly as he did so.

Once at the hospital Claire was wheeled in her stretcher to A&E and triaged. A doctor came along to check on Claire and said that she was going to be absolutely fine and that she should just rest for a couple of hours; he would come and do one final check and then he would discharge her from the hospital's care.

I sat next to Claire as she slept and, to my immense relief, her face seemed to have returned almost to normal, just her eyes still showing very slight redness and puffiness. I struggled to explain to myself how it happened, how I managed to get myself into these situations. Did anyone know that pesto contained nuts? Surely it should have nuts in the name if it contains nuts and can be this dangerous. My carelessness could have cost Claire her life, potentially. I had no idea what Claire would say when she woke up.

True to his word, in a couple of hours the doctor returned – blue scrubs on, clipboard in hand and stethoscope hanging around his neck, almost as if he were a doctor straight out of a soap – and woke Claire up.

'How are you feeling, Claire?' the doctor asked, shining a torch in her eye.

'Not massively enjoying the torch in the eye, but apart from that I feel fine, if not a little jaded,' Claire responded.

The doctor smiled. 'Looks like you're absolutely fine. Luckily your partner here did the exact right thing and called an ambulance immediately.'

'Well seeing as he was the one who attempted to kill me, I'm at least glad he managed to correct his cock-up,' she said, smiling.

'I'm so sorry, Claire,' I said, continuing to hold onto her hands but unable even to look her in the eye.

'Yes, your nut allergy is a reasonably severe one. Obviously today we've been able to treat your reaction and there is no harm done, but it is very important that you monitor exactly what you're eating. And you should always be in possession of your EpiPen'

'Yes, we're sorry,' Claire responded. 'I'll be far more careful in future; it was reckless of me to eat a spaghetti Bolognese with a twist without finding out exactly what went into it. And I do normally have my EpiPen on me, but I brought a different handbag out today of all days!'

'Indeed,' the doctor responded. 'Anyway, you're good to leave now provided you promise that you will not spend the night alone. Take these steroids and antihistamines with you and, if you experience any issues, come back. I very much expect you won't, but better to be safe than sorry.'

The pair of us thanked the doctor profusely and I shook his hand as he headed off down the corridor.

'Right then, Mr, we're getting a cab back to yours, and *you* are paying for it!' Claire exclaimed.

'Yes, no problem, we'll get a black cab from outside,' I responded. 'And, Claire, I really am so sorry.'

'Well it's done now, isn't it, but at least we know now how careful we have to be in the future. And it was reckless of me not to have my EpiPen on me so I'm not completely free of blame,' Claire said as we headed out of the hospital. I linked Claire's arm with mine in case she felt a little weak in her legs still, and we headed towards where a row of black cabs waited.

'This is a little awkward, but, in the interest of safety, I am requesting, no demanding, that you stay with me at my place tonight, it's literally doctor's orders?' I said to Claire, coyly, in the cab as we headed on the short trip back to my place.

'Hmm…they were literally the doctor's orders, I guess,' Claire responded as her head rested on my shoulder with my arm wrapped around her neck, 'I guess I'll have to stay the night, probably too dangerous for me to head home alone.' Claire rested her head on my shoulder and looked up as I turned mine down to hers.

'I promise to look after you. You will not come even remotely close to death again. Tonight I mean, obviously you're going to die sometime,' I bumbled on, ineloquently.

'That could be the sweetest promise anyone has ever made me,' Claire said sarcastically as the taxi driver pulled up outside my house.

Chapter 26

We both lay there exhausted and naked, Claire's head once again resting on my right shoulder, my arm once again wrapped around her neck, hand coming to rest on her breast.

'Well that was a pretty special way to end what has been an absolutely horrendous date, you undercover stallion you,' Claire gasped, her face a rosey-pink glow shimmering under a thin layer of sweat. I beamed back at her, heart nearly pumping out of my chest.

'Well, it wasn't my first time,' I replied with a wink and Claire smiled.

'Did you mean what you said back then?' Claire asked.

'About making sure you wouldn't come close to death again tonight?'

'No, silly! I mean what you said in the ambulance, when we were on our way to the hospital.'

I'd completely forgotten that I'd been talking to Claire in the ambulance, I'd thought she was asleep at that time.

'Oh...you heard me?'

'Yes I heard you. My eyes were closed and I was trying to rest, but I'd just been pumped full of adrenaline so it was actually quite difficult.'

'Well, yes, I did mean what I said, very much so.'

'So are you going to ask me then?'

'OK. I will. Claire, will you be my girlfriend?' Claire laughed and I frowned. 'Hey, what's so funny?'

'Sorry, nothing really, just you I guess. You're funny, you make me laugh. And that's a very good thing!' she exclaimed.

'Oh right, well good, I guess...are you going to answer? Or was that a diversionary tactic?' I questioned, thinking it was surely pretty harsh if she were to make me ask her the question secure in the knowledge that she was going to turn me down.

'Yes, my funny one, I would love to be your girlfriend!'

The Chronicles of a Malfunctioning Male

I pulled Claire towards me and gave her a big kiss, and I guess although the evening hadn't gone entirely to plan, what plan does? And the objective of the evening was to ask Claire to be my girlfriend and have her accept my offer, an objective that had clearly been achieved. So even though we'd ended up in hospital with my cooking nearly having killed her, the evening could be looked upon in no other way than as a success. We drifted off to sleep, Claire still resting on my shoulder and I felt entirely content and at peace with the world, and what a beautiful feeling it was.

Chapter 27

Something that may take you by surprise is that working in a call centre is sometimes not the most exciting job in the world. What makes it more bearable are the characters in the office. Many of those I'm referring to aren't even likeable characters. But spending parts of the day searching the deepest recesses of your mind to try to understand how someone like Jake from Accounts Payable ever managed to get through any kind of recruitment process given that I've never been able to stand within two yards of him without holding my breath due to the intensity of the BO seeping out of his pores and that I've yet to have a conversation with him which hasn't ended up with me being completely and utterly distracted when I've noticed a not insignificant-sized morsel of food resting snugly within his beard, actually provides the brain with a reasonable amount of stimulation to help the time pass.

Hardip, a rotund British Asian woman in her mid-forties had managed to climb to the heady heights of middle management, solely through from what I could see, possessing an ability to find an irrelevant and often nonsensical motivational quote for any given situation, sauntered over to the call team.

'A quick word, people,' she said, resting her ample right bum cheek on my desk. 'As you know on Wednesdays we down the phones at 4pm for training. Today we've got an external trainer coming in to provide some insights on motivation, something I'm a huge believer of and something which I have urged the powers that be to include on the training syllabus. Can anybody tell me why motivation is so important?' Hardip asked as the whole team simultaneously focussed their eyes anywhere in the room but on her. 'No takers? Well let me enlighten you then. Because, people, make no mistake about it, success is never owned, it is rented. And do you know what?' Hardip asked, scanning the team and resting her eyes on me causing me to hope desperately that this was a rhetorical question, 'the rent is due EVERY day,' Hardip said slowly for emphasis, staring hard at her audience. 'I'll leave you with that, people, back to those phones.'

I made sure to check that I was only shaking my head internally as Hardip sauntered back off to her office. I was reasonably sure she bought herself one of those motivational quote calendars every year and endeavoured to find a way to fit each day's quote into a part of work life every day. An external trainer. They wouldn't have asked her back, would they? I don't think I can recall an external trainer ever being asked back before, usually they were different. 'We are going to FUCK'. The words echoed around my head, and, for one disturbing moment, an image of Jan Straker entered my head, kneeling on my bed at home dressed only in black stockings and suspenders, peering seductively over the top of her glasses at me, a black whip in one hand and an enormous pink rubber dildo in the other. I shook my head to physically remove the image from my brain, mainly alarmed by the fact that I was a little aroused.

4pm came and the team made our way to the Beadle meeting room where the training was to be held. My relationship with the team had only just recovered from the embarrassment of Jan Straker's last training session, and I was praying that her arrival wouldn't stir up the memory of the incident in my colleagues' minds, and also hoping that I wouldn't have to make up any more imaginary meetings with friends and family to avoid being sexually assaulted.

Outside the meeting room I could see half of Rachel from Admin's head peeking just over the top of the frosted part of the glass walls of the meeting room. She was leading a shorter person across towards the meeting room whose hair I could just about make out. I let out a huge sigh of relief when I noticed that whoever it was she was leading over had dark hair. Rachel opened the door and entered the room, holding it open for the dark-haired lady to enter, her straw-like dark hair fell just below the level of her chin and she wore narrow black rectangular-shaped glasses, her skin was smooth but obviously heavily Botoxed.

The Chronicles of a Malfunctioning Male

She wore a very tight-fitting navy power suit on top of a white blouse and she scanned the room as she entered immediately, eyes resting on me, her eyebrow raising mischievously. And, suddenly, the whole room had turned towards me, most scowling, a couple grinning – of whom I was actually very appreciative – and one or two who looked like they could have actually spat blood at that particular moment in time. I sunk slightly lower down in my seat and hoped if I just closed my eyes maybe no one would be able to see me, sort of like the ostrich effect. Upon reopening my eyes, everyone had stopped staring at me; it had worked! I made a mental note to remember that useful trick the next time I was in a tricky interview or giving a presentation which wasn't going to plan.

'Guess who's back, ladies and gentlemen?' Jan Straker said whilst performing a curtsey once Hannah had left the room.

'Jan Straker,' Andy Sidebottom piped up.

'Rhetorical question, my friend,' Jan responded in her distinctive American drawl, 'but yes, you are correct. For those of you who couldn't remember, GET OUT OF THE ROOM NOW!' Jan roared, jolting everyone in their seats; a bunch of wide, slightly frightened eyes stared back at her as she giggled to herself. 'I'm only kidding, people. I'm here today to speak to you about motivation and, people, I want this to be an interactive session; the more you put in, the more you'll get out.' Oh god, I hate it when presenters say that at the start of a training session, 'What motivates you, what motivates me? Everything we do is motivated by something. When you go for a pee, you're motivated by your bladder telling you you need to pee, you're motivated by the desire to not pee yourself whilst sat at your desk, you're motivated by a desire to not experience that embarrassment.' Jan circled the room as she spoke, weaving in and out amongst the tables. 'What I want you to get out of this session is a) to work out what exactly it is that you want, now that could be in your work life, personal life, love life, in a sporting scenario, whatever you want, that is up to you. Then b) we are going to work out what motivational drivers you can install in your head so that when you come up against barriers that may prevent you from achieving your goal, thinking of these motivational drivers is going to help you smash straight through those barriers. Has everybody got that?' Jan discreetly dropped a folded-up piece of paper down onto my lap as she asked the question.

As Jan continued on her motivational spiel I picked up the piece of paper, tentatively unfolding it and wondering what horrors awaited me:

Wants: Gingey, naked, tied up, in my hotel room bed.

Motivation: The thought of Gingey lying naked and helpless, cock standing to attention like a sergeant major on parade while I sit on his cute little face, smothering it completely, slowly suffocating him in my pussy.

Below the words was a stick man diagram depicting a man lying tied to a bed, with a woman apparently straddling above the man's impressively large penis. The penis appeared to be longer than the man's legs which didn't bode well for me. Could this be construed as a death threat? She has expressed a desire to suffocate me.

My daydreaming was abruptly disturbed.

'Gingey!' The word made me nearly jump straight out of my seat. 'What do you want, Gingey?' The room turned to look at me and I looked at Jan as she leant over her desk at the front of the room, several buttons undone on her white blouse allowing a clear display of her ample cleavage. She took her pen with her right hand and slowly put the whole lot of it into her mouth before pulling it slowly out. *Oh god, think, think*, I thought as the pause got a little longer than would normally be expected.

'T-T-To be CEO of Hungry Kats,' I said, instantly realising I couldn't have given any answer that would make me look more like a wanker in the eyes of my colleagues.

'Excellent, Gingey, I can see how that would be…*one* of the things you really want,' Jan replied, raising that eyebrow above the top of her glasses at me once again whilst biting down on her lower lip.

Jan excused herself and left the room, returning a couple of minutes later with a large wheel about a metre in diameter propped up vertically on a tripod. The wheel was divided into segments much like the wheel of fortune from the popular nineties gameshow.

'Right then, people, we're going to play a little game which I hope will help with motivating you all to better yourselves. Because that's why we're all here, people, that's what winners like Gingey and I –' Oh god, please make her stop. '– tell ourselves in the mirror we're going to do, EVERY GODDAM DAY.'

I didn't even need to look up to notice the animosity being directed towards me from all corners of the room, but I appreciated the sentiment from the thrower of the crumpled-up piece of paper which bounced off my head, confirming that everyone hated me.

'So we're sat, roughly speaking, in a circle,' Jan began, 'and we're going to take turns going clockwise around the room to spin the wheel and whatever it lands on, you will direct towards the person to your left. You, boy,' Jan said, pointing at Graeme Phelan, a quiet Scottish man in his early twenties, the newest member of the team. 'Let's start with you.'

The exercise made its way round the room and I was asked to share with the group what motivated me to get this role. I thought 'Because I needed money' sounded a little unenthusiastic, but I didn't want to sound like too much of a wanker so I said, 'I've always enjoyed talking to people and helping to solve people's problems, so I looked for roles which combined these two elements and that directed me towards this role.'

'That's classic stuff, Gingey, note that one down, everyone, please, that's textbook material,' Jan responded, giving me a wink as she did so.

'Gingey, your turn. Step up to my wheel, put your hands on my curves and give me a spin, Gingey.'

I cringed as I stepped up to the front and spun the wheel, waited and watched as the ticker lay to rest on a segment:

Tell them one thing you don't like about them.

'Hit it, Gingey,' Jan said.

'Erm…really, I'm not sure that's going to motivate, surely it will serve more to divide the team won't it?' I asked.

'Gingey, the wheel must be obeyed,' Jan said, shaking her head as she did. 'Often people are unaware of flaws that others perceive within them and when they hear them out loud, this can motivate them to improve themselves. Now shoot, Gingey.'

I looked over at 'Office Speak' Andy, who was sat to my left, arms folded, head tilted slightly to the left, chewing on his cheek, almost daring me to tell him what I didn't like about him. Fuck it, it's true anyway, and maybe it will serve to make him less of a bellend.

'Erm… I guess, Andy, sometimes the amount of office-speak clichés you use can be a bit, not irritating exactly…but perhaps at times they might feel a little unnecessary. It kind of feels like you're making a point of saying something in a certain way, when it could be put in a far simpler way.'

Andy glared back at me, arms folded even tighter.

'Really, Jamie,' he spat, 'and do you have any examples of this?'

Fucking hell, Andy, just take the point and move on.

'It's nothing specific, Andy, it's just something I've noticed in the past. It's no biggie, I had to say something, it's nothing really, it's all personal preference, I guess,' I replied, realising now that I didn't actually care if Andy was content with continuing to come across to all sane people as a humungous bellend.

'No come on, I want to make sure we're all singing from the same hymn sheet here?' Andy probed and for a brief second I thought he was making what was quite a funny joke until I noticed the stern and serious look hadn't budged from his increasingly irritated expression.

'Come on, Gingey, there must be something, you need to back up your points with relevant examples. ALWAYS.'

'Well, I suppose, can't remember exactly, but you sent me an email the other week after I asked if you were able to help me organise the lunch rota because you have the most up-to-date list of people's holiday leave and it went something along the lines of this:

Jamie, hi.

Thanks for reaching out to me, am just now actioning the reversion to your email.

In relation to your request for assistance, I don't currently possess the necessary unused bandwidth for this.

Perhaps I'm just playing devil's advocate here, but might it not be an idea to kick this one into the long grass for the time being. To my mind there are a number of other current ongoing projects and I think I could see us picking up some low-hanging fruit from some of those a little easier.

I'm anticipating your next step and I can envisage you asking, how long is this one going to stay in the long grass before we bring it back onto the fairway and edge it towards the green. My answer to that would be, how long is a piece of string?

To summarise, thanks for alerting me to this, it's now on my radar and it is what it is. For now, though, I'm going to let you run this one up the flagpole and perhaps revert to me within a week or so to assess what value add we've achieved here.

KR

A'

'Textbook example of a professional email response to a colleague, I would say?' replied Andy, arms folded across his chest, seemingly genuinely pleased with my recollection of his absurd and at times nonsensical answer to a very straightforward request.

I scanned the room to see several nods of approval from the rest of the team. Am I the only fucking sane person in this place? That email screams *'I'm a massive bell end who doesn't really know what he's doing nor wants to do any work but if I use some fucking stupid office speak that doesn't really mean anything I hope I'll sound authoritative and clever!'*

'I just thought perhaps it could have been a bit more succinct, Andy, not a major criticism or anything, just seemed a lot of jargon in there which, if anything, confused me a little. I thought maybe you could have written: Sorry, Jamie, not got enough time at the moment, we'll do it some other time.'

'You seem to be suggesting I'm wasting time, Jamie? And, god knows, I don't have time to waste, I don't even have time to sign off my emails with my whole name, for God's sake, you said it yourself! I only have time to include the first letter of my name and I'm so busy I have to abbreviate kind regards to simply 'kr', so I think that means I'm pretty bloody busy don't you?'

'Well I—'

'And that's standard office lingo, Jamie,' Andy continued, cutting me off before I could answer and now standing up and taking steps towards me, growing increasingly accusatory in his tone and jabbing the air with his finger pointing towards me. 'I think what we might have all learned from this is that perhaps the issue lies currently with you, and maybe an action point for you going forward would be to brush up on your professional language skills, we are after all the call centre team. I mean, there's no need to re-invent the wheel, but I will let you get the ball rolling on that one,' Andy went on, tilting his head somewhat sympathetically I presume as he realised he was beginning to come across too aggressive; a condescending smile forming on his face. Then, for his pièce de résistance, he reached out and placed a hand on my forearm.

I wish we were on a floor well above the ground.

So I could throw Andy through the fucking window.

'OK, thanks, Andy. Maybe that's enough from us, perhaps we can "touch base offline" on this one,' I responded mockingly, beginning to get a little irritated that apparently no one could see the perfectly reasonable point I was making.

Andy frowned slightly and he sat back down in his chair. 'We are offline, Jamie?'

'It was a joke, Andy, don't worry about it. Let's just move on,' I responded as Andy slowly shook his head at me.

'Yes, people, let's move on,' Jan intercepted.

The rest of the session seemed to involve the dissemination of random nonsensical motivational quote after random nonsensical motivational quote. It was like the Instagram pages of every single personal trainer in London had instantly been sick into the room and we were drowning in a sea of their upbeat positivity. As we filtered out of the meeting room towards the pub at the end of the training session, it had definitely served its purpose to motivate me. The motivation however being to leave the company and do something which combined my passions with my qualities. Whatever that may be. Or failing that, to do absolutely fucking anything which wasn't working in a call centre for Hungry Kats.

The Marquis was packed again, although there were slightly less people outside this time as we headed deeper into the autumn months. I stationed myself inside this time, leaning on the end of the bar and breathed a huge sigh of relief as I took the first gulp of my beer; the first one always tastes so good, I thought to myself. Then I noticed Jan making a beeline for me, knocking all and sundry out of her path with a bottle of red wine in one hand and a full glass in the other, gradually becoming less full as she spilt it over random people as she marched over.

'Did you like my drawing, Gingey?' Jan asked as she arrived, squeezing in beside me at the bar and pressing her right breast up against my arm.

'It was an excellent drawing, Jan,' I said with pint glass held up towards my mouth, a slight nervous laugh, 'extremely graphic.'

'That was you and me, Gingey. Fucking.'

'Yes I got that much, J—'

'Fuck me.'

'Erm... I—'

'Fuck me.'

'Well, J—'

'Fuck me.'

'I mean in th—'

'In the wherever you want. Fuck me.'

'Jan, please!' I almost shouted. 'I have a girlfriend, Jan.' Then quietening my voice as people nearby turned their heads to find out what all the shouting was about.

'And I've got a husband. It's just raw fucking, Gingey, we ain't gon' run off and get married.'

'Jan, you're an incredibly sexy lady, and I am unbelievably flattered by the attention of such a magnificent woman. But I love my girlfriend, Jan, I could never hurt her like that,' I said in desperation, clutching at straws, but noticing Jan soften slightly and blush at the compliments.

'Oh, Gingey, you just know all the right buttons to push, don't you? I am tingling in all the right places and you know where I mean don't you?'

'Erm, well I...'

'My fanny Gingey. My fanny.'

'Oh...well...' I stumbled, utterly flummoxed, the awkwardness of the interaction thoroughly exhausting me and rendering me completely lost for words.

'I hope this girlfriend of yours knows how lucky she is.'

'She does, Jan, and I'm extremely lucky too. We're very much in love,' I said, doing my best 'genuine face' and hoping my bending of the truth wasn't screaming at her through my body language.

'Alright, Gingey. I get it. But believe me, Gingey, you and this broad of yours are gonna have bad times. Heck, maybe she'll fuck some other guy and you're gonna wanna get yours as well, and, believe me, Gingey, you're gonna get all sorts of revenge on that ho with this right here.' Jan pointed at herself and drew a circle around her body with her finger, 'We. Are. Going. To. Fuck.' Jan turned on her heels and marched off into the crowd, once more bouncing men and women off her as she went.

Chapter 28

That evening, Ozzy, Gary and I sat round a table by the bar in the Prince Albert.

'You should just fuck her, I think,' Ozzy said after I'd explained the events of today. 'If anything, you'd be doing it for the good of your career. To not do it would be like turning down a promotion including a pay rise and enhanced benefits.'

'Fuck her,' Gary cut in insightfully, coincidentally almost doing a perfect impression of Jan herself.

'Yep, deeeeeeffinitely should fuck her, innit,' Vijay added whilst delivering our drinks, obviously having been eavesdropping from the bar. 'You got der sexy older woman, ged a bit of experience innit, teach you a few things innit, make you a man.'

'I'm quite enough of a man as it is, thank you very much,' I replied beginning to get slightly annoyed that I seemed to be the only one thinking I'd done the right thing. 'I'm pretty sure I should actually want to have sex with someone before I have sex with them. And, most importantly, I have a girlfriend, with whom things are going really well, and I wouldn't do anything that could potentially jeopardise that.'

Ozzy and Vijay shrugged and screwed up their faces. Gary shook his head. Admittedly Gary could have been thinking of a different conversation entirely by this point, but clearly the consensus from the other two was that I'd had the opportunity to have sex and had let it slip through my fingers.

'On the plus side though, the more you turn her down, the more she's going to want you. She's probably at home frigging herself off over you right this minute,' Ozzy added.

'He's right innit.' Vijay nodded, having failed to leave our table after safely delivering our drinks.

'I have to admit it does seem to have that sort of effect on her.' And I shuddered involuntarily, making a note to give horrendous feedback on Jan's training to Hungry Kats in the hope that they'd never hire her again.

Chapter 29

The Chronicles of a Malfunctioning Male

As my relationship with Claire developed, it became more and more glaringly obvious that at some point in time she was going to have to be introduced to those closest to me, and that meant Dad, Ozzy and Gary.

Being that Dad was a big QPR fan and went to most home games, this year for his birthday he had suggested it might be an idea to head to see QPR v Millwall at Loftus Road. Dad had suggested I invite Ozzy and Gary also, which I had done. As the event approached though, I thought it might be the perfect scenario to introduce Claire to Dad. It wouldn't be too formal, should save the potential for any awkward silences; we'd be able to have a nice drink and it might be exciting for Claire to watch a football match too. The only issue was that I'd probably prefer it to be just Dad and Claire for the first meet and save the pleasure that would be meeting Ozzy and Gary for another time.

'So don't feel like you guys have to come tomorrow to see Rangers, just a little get-together with my dad for his birthday, you might be a bit bored. I mean, you will definitely be very bored, come to think of it, it is QPR we're going to see,' I said to Gary and Ozzy as we sat around a small table in the corner at the Prince Albert with our pints that Friday evening before the game.

'Oh no, wouldn't miss it, mate, will be nice to see your dad. And will be great to meet Claire, too,' Ozzy replied, taking a large gulp of his beer and glancing at Gary as he did so.

'Yeah, I'm still keen,' Gary added, returning Ozzy's glance with a nod.

'Oh…how did you know Claire is coming as well?' I asked, feeling pretty certain I'd tried to keep that under wraps from the boys so that they might think it would be just a boring day at Rangers with me and Dad and lose interest in the idea.

'Gary heard you on the phone to her last weekend. Don't think you've explicitly mentioned it to us, but we're happy she's coming and are very much looking forward to meeting the bird you've gone all soppy over,' Ozzy replied, taking another large gulp from his beer before glancing at Gary again and grinning.

'Oh…right…OK, then,' I replied, desperately trying to think of a reason which would dissuade them from coming along. It wasn't that I didn't want them ever to meet Claire, I really did. But I wanted to get to know Claire a lot better first, to have her deeply committed to the relationship so that it would be very hard for her to back out should she have significant doubts about my ability to make solid life choices after meeting my best friends. Right now felt some way short of that time.

'Yeah, we've been looking forward to getting down the Rangers, seeing your dad, meeting Claire. I'll probably bump into some of the old firm that I used to run with back as a youth, I usually do when I get down there, always nice catching up with a few of the old faces,' Ozzy continued. 'Your dad drinks in the Sceptre before games, doesn't he?'

The Sceptre was a very grotty, old pub sat on the Ellerslie Road, all the windows blacked out with paint where on matchdays fans could be openly seen snorting cocaine from the tables and in which I don't think a woman had probably set foot since the day it opened. In layman's terms, it was an absolute shithole. But it was where Dad had drunk since he'd been old enough to drink whilst going to QPR and he was very much a man of habit. He had his preferred stool by the bar where he would have three pints before the game and one pint afterwards before escaping the commotion to head back down the Uxbridge Road to home. Given that Claire was coming along, I'd suggested to Dad that it might be nicer to head to the Coach & Horses, a lovely old Victorian pub down a little back street off the Uxbridge Road which had been refurbished recently and generally didn't attract a matchday crowd.

'He does, Ozzy, but we're going to meet in the Coach & Horses instead tomorrow.'

'The Coach!' said Ozzy, his distaste apparent in the slam of his pint glass onto the table. 'I want to be with the lads in the Sceptre!' he protested.

'What do you mean you want to be with the lads?' I responded, beginning to get a little wound up at Ozzy's protestation against the plans I'd made which I actually didn't even want him involved in. 'You don't know any of "the lads", you never go to any of the games to get to know any of "the lads".'

'Course I know the lads! James Coyne's brother goes all the time with the Hanwell lot.'

'But you don't know James Coyne, let alone his brother! And how the hell do you know they go all the time?'

'I just know. I've got my ear to the ground, y'know, this is my manor, I know what goes on round these ends,' Ozzy responded, seemingly oblivious to the puzzled look which had formed on my face. 'Plus we want to be in with the matchday action, not tucked away around the corner in some gentrified pub where we're paying nearly double for the beers with the toffs and hipsters around us drinking single malts and vegan pale ales!'

'OK,' I responded.

'Thank you,' said Ozzy. 'Knew you'd come round, my son.' And he grabbed my cheek between his thumb and forefinger and shook it.

'Yeah, you go to the Sceptre, we'll meet you in there,' I replied, smirking and raising my eyebrows as I lifted my pint up to take a sip.

'Oh fuck you,' Ozzy responded somewhat harshly, nudging Gary as he did so.

'Yeah, fuck you,' Gary added, uncharacteristically aggressively.

'We'll come to the fucking wanky Coach then, but you can get the fucking over-priced wanky beers in.'

'No, Ozzy, you go and meet "the lads" in the Sceptre, talk about all the rows you didn't have down at the football over the years, it will be like a lovely, great big reunion with a load of people you've never met before; you'll really enjoy it.'

'Maybe I'll get the lads to come down the Coach?'

'Yeah, do,' I responded. 'Give them a call now, tell them to come down.'

Ozzy looked uneasy and fidgeted slightly in his seat.

'Nah, there's no way they'd be seen dead in that soulless boozer, I'll catch up with them some other time.'

Chapter 30

'Ahhhh!' Claire exclaimed exasperatedly. 'I think I'm going to have an *actual* meltdown! What does a girl wear to the football whilst simultaneously meeting her boyfriend's dad for the first time! This is a nightmare!'

'Don't stress, honestly,' I said, trying my best to calm Claire down and wondering how a usually relaxed and easy-going girl could get so stressed out by a decision as simple as putting some clothes on. 'Dad will probably barely register what you're wearing. I don't know, jeans, a top, trainers, scarf maybe, it can get a bit cold on the terraces at times.'

'I can't wear trainers to meet your dad for the first time!' Claire replied, as if I'd suggested wearing a Donald Trump wig with ski goggles and a bikini.

'OK, maybe stick some boots on or something, then?' I suggested tentatively.

'Yes, I'll wear my little black boots, with black jeans and this cream roll-neck jumper, with a little vest underneath, that should keep me warm. Are you sure I won't look weird at the football in this? Shouldn't I be wearing a QPR jersey or something?'

'No, you're absolutely fine, a lot of people don't wear QPR gear, and the last time a QPR shirt was referred to as a jersey I believe was 1967.' Claire laughed and the mood lightened somewhat, 'and if you're that desperate to show everyone you're a Ranger we'll get you a QPR scarf when we're down there, shall we?'

'Ooh yes, I think I'd like that actually!' Claire responded, clearly far happier now she had an outfit plan in mind. 'I've also got the strawberry compote I've made for your dad's birthday in my handbag. I've filtered it into one of these little pouches so it's easy to transport!'

'Ahh, thanks, Claire, that's really nice of you. Dad will love that.'

'Are you sure? He won't think it's really naff and wonder why I've made him a present and not bought him something decent?'

'No, of course not, this is much nicer, much more personal, he'll love it!' I replied enthusiastically.

Chapter 31

I could see that the Coach & Horses was busy but not packed as we jumped off the 207, crossed the road and headed down the back street leading towards the entrance.

'You OK?' I said, turning towards Claire just before we got to the entrance, taking both of her hands and squeezing them tightly.

'Yes, I'm OK, deep breaths,' she replied.

'You look beautiful, he's going to love you.' Claire smiled and we turned towards the entrance and walked through the large wooden saloon style double doors. The bar was on the left as we entered and curved round in a semi-circle with the pub space surrounding it. I saw Dad sitting on a stool around the other side of the bar and gave him a wave and proceeded to walk around the bar towards him, weaving in between the other customers as we went.

As we approached, Dad stood down from his bar stool, dressed in faded stonewash jeans, some old Reebok classics and a QPR badge emblazoned polo top, his fair hair was swept roughly to one side and he held a copy of what was presumably yesterday's *Evening Standard* underneath one of his arms.

'Alright, Dad,' I uttered first as we reached him and we shook hands and hugged awkwardly and briefly,

'Hello, Jamie.'

'This is Claire,' I said, gesturing in Claire's direction.

'Lovely to meet you, Claire,' Dad said as he held out his hand and leant in to kiss her on the cheek.

'And lovely to finally meet you too, I've heard so much about you. And happy birthday! I've made you a portion of strawberry compote, sorry it's a bit naff!' Claire responded as she pulled the pouch from her handbag and gave it to Dad.

'Ahh wow, thanks so much,' Dad responded, seeming to be genuinely enthusiastic. 'That's really nice of you, Claire, you shouldn't have gone to so much effort.'

Claire beamed, clearly happy that the gift had gone down well. 'No problem at all, I enjoyed making it so if you like it there's plenty more where that came from!'

'I'm sure I'll love it, thank you so much,' Dad responded, leaning in once more to give Claire another kiss on the cheek. 'Now, what are you guys drinking?'

'Pint of lager please, Dad. Claire?'

'A glass of white please,' Claire responded.

We stood there drinking and chatting and it all felt very natural. Dad was on form, doing his best to embarrass me with light-hearted stories of my youth and Claire laughed along, so it was almost a disappointment to see Gary and Ozzy slipping through the entrance and walking round the bar in our direction. Gary wore a woollen sweater with a zip-up collar, the zip coming halfway down the chest, black jeans and some kind of Nike trainers.

Ozzy wore what looked like a fake Burberry-style baseball cap, a navy Stone Island hooded jacket, dark denim jeans and black suede adidas trainers with white stripes.

'Yes, yes, my Rangers' boys,' said Ozzy as he approached, 'and my Rangers' girl,' he added as he acknowledged Claire, taking her hand and bowing slightly before giving her a kiss on the cheek. 'So this is the woman who has stolen our friends heart, ay?' Claire laughed and went ever so slightly red.

'OK, Ozzy, you been drinking before you got here or something?' I asked, slightly bemused by his overly boisterous greeting.

'Nah, man, just excited to get back down the Rangers. Millwall as well, gonna be lively.'

'Claire, as you may have guessed, this is Ozzy, and this is Gary,' I cut in.

'Lovely to meet you both,' said Claire as she kissed both of them on the cheek.

'Lovely to meet you too,' said Ozzy.

'Hello,' said Gary.

'How you doing, Steve, happy birthday,' Ozzy said with Gary echoing him.

'Thanks, boys, good to see you both.'

'You usually drink in the Sceptre before games, don't you, Steve?'

'Usually, yeah, just force of habit, to be honest. This pub is lovely, though, the architecture of the ceiling is incredible,' Dad responded to Ozzy.

'I usually drink in The Mitre,' Ozzy continued, 'by the ground pre game, but come to meet you guys in this poncey gaff, haven't I?' The barman glanced up at him whilst pulling a pint behind the bar and shook his head discreetly.

'The Mitre?' Dad questioned.

'Yeah right by the ground, think a load of the Acton lot drink in there.'

'Yeah I remember The Mitre, never drank in there, when was the last time you went?' Dad asked.

'Cor... I dunno, don't think I've managed to get down there this season, but would've been down there last season defo.'

'Oh right, you must be thinking of somewhere else I think because The Mitre was demolished about five or six years ago. There's a kids' playground there now,' Dad answered as Ozzy looked flustered and took a big gulp from his pint. Claire began to snigger and turned towards me, hiding her face from Ozzy, and I started laughing out loud.

'Were you having some beers with the Acton lot while you were on the merry-go-round? Were you lining up the sambucas as you went down the slide? Cheeky glass of whisky after the game whilst seeing who could go highest on the swings? All having great fun until the Acton lot's mums shouted at them for staying out in the playground too late?' I continued, really enjoying Ozzy's growing embarrassment.

'Shut the fuck up, alright. I must've been thinking about a different pub, I get confused,' Ozzy spat back, gradually regaining his composure and bravado.

'That's right, Ozzy, you are a very fucking confused little man,' I responded gleefully.

'Language boys, language,' Dad said, calmly.

'Sorry, Steve, I must've been thinking of a different pub.'

'There's the Kings Arms over the other side of the ground?' Dad said sympathetically, seemingly trying to allow Ozzie a way out of his tangled web of lies.

'Yeah, yeah, that's it I think, the Kings Arms, now I come to think of it. Big bar as you go through the entrance?'

'That sounds like the one, mate,' Dad responded.

'Yeah, yeah, knew it, that's the one. The Mitre was round the other side, weren't it. I never even look at the names when I head in these places, I just know them from being in them y'know, and I'm usually stumbling out of them by the end of the day, know what I mean?' Ozzy said, the full display of faux-machismo returning to his words, nudging Gary to ensure at least one person responded with a nod and a grin.

We entered the lower loft behind the goal and took up our seats. I'd not been to a game in years and was surprised at how much I realised I'd missed walking up the concrete steps and emerging inside the stadium, the large expanse of pitch spread out before us like a sea of emerald green, the excitement building instantly inside as the noise of the supporters rattled around the ground, rebounding off the old tin barriers at the back of the stands before floating out of the ground to echo faintly across the surrounding streets of Shepherds Bush. It was just a few minutes to three and the ground was virtually full. Chants of 'Rangers, Rangers, Rangers…' would start in a small section of the ground before catching almost contagiously and spreading rapidly until all areas of the ground except amongst the section of away fans behind the opposite goal were in full voice. I'd seemingly forgotten what a good atmosphere could be like in a London derby against a team that, by their own admission, no one likes.

I'd never been much good at football. I'd liked it, and I'd wanted to be good, and I'd been taken to football training with different kids' football teams, to soccer schools in the summer, put myself forward for school teams, but I just wasn't particularly coordinated. Dad had been a very good player and had played semi-professionally and maybe it's just my imagination but the image of his face growing more and more disappointed each time he watched me at football training is seared into my memory. It left me thinking that Mum must have been terribly un-coordinated and un-sporty.

'Wow,' Claire exclaimed as we got to our seats which were pretty much dead centre behind the goal, on the end of row N, 'this place is buzzing. It's a little bit scary.'

'Yeah, it's a good atmosphere today, isn't it!' I replied, happy that we'd come to an exciting game. 'Now we're fifth and Millwall are sixth, so it's quite a big game, only early on in the season really, but it's around this time that the league starts to take shape. And there's no need to be scared! It's not like thirty or forty years ago where maybe there was cause to be a bit worried, it's all very safe these days.'

'OK, I'll not be scared then! And Claire grabbed onto my arm with both of hers and leaned in towards me, and something told me this was going to be a good day for us and for the Rs.

I think twenty-two minutes had passed because I remember looking up at the scoreboard as the group of guys to our left began arguing with the group to our right, and Rangers were four nil down.

'You're a fucking embarrassment, you absolute bunch of cunts, you're not fit to wear the shirt,' screamed one of the men on our left.

'Why don't you shut the fuck up and get behind the team,' responded a large gentleman to our right.

'Who are you telling to shut the fuck up, you fat cunt, they're a fucking embarrassment to the club and if I wanna I'll tell 'em so,' shouted the man on our left in reply, walking out into the concrete walkway in between the two sections of seating as he did so. 'If you've got a problem with that, I'm here now if you wanna go.'

Claire had grabbed onto me a little tighter and I looked around vaguely nervously, unable to see any police officers about and noticing that the stewards were down too far below seemingly paying little attention to what was developing.

'If that's what you want, pal,' said the larger gentleman as he squeezed past Ozzy and Gary before passing myself and Claire.

Before the gentleman could get out of the row, Dad stepped out into the central walkway himself.

'Alright, boys, we're all Rangers here, aren't we? It's been a shambles of a first twenty minutes, but let's not make things any worse, shall we?'

'The fuck's it gotta do with you?' the guy from the left said aggressively, puffing out his chest and taking off his jacket as he did so, throwing it back onto his seat. No one in the vicinity was watching the game now yet still no police officers or stewards seemed to have become aware of what was developing.

'Stay here, Claire,' I said and walked out of the row to where Dad was trying to placate the angry man, the guy from our right edging around Dad as he spoke.

'Come on, guys, there's no need to make this day any worse,' I said, directing my comments at the guy from the left who had become aggressive towards Dad, edging Dad out of the way as I did so.

'What the fuck's it gotta do with you, ginger bollocks?' came the response.

I stepped forward and went to reply that it had nothing to do with me and that I just didn't want to see the situation turn violent, as it happened though, I don't remember any words leaving my mouth.

The next thing I remember is opening my eyes slowly and seeing the faces of Claire, Dad and a woman in a police officer's uniform leaning over me.

'You alright, Son?' Dad asked.

'Oh god, Jamie, are you OK?' said Claire, kissing me as she did so.

'I'm fine, why am I lying down?'

Claire and Dad glanced at each other.

'You got punched in the face, Jay, and you went down. Luckily you came down on the seats so you didn't bang your head off the concrete or anything' explained Dad.

'Ahh, that's embarrassing,' I replied.

We didn't stay to watch the rest of the game; the St John Ambulance people gave me a quick assessment and I said I felt fine and we made our way back to the Coach. Claire and I walked arm in arm, my legs still feeling a little unsteady, and she explained what had happened.

'So you went down because that awful man punched you in the face, are you sure you're OK?'

'I'm fine, massively embarrassed but physically fine, ego terribly, potentially irreparably damaged,' I replied.

'Why are you embarrassed, you were just trying to keep the peace and that horrible, ugly, nasty man punched you in the face for no reason at all. You weren't being aggressive, what an absolute shit! And to be embarrassed for being attacked seems absolutely ludicrous. I would hate to be with someone who believed he could prove his manliness through overt displays of violence, it's literally sickening.'

'Are you sure you're OK? You must be shaken up?' I asked Claire.

'I am a bit, I guess. It was horrible, my instinct was to jump on you because the horrible man went for you again as you went down on the seats but luckily your dad grabbed a hold of him and threw him what seemed like halfway across the stadium. And then, luckily, after what seemed like an eternity, the police were there and they grabbed hold of the man. They tried to grab your dad but others in the crowd told them he was just trying to keep the peace so they let him go.'

'Jeez, what did Ozzy and Gary do?'

'Hmm… They seemed to hide behind me, to be honest. Not that I blame them particularly, it was awful, but I thought they might have tried to help get you out of the situation.'

'Bloody hell, well thank god for Dad, I guess. I'm so sorry this has happened on your first trip to the football. That has literally never happened to me before!' I said as we arrived at the Coach, pulling Claire a little closer to me.

As we entered, I could see Ozzy and Gary were already at the bar.

'You alright, Jay?' Ozzy asked, Gary echoing him.

'I'm alright yeah, thanks for jumping in and helping,' I replied.

'Erm, yeah…no probs,' Ozzy responded hesitantly, looking at Gary whose face bore an expression showing even more bewilderment than usual.

'What's up? You did jump in and help me, didn't you? Or at least you must've given the Hanwell or Acton lot a shout so that they could help out?'

'It was over very quickly, mate,' Ozzy replied, 'you went over to chill things out and I thought that would be that, then you got smacked in the boat and before we could get involved, the Old Bill was pulling everyone apart.'

'So you're saying you didn't help me out? I got punched in the face and you stood there and watched?'

'No, it weren't like that! Tell him, Claire, it was over too quickly, we couldn't squeeze past to get at them.'

'It's true, Jay.' Claire turned her back to Ozzy and Gary, faced me and gave me a little wink, 'I think they were trying to get through but then the policemen turned up.'

'See!' shouted Ozzy, clearly elated that his version of events had been vindicated. 'I'll have a word with a few of the chaps though, find out who those fellas were. I'm not just leaving that there, I ain't having it,' Ozzy continued, oblivious to the fact that absolutely no one believed a word he was saying.

Dad entered the pub and immediately walked up to Claire and gave her a big hug.

'Are you OK,' he asked, hands on Claire's shoulders, looking straight into her eyes.

'I'm fine thank you, Steve, just a little worried for this one,' Claire said, pointing at me, 'but I'll keep an eye on him for the rest of the day and any sign of headaches or nausea and you're going straight to the hospital, no ifs no buts,' she continued.

'People like that put me off the football, they really do,' Dad continued, shaking his head. 'I think I'm in need of a whisky to be honest, anyone else?' Dad asked.

And so we settled in for the next couple of hours, a few whiskys to settle our rattled emotions. Claire and Dad had met and, being punched and knocked unconscious by a violent thug aside, I thought it had gone really well. I'd never been in any doubt that Dad would love Claire but they seemed to really get on well; they were laughing and joking and it was nice to see Dad like this. It was like Claire brought out a hidden part of his personality which warmed my soul to see. Claire had also met my best friends and for all their many, many faults they had been generally quite charming throughout the day. They'd made sure to include her in all discussions, shown genuine interest in her life story and Claire, in return, had been in fits of laughter at some of the tales they had recounted, many of them giving only the briefest of nods to actual facts. That night, Claire and I walked back to my flat, jaw sore but my heart filled with warmth.

Chapter 32

The annual Hungry Kats Office Ball was approaching and, for once, I was actually genuinely excited about it. Claire had agreed to accompany me as my date. For the first time in the history of my time at Hungry Kats I was bringing a legitimate date to the ball and I didn't have to lie to Ozzy and Gary that due to health and safety restrictions on numbers allowed in the venue I wasn't allowed to have a plus one at the event.

'So this year you're allowed a plus one to the ball, are you? That's convenient seeing as you've started going out with Claire this year; every other year they didn't give you a plus one?' Ozzy had asked.

'Yeah, guess I'm just lucky this year. I think they've chosen a bigger venue so that they don't have the same issues they've had previously.'

'And it took them five years to work this out, did it?' Ozzy continued

'Yeah, dunno why it took so long. You know what the bureaucrats are like at the top of these organisations with red tape and the like, they've probably had five years' worth of meetings to come to this decision,' I replied hoping that this would satisfy him, feeling like my web of lies was dangerously close to being torn apart.

'True, those pricks in charge of these big firms couldn't take a piss without someone holding their dick.'

'Exactly!' I responded enthusiastically, grateful that Ozzy's disdain for authority seemed to throw him off the scent of deceit.

We arrived at the venue, a bar/nightclub in Bank which had been hired out in its entirety, something I gathered was not too unusual for venues around the City of London which might otherwise be left quiet on Saturdays without the throng of city workers passing through the doors like they do on weekdays.

'You sure you're OK, Claire, not nervous?'

'I'm fine, it feels like you're more nervous than me!'

The Chronicles of a Malfunctioning Male

'Yes, nervous is my default state though I think, I need to drink several gallons of fluids a day just to compensate for the sweat which pours out of me daily as a result of nervous exhaustion.'

'Relax, you idiot, these are your workmates, you see them every day, have a drink and enjoy yourself. Just don't run off and leave me on my own for too long!'

It was hard to relax, though. I wanted Claire to think I was popular at work and that people liked me and that people thought that I was good at my job. And, most of all, I didn't want her anywhere near Miles. I know nothing would please him more than an opportunity to flirt with my girlfriend and piss me off.

We entered the nightclub, an open doorway which could easily have been missed had it not been for the two burly doormen stood dressed completely in black on guard outside. We dropped our coats at the cloakroom and walked downstairs and through a curtain which led into a huge ballroom-type venue, a large circular dancefloor down below us, skirted by a balcony above. Some awful current artist from the charts was blaring out of the speakers, offending my eardrums.

The evening was going well. Claire and I had mingled with my various colleagues and, somewhat to my surprise, everyone from work that we spoke to was extremely complimentary about me, causing me to say stupid things like:

'Oh, Jeana, you're far too kind.'

'Lyn, do you want me to give you the fifty quid in cash or shall I do a bank transfer?'

And ,'Well I'd be lost at sea, to be honest, if it wasn't for your help, Dave!'

A perfect mix of humility whilst not disagreeing or seeming surprised by all the praise being heaped upon me.

'Your colleagues seem to love you!' Claire said into my ear so I could hear over the music, 'everyone seems to think you're an absolute star!'

I chuckled, raised my eyebrows and jerked my head upwards before nodding a few times,

'I think everyone's clearly had far too much to drink,' I replied, sufficiently self-deprecatingly.

'Oh stop being so modest,' Claire responded, gently pushing my cheek as she did so. 'You're clearly a superstar round here and you know it. It's great, I think you're great!' she said, pulling me in and kissing me on the cheek as she did so.

Mission accomplished! The woman I love thinks I'm a superstar!

'Right I said,' high on a mixture of pride, love and alcohol 'let's step this evening up a notch, I'm off to get some shots!'

'Alright, party boy! If you insist, but no sambuca, I will be sick instantly on the floor and you'll never bring me back to a work event again.'

'That might be quite funny to see actually, but OK, no sambuca.'

Chapter 33

I awoke the following day fully clothed and alone in my bed, the events of the evening before a hazy, jigsaw of mish-mashed pieces which I struggled to put together in the correct order. One thing I was sure of was that I had an overwhelming feeling of doom and I couldn't quite put my finger on what had happened.

I checked my phone to see I had a WhatsApp from Claire from 01.42 this morning and the feeling of dread rose as I opened it.

One of the things I've really liked about you is how different you seemed from every other man. I never thought you would behave like you did this evening, you hurt me like I thought you never would. I felt humiliated tonight. Just as I was opening up and letting myself fall for you, you slammed the doors shut in my face, hard. Please don't contact me again. C

I felt the overwhelming urge to be sick and rushed to the bathroom. What had I done? How could I have messed this up so badly? I gagged and heaved violently before a large torrent of yellow liquid poured from my mouth into the toilet. The smell of warm sick, mixed with stomach acid made me gag and I was sick again, hands left resting on the rim of the toilet, dribble coming from my mouth and eyes streaming. Is this the lowest, I suddenly thought? Is this rock bottom? What the hell did I do? How could I have done something so bad? I felt an overwhelming urge to call Claire right there and then. More than anything, I wanted to check she was OK. It cut like a knife to the heart when I read the words that I'd upset her and the thought of never speaking to her again felt like absolute agony.

I racked my brains for evidence of my behaviour and slowly very hazy memories began to form in my head.

A vision of Miles whispering into Claire's ear while I was at the bar, her back to me, his hand resting on her lower spine as he lent in towards her, him looking over her shoulder and grinning at me bubbled to the surface of my mind and the recollection of rising anger swelled within my chest once again.

Oh god, I'd hit him. Had I hit him? No, that didn't seem right, that's not ringing any bells. I racked my brain but nothing was coming back to me. I had various memories of drinking shots with various people, but nothing that I could pin my hat on and say: that's what I did. Every memory that trickled back to me left me feeling that something was being overlooked, I still wasn't recalling the whole picture.

I needed to speak to Claire. But she had said never to speak to her again, shouldn't I respect her wishes? No, Jamie, on this occasion you shouldn't respect her wishes, this is one of the rare occasions where you have to overrule her decision because there is a very good chance that you might have royally fucked this up and lost the girl of your dreams, the woman you love, for ever. If you respect her wishes and never contact her again then you will definitely have lost the woman you love for ever. Now is the time to fight for her and show her how much she means to you.

Right. Fight for her. How do I fight for her? Give her a call. The phone rung eight times before it clicked onto voicemail. Shit. I hung up. Send her a message. She'll have no choice but to read the message. What should I say? I started typing.

Claire, I am so sorry for my actions last night.

Just be honest.

I've woken up this morning with a huge sense of dread filling every part of me. Reading your message actually broke my heart; the thought that I've hurt you in any way kills me. I had far too much to drink and I have no memory of what happened after a certain point last night. I know you said you never wanted to hear from me again and I will always respect your wishes but that is one wish I can't comply with. I've never felt remotely this way about anyone before and I cannot give up on us. I'm not perfect but I never want to hurt you. Please can we meet and can you give me a chance to apologise properly for however I hurt you. xxx

An hour passed and no response to my message. I could see that she'd been online so she must have read it. It was killing me not knowing what she was thinking. Was she still upset? I could picture her just sitting at home alone in her flat, crying to herself, tissues strewn all around her. The thought actually made me feel nauseous.

My phone buzzed, it was Claire.

You feel like a completely different person to me now. I feel like everything is ruined, my whole picture of you is clouded. You felt like a man who I could depend on, I felt so safe with you and that image has been completely shattered now. I do know you're not a bad man but I can't allow myself to be drawn any further in by someone who is capable of hurting me so deeply and making me feel so small, I need to respect myself enough to ensure that. I've booked a holiday, I'm going away today to clear my head and to put this behind me. C

To put this behind her. I don't want her to put this behind her. The clock in my front room ticked quietly by on the wall of my front room as I sat and considered my options. Do I let her clear her head? Wouldn't that be the right thing to do, to respect her wishes and give her some time? As much as this felt like it was the right thing to do, I couldn't escape the fact that a monumental chunk of me was screaming at me: 'Show her you will do whatever it takes to fight for her. Show her how much she means!'

Fuck it. I grabbed my phone, ran outside, still wearing the grubby tracksuit I'd jumped into, and ran down the road trying to flag down a cab.

'Where to, fella?'

'26 Benstalton Road, Balham,' I replied, having to refrain myself from saying 'and step on it'.

'Right you are, guvnor.' And he performed a tight U-turn in the middle of the road and we were off on our way.

I worried frantically on the journey about what I would say when I got there. What can I do but apologise again? Say that everyone makes mistakes and that I wanted one chance and if I hurt her again I would not have the gall to even attempt to stop her from walking away from me.

It would help if I knew what I'd done to upset her. That was a real sticking point. What if I didn't necessarily think what I'd done was wrong, the stubborn side of me suddenly pointed out. No, I would not have this inner feeling of dread if that were the case; I've been a complete dick, there's no doubt about that. Claire is a perfectly reasonable girl and she would not be this upset if I hadn't done something awful.

After being stuck in traffic for about half an hour around Putney Bridge, we finally arrived at Claire's address. I jumped out and ran to the front door of the small block of flats and pressed on the buzzer for flat 3. I waited. Shit, she's not answering. I tried again and waited again. Shit, I need to get into the block. I tried flat 2.

'Hello,' a voice came through the intercom

'Hello, sorry to disturb you but I really need to get into flat 3 to see Claire but I can't get through to her at the moment.'

A window above me opened and a man in his forties poked his head out of the window and peered down at me.

'Hello, mate, bumped into Claire on the stairs earlier. She headed off in a taxi a couple of hours ago, I'm afraid, mate. Had a suitcase with her, said she's heading to Crete for a few days to relax. Wish I was going with her. I offered to give her a lift but she said she'd already ordered a cab.'

'Do you know what airport she was heading to?' I asked

'No, she didn't say actually. I guess maybe Gatwick. Or Heathrow. Could be Luton, I suppose, or Stanstead. Probably not Southend, would be surprised if it's Southend.'

'OK, thanks a lot, mate,' I replied, making a mental note to try and avoid him in the future as he seemed borderline odd and was definitely in love with Claire.

'Cheerio, mate, sure she'll be back soon enough.' And he closed his window and disappeared back into his flat.

Shit. Even if I ordered a cab now and by some miracle of fate picked the right airport and the right terminal, realistically I still wouldn't catch up with her. And I know I am not nearly lucky enough for all that luck to go my way.

I wandered towards Clapham Junction station to make the lonely trip home, despondent and with a sickening feeling in my stomach that I'd single-handedly managed to completely cock up the best thing that had ever happened to me.

Chapter 34

'You've got to go after her, mate!' Ozzy urged, having come over uninvited with Gary in an attempt to apparently 'cheer me up' but managing to do absolutely nothing of the sort.

'I think I should just give her some space,' I replied, 'I've been a big enough dick as it is, now I need to let her have the relaxing holiday she intended to have and try and deal with the consequences when she returns.'

'You're nuts,' Ozzy exclaimed and physically shook me. 'I know what you're saying has some sort of logic to it, and you're saying it because you're a good guy who respects people's wishes, but you've got to trust me on this one, this is the one time you have to show that there's nothing that will stop you making this right.'

And I had to admit that he did have a certain amount of logic in what he was saying; this was the time I needed to show her how much she means to me, show her that oceans cannot keep us apart, just like they would in the old days. And these days with EasyJet and Ryanair it was far easier to show a woman that oceans couldn't keep you apart.

'Regrettably and weirdly, you seem to have a point,' I replied, reluctantly.

'Course I've got a fucking point, you nutter! You don't gain Lothario status such as mine without knowing what women want, and, believe me, she wants you to chase her.'

'Alright, don't get cocky – even a broken clock is right twice a day,' I pointed out, eager for him not to recall this moment at every possible opportunity over the next decade.

'Whereabouts in Crete is she?'

'I don't actually know,' I replied, momentarily realising the absurdity of the situation and picturing myself running around Crete frantically screaming 'Claire' over and over again until I was picked up and given a hiding by the local police for causing a public nuisance. 'But come to think of it, I do know that she has a friend who lives in Crete.'

'That's a good start, then,' Ozzy responded enthusiastically, evidently the excitement of what appeared to be a big adventure to him building.

'I can't remember the name of the town though, but maybe if I had a map I'd see the town and recognise the name. I could really do with a helper on the trip, to be honest.'

'I can come with you,' said Gary.

'Really, Gary?' I questioned, pretty unsure as to whether I actually wanted Gary to be able to come with me. 'What about work? It's very short notice.'

'It's fine, I haven't been on holiday for ages, the bosses keep telling me I need to take some so I'll take some.'

'Ohhhhhh-kayyyy. Fine, me and you to Crete it is then, I'll look up flights now.'

And so, less than twenty-four hours later, Gary and I boarded our flight from Heathrow terminal 2 to Heraklion airport, feeling part Hugh Grant in a romcom, part stalker and part complete wanker.

As we settled down in our seats a middle-aged woman wearing a bizarre, furry jumper approached us and looked at Gary who occupied the middle seat of the row, myself on the aisle. She spoke briefly to the man sitting next to Gary and then turned her attention to Gary.

'Excuse me, are you on your own?' she asked.

'Yes,' Gary responded, 'but I'm hoping to get back with my ex-wife soon.'

The woman laughed politely but nervously as Gary stared back, stone-faced, seemingly unsure of what the woman had found so funny.

'Riiight,' she replied.

'Erm, no we're actually together.' I cut in, 'Well, not together like that, just, we're flying together, school friends, going to find my girlfriend in Crete. Not searching for a new one, I have one, she's out there, just not sure exactly where, so on the hunt.'

The woman looked at me as if I were talking ancient Greek.

'It's a long story,' I added, turning my face away from her as I did so, hoping to wrap the conversation up quickly without making the pair of us look any more freakish than we'd already achieved in the space of two sentences, quite the accomplishment.

The woman left and came back eventually calling the man next to Gary out of his seat and in his place sat an attractive girl with short dark hair, a short pair of denim shorts and an impish smile.

'Emma,' she said as she sat down and held her hand out to Gary to shake it. Gary looked at her initially as if she were offering him a dead cat to eat but eventually, after a slightly uncomfortable pause, took her hand and shook it.

'Gary,' he said, refusing to break out into a smile.

'Jamie' I proffered my hand, giving a big smile to the girl to try and make up for the lack of one on Gary's face.

'So are you two together?' she asked.

'No,' I shouted quickly and altogether too loudly, as I tried to intercept before Gary had a chance to speak, 'we're friends, just coming out to Crete for a holiday.'

'His girlfriend's run away from him and he's coming out to Crete to win her back and take her home,' Gary added.

'Are you now?' Emma said, a cheeky smile appearing on her face. 'I'm not sure whether that's spectacularly romantic or unbelievably creepy. What are you planning to do, club her over the head and drag her back onto the plane?'

'He would never club a girl over the head,' Gary answered, accurately in all fairness but very clearly missing the intended humour in the line. Emma laughed.

'You're funny,' Emma responded and Gary smiled at this and laughed before his face returned to deadpan expression and this made Emma laugh even more.

'I can't work out whether you two are the oddest people I've met for a while or the funniest, but either way you're making this plane journey a lot more enjoyable. Now, where's the drinks trolley?' Emma asked and peered over the seat in front of her down the aisle to where the flight attendants were slowly making their way down towards us.

'So what are you doing in Crete?' I asked.

'Funnily enough, something not too dissimilar from your girlfriend,' she replied and laughed, 'my ex-boyfriend is a complete tosser and last week I came home from work to find his wardrobe empty and a note saying 'he needed space and time to think', and that he'd be back for the rest of his stuff at the weekend. So I thought I'd do him a favour and pack all his stuff neatly into one bag. But to get it all into one bag I needed to build a bonfire and chuck it all on there to reduce it to ashes, and then – just as planned – it fitted into one bag. And like the good girlfriend, or ex-girlfriend I should say, that I am, I put the remains in one bag, left it on the doorstep with a name tag on it.'

'Oh no' I replied, 'I'm really sorry to hear that, sounds like a difficult situation.' Not really knowing what to say about the borderline psychotic episode of burning the remains of her ex-boyfriend's possessions, and so choosing to continue as if not having heard that part of the story.

'Don't be sorry,' she replied assertively, 'he's a cock, he was always a cock, I always seem to go for cocks, I love cocks.'

'That sounds a bit odd,' I replied, noticing a few sideways glances and raised eyebrows from other seats in the plane.

'Yeah that really did, didn't it, didn't think that one through. My mouth can get me in trouble; it seems to run on a very slightly higher speed than my brain so that by the time I've realised I'm saying something unwise, it's already out in the open.'

I chuckled. 'I like people like that,' I replied, 'they tend to be the most honest of people.'

'And how about you, funny man, what are you doing coming to Crete? Going to help him if she struggles?' Emma directed to Gary.

'Jamie needed someone to give him a bit of support so I said I'll get a few days off work and come along.'

'Well isn't that a lovely thing to do for your friend.'

'Is it?' Gary replied in all honesty.

'Well yes, I think so, you've put your own life on hold to help out a friend. I hope he appreciates it.'

'I do,' I replied.

'He does,' Gary seconded.

And I started to wonder whether I'd been supportive enough of Gary during his breakup. He was quite plainly a strange individual, but that didn't mean he didn't have feelings, didn't mean his heart didn't ache as bad as anyone else's would when the love of their life walked out the door.

'Plus I don't have much of a life to put on hold,' Gary added and I winced at his honesty. He was going to have to stop saying things like that if he wanted to find a new woman, but Emma laughed again.

'You're like a young Jimmy Carr or something, you, so deadpan, so serious.'

And I knew Gary would be wondering what the hell this woman was going on about, but he smiled – apparently sincerely – and I felt relieved he'd decided not to make comment.

'So what did you do that's made your Mrs run off to Crete, must have been something pretty bad. I have to find out before I decide whether we can be friends or not.'

'Hmm…well that's the worst thing, really, or at least I hope it's the worst thing. I can't remember what I did. Maybe I got drunk and killed her cat, maybe I set fire to her curtains, I really don't know.'

'Go on then, tell me what you do know.'

And so I retold the story of the work night up until the point I could remember and then relayed Claire's reaction the following day.

'And do you have any former flames at work?' Emma asked.

'No, none at all, I'm actually pretty universally unpopular, amongst the men and the women to be honest.'

'So you said you vaguely remembered her talking to some prick that you hate and feeling anger.'

'Yes, very vaguely before I lose all memory. I can remember him coming over to her while I was at the bar and I remember the green-eyed monster rising up inside me.'

'And then the next morning she said you'd humiliated her. Now as a woman, using that sort of language when you've been invited to an event with a boyfriend where you don't know anyone else I would say it probably means one of two things.'

'Really?' I replied eagerly, keen to get any further insight into what I might have done.

'Yes. Either you gave her a dressing down in public for talking to the dickhead –' I thought but that didn't ring any bells and I couldn't really imagine myself doing that, ' – but that doesn't seem very you, to be honest. Or you felt so jealous you thought two can play that game and tried it on with another girl at the do while she stood there feeling absolutely humiliated because you're with her but are trying to play tonsil tennis with someone else so she feels like a prize prat when all she has tried to do is be polite and friendly to the people you work with.'

Suddenly a fresh wave of nausea washed over me.

'You've gone a bit pale there, matey. You OK?' Emma added, but I couldn't respond.

Flashback to me speaking to Colette at the bar, drunkenly hoping that Claire would look over while she was talking to Miles. Look at her laughing at his jokes, he's not funny, she fancies him.

'So look at you with your girlfriend…' Colette said teasingly whilst putting a finger in-between my shirt buttons playfully.

'I guess the dream of me and you is just a fantasy after all then…' And I remembered her moving in close, a breast squeezing against my chest, her cheek against mine as she whispered in my ear. I glanced up and saw Claire watching at this point, alone, Miles gone, no smile on her face, and I felt glad that I'd got one back on her for flirting with Miles in front of me; this will teach her and I turn Colette's head and go to kiss her, she lets me kiss her briefly and then pulls away, wags her finger and says, 'Naughty, naughty.' Instantly I panic and think what have I done? I turn my head towards Claire, who seems frozen to the spot, tears filling her beautiful eyes. Shit, what have I done? I turn away from the bar but trip on a coat left on the floor and stumble over. As I look up from the ground, Claire composes herself and walks away from me.

'Oh my god. I remember. Oh my god, I can't believe what I've done. I'm a horrible person, a horrible, horrible person. I don't deserve to be begging for forgiveness. I need to jump straight back on a plane home, Claire is too lovely to deserve an absolute prick like me. How could I have done that?'

'What did you do?' Gary and Emma asked in unison, both leaning in closer, eager to get the details.

'She was speaking to Miles while I was at the bar. God, that guy's such a dick! Why does he bother me so much, literally no one else does!'

'And…' Emma probed.

'And… Colette came over…'

'Colette the girl who you used to like but now think is a dick Colette?' Gary asked.

'Yes, that Colette. She started being all flirty, saying me and her was just a fantasy after all now that I've got a girlfriend. And I leaned in and…and kissed her.'

'You prick,' Gary exclaimed, succinctly and accurately.

'Oh god, pretty girl from office misses attention from formerly lovesick idiot because he's actually found a nice girl to go out with, tries to mess things up because she misses said attention, even though she has no interest in lovesick idiot whatsoever, and lovesick idiot falls for it hook, line and sinker,' Emma added.

'I know. I'm a fool, an absolute fool. I don't deserve to be following her to Crete, I can't believe I could have been such a dick. I never thought I'd do anything like that.' I felt absolutely desperate with shame and disappointment in myself. I'd always prided myself on being a decent person, on having a strong moral compass; I'd felt it was one of my strengths. Never in my wildest dreams had I thought I could hurt someone that I love so much in such a callous and humiliating way.

'Look,' Emma started, reaching across Gary and placing a comforting hand on my arm which momentarily made me jump slightly. 'Easy there, laddy, I'm not little Miss Prick Tease from the office.'

'Sorry, I know, I just…'

'Look, you've made a mistake, a bad one, but personally I think this is salvageable. Nobody is perfect, but if you do manage to fix things you have to learn from this. You have to learn to trust the one you love. Everyone struggles with jealousy issues, you're talking to someone who by my own admission can go absolutely batshit mental with jealousy, especially when you're with someone who knows this and will play on it. But when you find the person you love, and it does sound to me like you have found that person, then you need to trust in their character to do the right thing. Had you mentioned disliking this particular guy before?'

'No, never.'

'So from an outsider's perspective, she was probably feeling a little nervous meeting all your work colleagues, a friendly guy approaches and she talks amicably with someone as any girlfriend trying to make a good impression would do, and that prompted the jealousy?'

I bowed and shook my head. 'Yes, that's about right.'

Emma stroked my arm as a teardrop fell from my eye onto my jeans. I bowed my head deeper, trying to disguise the fact that I was crying.

'It happens; live and learn. She'll understand. Judging by your reaction, it certainly doesn't look like this is a regular kind of occurrence; forgive yourself and ask for her forgiveness. Explain everything, don't be afraid to show that you have a weakness, and I think she'll understand. Good people understand because they understand weakness in others through recognising weaknesses in themselves.'

And I wondered there and then about the magic of the universe we live in, the fact that fate had placed someone like Emma beside us on the plane who had managed to put so perfectly into words a feeling of hope for someone such as myself who at that moment had felt without hope.

As we departed the plane, a strange thing happened. Gary asked Emma for her number and she gave it to him and they said they'd meet up for a drink in Crete. I smiled briefly and then my mind turned back to the serious business of finding Claire and apologising for the complete mess I'd made of our relationship.

Chapter 35

I'd never been a stalker. Unfortunately, it turns out, given the predicament I was currently in, as some stalking skills would definitely be necessary to track down Claire right now.

Confusingly, when Claire had first told me about her friends who lived in Crete, she had told me that they lived in Bali. It took several back and forths before I was able to establish that Bali was actually also the name of a seaside village on the island of Crete as well as being an island of its own in the Indian Ocean.

'We've got to think, what would we do if we were in her situation, i.e. sad and depressed because her boyfriend is a wanker?' Emma had made it clear that as she was involved now, she wanted to see this through until the end, and her help was appreciated – when she wasn't making sarcastic comments. She had come over to the villa that I had rented for the week to make our plan of action. We sat in the kitchen area at the island which was in the middle of a large marble floor which led directly out onto the shaded terrace which followed onto the unshaded area with a swimming pool, shared by several near identical villas, and a BBQ area. I sighed silently for a second, thinking how lovely it would have been to be here just with Claire, enjoying the sun, the peace and dipping into the pool on occasion to cool down. With a cup of tea each to help the mind think, we put our heads together to work out how we were going to find Claire.

'I imagine she'd mainly want to just relax at her friends' place,' I suggested,

'She'll have to come out sometime,' Gary added.

'She will, you're right, Gary. I guess we could just head down to the village and do the rounds at lunch times, and dinner times, just sort of hop from place to place. From what I remember Claire saying, it's quite a small fishing village so I can't imagine there are that many places. We could probably do the rounds at lunchtime and then again a couple of times in the evening?' I added.

'I think that sounds about as good a plan as any, do you agree, Gary?'

'Yes I do, Emma, and maybe a couple of piña coladas while we track her down!' Gary replied cheekily, with a mischievous grin on his face.

'Well these bar owners aren't going to allow us just to sit in their bars and scout for Claire without buying anything, it would literally be rude not to,' Emma replied and held her hand up for a high-five which, amazingly, Gary acknowledged.

And so that's what we did; we wandered down to the small seaside village of Bali in Crete and basically did a bar crawl around the tavernas and restaurants which clung to the hills looking out to sea. I stuck to cokes and waters so that if we did find Claire I wouldn't be slurring my apology whilst reeking of booze, whilst Emma and Gary proceeded to get gradually more and more pissed as we went; the flirtation and tactility between the two of them seemingly increasing with each piña colada they threw down their necks.

Two days of bar crawling around the small village and the only major development had been a significant decrease in the size of my bank balance. Annoyingly in any other situation it would have been a delightful way to spend some holiday, boozing in the afternoon sun and sampling the local foods on offer, but given the situation it was impossible for me to enjoy. Also I figured it would be just my luck if the one time I turned to join in the conversation and tomfoolery that Emma and Gary were indulging in, Claire would turn the corner and see me sat with my friend and a random girl who she would never have seen in her life before, Emma's hand would have momentarily found its way onto my leg and we'd be laughing heartily whilst staring into each other's eyes. It may sound a little far-fetched, but, believe me, it was inevitable. I had to stay focussed, keep my eyes on the game and, importantly, always keep Gary between Emma and I just to make doubly sure that no misconceptions could occur if we did finally manage to find Claire.

It was our third day of searching and we were sat in George's Taverna when I looked up at the entrance, looked away momentarily, before sharply returning my gaze. There she was. She had floated into the taverna, was briefly perusing the menu before a brief interchange with the waiter and she began to head this way. As her head lifted and caught sight of me, she literally froze. I've never seen anyone at the precise moment they've seen a ghost so I'm a little unsure as to how they would look, but everything in my body screamed the picture of Claire right then would be the textbook definition: frozen, turning pale and seemingly unable to function.

For a few seconds we both just remained totally still staring at each other as Gary and Emma continued to natter semi-drunkenly, completely oblivious to the fact that she was there. The waiter had by this point noticed that Claire had ceased to follow him as he beckoned to a small table in the corner of the decking. I lifted myself up from my chair and this seemed to be the signal for Claire to unfreeze; she turned on her heels and immediately headed out of the restaurant.

'Claire, wait,' I called after her. 'Please, Claire,' I said as I caught up with her just outside the restaurant, placing my hand on her shoulder and causing her to spin round sharply. By this point, Gary and Emma had realised what had occurred and caught up with us.

We stood there on the gravel path leading away from the taverna, a small wall made of large stones separating us from a vast drop, the large expanse of the beautifully blue Mediterranean Sea stretching out as far as the eye could see until it met the lighter blue of the sky, darkening slightly as late afternoon faded into evening.

'Claire, please!' I almost begged. 'Could we just talk for a minute? I know I've got a huge amount of explaining to do and a huge amount of apologies to make, but I can't leave like this.'

The Chronicles of a Malfunctioning Male

'Why have you followed me all the way to Crete? I came here to get away from you in case you'd not worked that out?' Claire responded angrily.

'I know, Claire, and I do respect that, really I do, but this time I needed to see you and to let you know how sorry I am.' Emma had gradually edged her way closer towards us so that we were now stood as a three rather than a two. Out of the corner of her eye Claire eyed Emma suspiciously, and I half expected her to ask her who the hell she was and why the hell she was encroaching on a very clearly private conversation. There was a pause in conversation as I wondered how to continue and Claire seemingly pondered how to respond to my apology. The silence was filled by the lady whom I'd known for a little less than three days who seemed quite determined to make her feelings on the matter known.

'I know you don't know me, but do you mind if I say something?' I detected a very slight slur in her voice, no doubt induced by the several piña coladas she had knocked back in the sun. Claire turned her head to me, arms out by her side, her palms turned upwards, hunched her shoulders up slightly and shook her head slightly.

'Oh, this is Emma. Gary and Emma met on the plane and she's been helping us look for you,' I explained, given that Claire was clearly thinking who the hell is this weirdo. 'Not in a hired way or anything,' I decided to clarify, 'she just heard the story and wanted to help. For some reason.' And Emma took this as her cue to continue.

'Look, I know dicks, I'm attracted to dicks. God, I've got to stop saying that! Jamie is not a dick. He told me what happened, which he could barely remember by the way, and he was an absolutely massive dick, but he's not a dick. If that makes any sense at all,' Emma explained in an unconventional manner but in a way in which I understood what she was trying to say, even if no one else did. Claire continued to look confused, upset and drained in equal measure.

I felt hugely awkward standing there like a lemon whilst to all extents and purposes a complete stranger tried to argue my case as to why I'd behaved like a complete and utter cock and didn't know what to do with my hands, whether to put them in my pockets, on my hips or behind my back, so I settled on folding my arms, with one hand reaching upwards so that my chin rested between my thumb and my forefinger in what I hoped was a conciliatory manner.

'Look,' Emma continued, clearly deciding to fill yet another awkward silence after she had made her rather unconventional defence of the accused, 'I don't blame you if you're thinking who the hell is this person and why doesn't she just bugger off, but I can already see that you're too decent a person to say that,'

'Hmm.' Claire sighed, raising an eyebrow, seemingly seriously considering proving Emma wrong.

'But I'm an impartial outsider, have been through similar things in my life, and I would hate to see something special ruined because of a mistake.'

'He didn't hire you to say all this, did he?' Claire asked.

'No!' Emma and I both proclaimed in unison. 'Emma has not been hired as private detective nor in any other form, she is here completely of her own free will,' I pleaded, the strain in my voice seemingly demonstrating that I was worried Claire would actually believe I'd hired someone to make my case for me.

'Sorry, I'm joking,' Claire continued, her expression softening as she placed a hand on my arm. I wanted to grab her and hold onto her so she could never move away again, never again take her lovely hand away from my arm, but I was aware this would appear strange and was technically extremely impractical.

'Look, I don't know if I'm mad saying this because, in all honesty, I haven't quite worked out yet whether you're a very nice person or just a bit insane, but thank you very much. I realise when you booked your holiday you wouldn't have thought what an amazing chance to get away and solve some domestic disputes, but do you mind if I speak to Jamie alone for a sec?' Claire asked Emma.

'Not at all,' Emma responded and drifted off towards Gary who was stood back by the stony wall seemingly trying to make out that he wasn't listening.

'Look,' Claire started.

'Can I speak first?' I cut in.

'No!' Claire responded firmly, seemingly exasperated and somewhat exhausted by the situation. 'Look, I know you're not a bad person. I've been with you and around you for more than long enough to know that.' I went to speak, but thought better of it and closed my mouth again.

'But what you did absolutely humiliated me, and it turned you into someone I never thought you had the capability of being. And that has really thrown me. Which is why I need this space and time away to think things over, because potentially we're walking into what will be the biggest decision of our lives, so I for one think it's important to try and make sure we get the decision right.'

My heart wept as I heard the emotion and the quiver in Claire's voice and for the millionth time I kicked myself for being such an arsehole.

'Claire. I'm so, so sorry. There are no excuses for what I did, I have nothing I can say that will justify what an absolute berk I was… I am. I was extremely drunk, and the guy you were talking to is probably the only person in the world that I despise; he's a really arrogant twat, to be honest.'

'He did come across like a bit of an arrogant twat, to be honest, he kept telling me about the terrific views of Hyde Park from his apartment, *top-of-the-range appliances*. He sounded like a bad estate agent, even invited me back to take a look at it.'

'He did what!?!'

'Perspective! Jamie, not talking about that are we?'

'No. No. Course not. As I was saying, when I saw you two talking and laughing, a lot of insecurity which sits just below the surface bubbled to the top, and in my drunken state I thought you were trying to make me jealous, so I reciprocated.'

'Jamie! Why would I try and make you jealous?'

'I don't know. Not everyone is as nice as you. I'm sure you've come to recognise that during your life.'

'I'm no angel,' Claire cut in.

'I know, but you have such a good and well-meaning heart. In the past, people I've been with maybe haven't had their hearts in the same place as yours, and maybe this has developed insecurities in me. I realise now all you were doing was trying to make a good impression on my colleagues. But the dick in me came out.'

'I sincerely hope it didn't,' Claire responded and we both giggled together, the mood lightening somewhat.

'I'm so sorry, Claire, I don't ever want to hurt you. I've felt awful for what I did.'

'Tell me something,' Claire cut in, 'have you and the girl ever had a thing?'

I almost burst out laughing, but quickly suppressed the urge; don't make it look like such an absurd notion.

'I promise you, Claire, never. Look, I don't know what your thoughts are but I just want to say I don't think I've ever been as happy as when I've been with you. I love you with all my heart and I don't want to lose you over this. But I know I've put you in an awful position—

'You love me?'

I'd meant to say it so many times already, lying in bed just looking at each other, on messages when I couldn't wait to see her, suddenly realising that I couldn't put it in the message because I'd never actually said it before. Singing along to a song with Claire beside me and suddenly becoming self-conscious because the words 'I love you' were in the lyrics and suddenly stopping singing.

'I do. I love you. And please don't think I'm only saying it because of the situation, I kind of thought you might already know, to be honest. I've wanted to say it so many times before, but have been scared it was a bit early on for us to be saying it. I even Googled how long should you wait before saying I love you to a new girlfriend. If you're interested, various surveys have been carried out and the consensus was that one to three months is the optimum time period. I believe we're safely within that timespan now; conservatively within it you may even say.'

Claire smiled and with her left hand brushed her hair which had dropped down over one of her eyes away from her forehead.

'You're such an idiot,' she said, smirking, not exactly the response I had envisaged upon telling my girlfriend I loved her. 'But I love you too, I did, I don't know, everything feels so confused in my head now. I'd had time alone, and I had begun to feel so strong on my own and then I began to give my trust to you and now I feel back to square one. I can't have someone destroy my confidence again, I won't let it happen!' Claire said, getting more agitated as she did so.

My heart sunk and my stomach felt like it had tied itself into a thousand knots. I was absolutely disconsolate that my stupid, drunken actions had caused such pain and anguish to someone that I loved. I gripped each of Claire's shoulders with my hands and looked deep into her beautiful green eyes.

'Claire, there is nothing I can say, literally nothing. Words mean nothing really without actions to back them up. But if you do end up deciding to be with me for five years, or ten years, or fifty years, then I'll show you over time that you'll never feel this kind of pain again. Because it's true what they say: words are cheap, and anybody can say anything, and lies, false truths, false intentions are all too easy to throw around, but it's what we do that really matters, not what we say.'

'You're right. I know. But I just don't know whether I can take that chance and give you that time to potentially let me down again. It's easier for guys; you don't have a body clock hanging over your head like a ticking time bomb.' Claire looked down towards her feet, which she shuffled nervously. 'That could be it for me then; I could literally be putting all my eggs in your basket. I don't think you can possibly have any idea how scary that is.'

I bit the bullet, moved forward and pulled her into my chest. She turned away slightly so that her arm and side were resting on my chest, her head facing away from me looking out into the distance, my left arm wrapped around her, stroking her arm.

'You're right, I don't think I can, it's not something a man will ever really have to take into consideration. I can see your point entirely, but I don't think I'll ever fully understand how that feels, and I realise it must be a scary prospect, but I know that it's not a risk that you'd be taking.'

Claire pulled away and looked up at me. 'But how can you say that? A week ago you knew you'd never hurt me and now look where we are.'

And she was right, of course she was right. How could I stand there and expect her to believe me when my actions had betrayed any trust she could have previously had in me.

'Look, I think I need to give you a little bit of time, because by chasing you to another country I obviously haven't done that, but I'm going to stay on the island and maybe after you've had some time to yourself we could meet up?' I asked tentatively.

'I think that sounds like a good idea. I feel exhausted, drained. I need to sleep for about seven years. I need some time to think, to decide what's best for me, and then maybe we can meet or maybe we'll just call it a day.'

'OK, beautiful one,' I replied, the back of my throat suddenly feeling tight and my eyes starting to fill very slightly with tears on hearing Claire's words. I pulled her into me, gave her a kiss on the top of her head, turned and walked away, the now-familiar feeling of nausea eating away at my stomach as I went. And so, I returned to our home for the week alone, disconsolate, but hoping upon hope that Claire would give me one chance to prove to her that I was right. Because it takes an exhalation of breath, and a flick of the tongue to say I love you; almost nothing could be simpler. But to show it takes years of devotion, of loyalty, of caring, of doing things that you don't necessarily want to do because you know it means a lot to the one you love, of sacrificing what you want for the sake of what they want and of holding that person above all others in your thoughts and in your actions. Three little words prove nothing, that's what love is.

Chapter 36

The Chronicles of a Malfunctioning Male

And so, I waited, nervously, back at the villa we had booked for the minimum stay of a week, with Gary for company and with Emma a frequent visitor. Me being in a mood which was pretty incompatible with basic socialising, Gary and Emma spent most of their time alone together. I'd watch them from the safety of a sunbed in the shade (ginger problems). They'd be laid out by the pool, laughing together, Gary, resembling an overgrown yeti, bombing into the pool beside her while she was practising her breast-stroke, her pulling up from her stroke abruptly seemingly gasping for air in a state of panic, the various kids in the pool shouting at him to do it again so that they could ride the waves caused by the impact. Him coming back from the pool bar with a couple of afternoon piña coladas which they'd drink before sinking into a hazy afternoon nap beside each other.

I was actually envious of Gary. Not because of the friendship he'd struck up with Emma, but because of his character. I actually thought he was one of the most selfless, most kind and decent people I'd ever met. Everything he did was well meaning; he didn't have a bad bone in his body, I genuinely believed that. If he did something which ended up hurting somebody, it was through pure unwitting ignorance rather than an intention to be nasty. And I think this knowledge that he only had good intentions in everything he did, gave him a sort of self-confidence that was difficult to replicate for others. For the second time in a week, I figured that perhaps I'd not been the sort of friend to Gary that he had been to me in the past, and I resolved to make sure I was a better friend to him in the future.

What advice would my mum have given in this scenario, I wonder? Maybe she'd have had a way with words which would make everything seem better, would clear my head and make my mind less fuzzy. I don't know. Maybe.

A full four days after we'd parted ways on the dusty walkway looking out to the ocean, my phone buzzed and I looked down to see 'Claire ♥'. As I picked up my phone and unlocked it with my passcode, my body was a shivering bag of nerves, terrified that it would be Claire saying she'd had time to think and wouldn't be able to get past what I'd done.

Hey, thanks for giving me some space, do you want to meet up this evening to talk?

I gave a huge sigh of temporary relief, my shoulders relaxed and my head tilted backwards as a huge rush of tension swept out of my body. For a split second I wondered if it would be funny in my first response to say I was busy, but obviously that idea was placed into the bin along with all the other stupid thoughts I have.

Hey, no problem, have missed you but wanted to give you all the time you need. This evening sounds good – shall we meet at George's Taverna at 7pm? X

Yes, will see you there then.

I spent the bulk of the rest of the day before we were due to meet overanalysing Claire's messages. No kiss. On either message, what does that mean? Does that mean she never wants to kiss me again? Is she preparing me for the bad news she's about to deliver, not wanting to get my hopes up?

To the impartial observer, surely they would be described as reasonably cold messages. Especially the second one, the first one expresses gratitude which seems pretty genuine, but she's a genuinely lovely person with exemplary manners, so perhaps that's absolutely nothing to do with her feelings towards me. The second one is purely a confirmation, the layman would be excused for thinking it was a response to a business meeting request, succinct, to the point, like the sender has a million other things to consider at that moment in time, all of far superior importance.

That evening I got ready to meet Claire, putting on my smart grey shorts, my navy boat shoes and a navy polo top, doing my hair as neatly as I could, wanting to at least look presentable when we met.

'Good luck,' Emma said, placing a hand on my shoulder as she did so, the leaving committee of Gary and Emma having come to show me some support as I headed off to hear my fate.

'Thanks,' I replied.

'Good luck, mate,' Gary added, one arm wrapped around Emma and one arm wrapped around my shoulder as he said it, somewhat bizarrely leaning down slightly and placing a kiss on the side of my head as he said it.

'Erm... Thanks, Gary,' I replied, deciding just not to mention the kiss.

I trudged away from the villa, feeling almost lightheaded and dizzy at the thought of being told by Claire that my one stupid, drunken, three-seconds-in-duration mistake had cost me the most important and best part of my life.

I walked along the dusty track which followed the perimeter of the island, the stony wall at the edge the only thing separating me from the huge drop to the sea rolling gently into the rocks below. The sun was just setting and the lower part of it was just skimming the horizon, the sea turning almost pink in its reflection, the sky and the small number of clouds in it displaying a vast array of shades of purple, the sun itself a ball of yellow tinged white, fading gradually from the bright white which had dominated the sky hours prior. Somewhat ironically, it was possibly the most beautiful and romantic setting I had ever seen in my life.

I arrived at George's Taverna ten minutes early. Perched on the edge of the cliff face looking way out to the Mediterranean Sea, the sun was just taking its last breaths before dipping completely below sea level. The outer perimeter of the restaurant sat almost perilously on the edge of the cliff, just some old wooden boards for flooring, the numerous cracks in-between them clearly showing the rocky surface below. Wooden tables and chairs were spread out across the floorboards, red and white check table coverings adorning each one, and each table was decorated with a small candlelit lamp and a small vase with a single rose in it. It being relatively early in terms of the traditional time that the locals tended to have dinner, the taverna was fairly empty, just a few tables occupied by pairs of tourists dotted about the venue, holding hands, giggling amongst themselves, taking selfies, making sure they picked up the incredible view in the background to ramp up the likes on Instagram. I picked a table at the edge of the restaurant, away from the other diners, one which looked far out to sea, and I waited.

I began to worry slightly that Claire might have changed her mind and decided not to come, but at just gone ten minutes past seven I saw her arrive at the entrance and after a brief exchange with the waiter he directed her to my table where I stood waiting to greet her.

I'm not sure whether it was the intensity of the situation, or the adrenaline coursing through my veins, but she glided over, looking more incredible than I'd ever seen her look. In the days she had spent here she had clearly been making the most of the sun; her skin had turned a rich mahogany and the light from the numerous candles dotted around the taverna clung to her skin seemingly attracted only to her, putting everything else in the shade. She had curled her hair slightly so that it bounced gently off her shoulders, and she wore a floaty white dress which fell just above the knee. Making her way through the haphazard maze of tables on the outer terrace, her eyes made contact with mine and she smiled briefly before seemingly remembering why she was there, pulling back from the smile.

'Hello,' I said as she approached, greeting her with a kiss on both cheeks and pulling out her chair as I did so. 'The sun clearly agrees with you, you look amazing,' I continued.

'Or maybe it's just not being around you that agrees with me?' Claire responded coldly as she sat down opposite me. The stubborn part of me spiked, urging me to strike back, but the more rational side of me caught my tongue before it could do any damage.

'Yeah, I guess it could be that, I suppose,' I responded, undoubtedly unable to hide the flicker of pain from my face. The young waitress who had been totally focussed on her phone up until Claire's arrival had trudged wearily over to our table and with a face that looked irritated that our arrival had disturbed her scrolling through twitter or checking her WhatsApps or whatever it was, asked with a strong Greek accent, 'Can I get you any drinks?'

'I'll have a large whisky, please,' Claire responded swiftly.

'Erm…yeah why not, I'll get one of those too,' I added.

'Perfect,' the waitress responded, her face suggesting it was anything but as she collected our drinks menus and retreated from the table.

'So how have you been over the last few days?' I asked, hoping that Claire's responses to my questions would soften slightly.

'Good, actually. I think when you're in London and you're working and you're crammed face-first into someone's armpit on the Tube every day and you're constantly rushing to get to work on time, to get to your gym class on time, to get to your hair appointment on time, the doctor's, the dentist, to get home quickly so you can get dinner on and have it done so you get a reasonable amount of time to relax before you head to bed and have to do it all over again, you forget how much your body just needs a break and a rest.'

'Very true. So you've just chilled out at the villa, have you?'

'Yeah, just chilled out with Elena and Nikos. You've not been flavour of the month with them, to be honest. Nikos has actually threatened physical violence on you if he sees you'

Oh yeah, well Nikos didn't see me down at the boxing speed dating event did he, maybe he'd reconsider his words if he'd seen me take it to the bags. Or maybe not, thinking about it, most of my female partners that night did more damage to the bags than me.

'He's a very fiery, Mediterranean, hot-blooded type of character, y'know,' Claire continued, 'very different to you.'

And my heart sunk a little as I detected a thinly veiled dig at my character and personality.

'I see,' I replied after a slight pause, 'well hopefully it won't come to that.'

'It's just so difficult, you see. I want all my friends and my family to love you. Like I love you. Loved you. And I haven't told anyone about what happened, but obviously I had to mention it to Elena and Niko given that I was staying at their place, moping around with a face like a slapped arse and sporadically bursting into tears.'

'I know, I'm so sorry, Claire, my terrible actions have put you in a horrible position, I'm aware of that.'

'Now, if we were to get back together, I don't know how my friends would be with you, knowing how much you'd hurt me.' Claire shuffled her chair sideways slightly, turning her head and body away from me

'Well hopefully they'd get to know me, get to know that I'm a decent person, acknowledge that nobody's perfect and that everyone makes mistakes. They'd get to see all that, I'm sure of it, beautiful one.'

'Maybe you're right, I suppose,' She responded, her eyes swiftly shifting position any time they were caught in my glare.

'I'm sure I'm right, Claire. I do doubt myself a lot, you know I do, but I'm backing myself on this one. Have you had any thoughts about what you want to do?' I asked tentatively, having plucked up the courage to grab the bull by the horns, waiting for the answer that could potentially determine my destiny.

'I've given it a lot of thought. A hell of a lot of thought,' Claire responded, turning her body in to face mine and looking up into my eyes, 'I don't think I need to reiterate how much you've hurt me, I think I've made that plainly clear, and I do get the feeling that you understand that.'

'Totally,' I replied.

'And you coming out to Crete after me, although borderline stalkerish, has definitely let me know how sorry you are and how I must mean a lot to you. And I appreciate that you've given me space and just waited. And the truth is I love you, still, and that feeling really doesn't come along very often, true love can be a very tricky thing to find.'

Typically, at the most ill-opportune moment our waitress arrived and dumped our drinks down somewhat angrily on the table. Both of us immediately grabbed our glasses and took large gulps.

'Could we get another two, please.' I asked after the retreating waitress who nodded, whilst raising her eyebrows clearly thinking she'd been stuck serving a couple of English alcoholics for the evening.

'Sorry,' I said to Claire, 'go on.'

'As I was saying, I've thought a lot and it has boiled down to this. I genuinely don't think you find love often, and I do believe that everyone can make a mistake and I do believe that you are a really good person.' My heart soared a little and I struggled to keep a smile from appearing on my face.

'And so I think it would be a real shame to let something slip away and not fight for something which I believe has the potential to be something really good and something that could last forever.' I was slightly taken aback and at the same time over the moon to hear Claire's words and I reached forward on the table and grabbed Claire's hands and she finally retained eye contact with me.

'And if I'm honest, these thoughts have been brought forward massively because of your actions. I kind of had to ask myself, well is this something that might be nice for a year or is this something that could be meaningful to your whole life? And now I feel extremely self-conscious that I've laid my cards on the table, angry that your horrible actions have brought it out in this horrendous scenario, and worried that it's all too much too soon.' Claire pulled away and looked down to the ground.

'No, Claire!' I exclaimed, taking her hands back in mine whilst lifting her chin with my finger to return her gaze to mine, 'not in the slightest. That is exactly how I feel and is exactly how I've felt for a little while. I know we've been together a very short amount of time and I'm sure we're still learning about each other, but sometimes I think your gut is a better indicator than anything in this world, and my gut tells me that I will never meet another woman as special as you.'

Claire's expression softened a little and she allowed a slight smile to form on her face.

'You have always made me feel special, to be honest. And my gut says the same about you.'

'Then please, please listen to it.' And moving my face closer to hers we kissed, and I breathed out for what seemed like the first time since I'd been on the island.

The rest of the evening felt almost euphoric as the tension in my body ebbed slowly away, we relaxed and, very slowly, we slipped very slightly back into something which more closely resembled our more natural interaction with each other. We ate delicious seafood and Claire laughed when I told her about Gary meeting Emma and she got very excited when I told her that they seemed to be hitting it off. And that evening Claire decided to come back with me and, once again, I felt like the luckiest man in the world.

We can get bogged down just dealing with life sometimes. Strangely, particularly when life is good, we have a natural propensity to worry and our minds will search for something to fixate upon, something to gradually nibble away at our well-being. We worry incessantly about our weight, our hair, our skin, about whether we'll meet a deadline at work or whether we look good in our new jeans, but, in reality, none of this really matters. What matters are the people we love, those people whom without, our world would always be that little bit less happy. So we need to hold on tight to those people, let them know how important they are to us, and show them that our happiness is eternally intertwined with theirs, tied together by a bond of emotion, love, friendship and feeling, in such a web of knots and cords, that nothing could ever break it.

Chapter 37

Once back in England, Claire and I seemed to become closer than ever. Most evenings we would be together and stay either at my place in Acton or at Claire's place. It was like our relationship had been tested and we'd both decided what we had between us was worth all the effort. Claire had decided what we had together was special enough to merit giving me another chance, even after I had proven myself to be a massive, drunken dickhead. And in a weird way it had proven to me exactly how much Claire valued our relationship; if she didn't then I'm sure after that she would've thought *sod this* and got herself out of there.

I loved going to Claire's place. She seemed to have a way of making a place seem amazingly homely and comfortable. She was always complaining that the place needed a really good clean, and I'd look around and think the flat looked absolutely spotless without one thing out of place. She would say it wasn't *'me clean'* though, whatever that meant.

'I'm going to pop to the loo quickly,' Claire said one sunny Saturday morning when we'd ventured down to the Northcote Road for some breakfast to a little pop-up café run by a local community group in a venue which was a wine bar in the evenings. 'Now, while I'm up, there's a possibility I may have a conversation with a waiter, and he may say something to make me laugh. If he does, please can you promise not to snog the girl on the table beside us?' she said whilst getting up from the table and nearly knocking the wine bottle with candle in it from the table as she swung her bag round her shoulder.

'Yes, yes, very good, now bugger off, make sure you don't fall down the loo or do yourself any other kind of mischief,' I responded lamely, steadying the wine bottle and wondering when the jokey remarks would die off but at the same time acknowledging that they were more than justified.

When Claire returned we had started discussing her parents and when it would make sense to introduce me to them when the conversation took a turn towards my family life.

'So you've never tried to find your mum?' Claire asked.

'No, never,' I replied.

'Have you never felt curious? Do you not want to find out where you come from? Do you know why she left?'

'I think I *was* curious. When I was younger I would occasionally ask questions of my dad about her, but it seemed to agitate and annoy him hearing me talk about her and so gradually I stopped mentioning her. So no, I don't really know why she left, and I haven't given it much thought as I've grown older, I guess you sort of don't miss what you've never had.' I replied semi-honestly, thinking back over the thousands of times I'd daydreamed about seeing her.

'I think your dad is one of the nicest and most genuine men I've ever met, I just can't imagine him getting agitated over something so important like this. Do you not see people with their mums and wonder?'

I paused for a moment, thinking about all the times I'd wished I could tell my mum something like when I'd passed my driving test, or like when I'd gotten into university, and the times I'd wished I could ask someone questions about girls but had had to rely on Ozzy and Gary instead who gave advice that in all honesty I thought was at best questionable and at worst very dangerous.

'Yeah, I suppose so. I guess I don't like to think about it or talk about it, because I suppose it is a little bit painful and not thinking about it makes things a bit easier. And I don't ever want to upset Dad, really.'

'You're nuts!' Claire exclaimed, somewhat unjustifiably I thought, 'that's literally the worst thing to do with thoughts that hurt you! You need to talk about them, you need to face them, otherwise they won't heal and you won't work through them, and by the time you're forty you'll have a metaphorical treasure chest of pain lodged in your chest, shut tight, but weighing you down every day of your life. Serious question, if you knew where your mum was, would you go and find her?'

I looked at Claire. I half wanted to tell her to shut up, to stop talking about this, let's change the subject, it was making me deeply uncomfortable. But there was sense in what she said, I knew that, and I knew she wouldn't be doing anything to deliberately hurt me.

'Hmmm... I guess so. But I don't.'

'But you've never looked?'

'No.'

'I just think that's nuts! How can you not be curious? How can you not have a million questions? Your dad will understand, he's a good man. Sometimes in life you have to do things that won't necessarily please absolutely everybody, sometimes you've got to think of number one, and I really think this is one of those times,' Claire said passionately, placing a comforting hand on my shoulder as she did so. 'Obviously it's not my decision, and if you really don't want to then that's your decision, but don't make the decision based on whether you'll hurt other people. This is something you're fully entitled to do.'

I considered Claire's words and knew she was right. I tried my hardest to push thoughts of my mother out of my head, any questions that surfaced on occasion I'd immediately send back into the murky depths of my mind to avoid the scenario of having to confront these thoughts and through fear of these thoughts leading to further and more unsettling questions which might lead me to decide to take action and try to find my mother. At present I could paint the picture in my mind, my own picture, one that suited me, a picture which had my mother loving me unconditionally but being forced to leave by some sort of evil. The knowledge that she had a terminal and degenerative disease was one which was painful but so bitter-sweet simultaneously: my mother leaving in the dark of night, kissing dad, kissing me on the forehead and walking out of the door, tears streaming down her face in the knowledge that she was wasting away and that within a couple of months she would be dead, but in her heart knowing she was doing the right thing rather than staying and placing the burden on my dad of looking after a new-born baby and at the same time caring for the woman he loved while she slowly and painfully slipped away, gradually forgetting who he was in the process.

That way I could love my mother, even without remembering or having ever met her, rather than find out the truth and being forced to deal with whatever emotions that should kick up.

'Yeah, I guess I'll have a think about it,' I said, hoping this would be enough to change the subject as the waitress interrupted with my order of poached eggs on smashed avocado and sourdough.

'AKA let's change the subject,' Claire responded, astonishingly intuitively, as she placed her napkin onto her lap.

'No, I didn't mean that!' I lied. Badly.

Claire took my face with both hands and looked me straight in the eyes. 'You need to face your demons, chase them out of the shadows,' she said, giving a surprisingly good impression of a superhero in a Marvel comic film.

I bristled momentarily with irritation, agitated at the implication that I was someone who runs away from their troubles and the stubborn streak in me really wanted to tell her to bugger off and that I'd face off any demon she liked. But could that be me? Could that have been my mother? Could it be a trait I've inherited from her? The conversation was really beginning to become deeply unsettling, and I wanted to get up and leave the room, go and make a cup of tea, go for a jog even though I never go for jogs, do anything just to get away from these thoughts and the horrible, nauseous feeling that was developing deep in the pit of my stomach.

'I'm sorry, I shouldn't be so forceful,' Claire said mercifully, as if reading my thoughts.

'No, no it's fine, this is something I should have given more consideration to. If I'm honest, it's just quite painful to think of and to talk about,' I replied. 'But I'm not running away from anything,' I added, forcefully, desperate to try and prove that I wasn't scared.

'You're crazy! You must be so scared,' Claire responded, again almost worryingly, telepathically accurate. 'This is something that must be so difficult for you that I can't even begin to imagine. I had such a fortunate upbringing with two parents and a brother and a sister in a household that was filled with love and laughter and energy. I simply can't imagine what it would have been like to have grown up with just one parent and no siblings.'

'Well it was—'

'Not that I'm saying it can't have been great, I'm sure you and your dad had great times,' Claire added, clearly keen not to upset me.

'We did have great times. We were like a team, y'know. We did everything together. I've got so many happy memories and not having a mum didn't feel like a major issue on most occasions. Sometimes kids at school would pick on me, I suppose, would laugh at me. *Your mum left you because even she was sick of the sight of your ginger hair; what did you get your mum for Mother's Day, Jamie?* That sort of general hilarity. But, if anything, it did me a favour. I learned to stand up to people, to stand up for myself, something which I don't think came naturally to me.'

Claire placed her hand on my bicep and, for some reason, I instantly tensed it slightly, trying to make it feel bigger and stronger in her hand.

'It was a really happy childhood, but when I look back now I feel slight guilt because I was literally Dad's life. He didn't have any friends he went out with, I don't remember him going on dates. And those are things he should have been doing; I shouldn't have completely monopolised his time, but obviously as a kid you have absolutely zero concept of that being the case.'

'It sounds like you're massively worried about treading on anyone's toes?' Claire responded as she took a bite out of her bacon butty, a dollop of brown sauce dropping out onto her plate as she did so.

'No, not really, I'm worried about treading on my dad's toes, making him feel shit.'

'He'll understand,' Claire cut in, stroking my arm gently and leaning forward on the table between us.

'I know. I think you're right. Maybe it's a bit of both. Maybe I'm using it as an excuse because it's… well it's—'

'It's scary. You can say it. I won't think any less of you for admitting to being a little scared on occasion. It's called being human.'

Again she was right. She continued, 'Everyone is scared at some point in life. Everyone has places, people, situations which push them slightly outside of their comfort zone and make them feel uncomfortable and often we avoid them because of this very reason.'

Claire moved the candle-topped wine bottle out of the way, took both of my hands in hers and pulled them towards her. I felt the comfort that was always provided by her warm, soft hands, 'It's natural to want to avoid scenarios which cause us stress. But by avoiding these situations we empower them. I used to be so self-conscious about my weight. To the extent there is not a chance in hell that I would have walked through that door into that lecture theatre that evening we met for the second time, knowing I was late and knowing that the opening of the doors would be likely to cause people to swing round and stare in the direction of the door. The thought of the instant judgement, *oh she's fat, bloody hell, look at the size of her?*

I went to interrupt, but Claire released one of my hands from her grip and held up her index finger to my lips,

'Just give me a sec. And so I forced myself to do those things that scared me, to walk into the lecture room, to go and dine out alone, to march down to the beach on holiday in my bikini. And do you know what? I'd get the odd comment. The odd comment from some absolute dickhead who was miserable, weak, unsure of themselves and unhappy with their own lives, but that's life, and by doing these things you learn to brush off these little knocks and wish the small-minded individuals in question a good day and march on feeling fabulous. And do you know what? If I'd not pushed myself out of my comfort zone, I wouldn't have walked into that lecture room, and I wouldn't have met you and I wouldn't have fallen in love with a man who makes me happy.'

I reached across the table, put my hand behind Claire's head and pulled it gently towards me before kissing her on the lips, as the sleeve of my shirt rested perfectly in the yolk of the egg on top of my smashed avocado.

'When he's not snogging other girls,' Claire added and I grimaced.

'So what are your thoughts?'

'Thoughts on what?' I replied instantly, realising this was a stupid question given our most recent conversation. 'Oh, on trying to find my mum.'

'For someone I know to be very clever, you do genuinely astound me at times!' Claire responded sarcastically.

'I need to have a think about it. I've spent so much of my life without my mum that giving myself a bit of time to think won't make any difference. But I have a feeling in my stomach that you're right, and I think you've hit the nail on the head; it's something that I really don't want to get into because of the potential pain, but I think doing it will make me a stronger person, not to mention answering a few questions which I've had ever since I was little.'

Claire placed a hand on my hand on the tabletop.

'I think that sounds like a good idea. And your sleeve is covered in egg yolk.'

I placed my other hand on top of hers.

'I know. And thank you, Claire.'

'There's no need to thank me,' Claire responded, taking her hand from underneath mine and placing it back on top as if we were playing a huge game of one potato, two potato, three potato, four.

'There is though,' I responded, deciding I'd leave my hand resting underneath Claire's. 'You make me feel a lot stronger, and, with you by my side, I genuinely don't feel there's anything I can't do.'

Claire looked down at her by now empty coffee cup, picked up her spoon and started stirring the non-existent contents. After a brief pause she raised her head again to look back at me.

'Well you make me feel loved, secure and happy, so I guess we're both lucky to have each other.' And I leant forward across the table and kissed her once more, dipping the other sleeve perfectly into the remains of my egg yolk and wondering when I'd transformed into the type of lovesick sap that used to physically repulse Ozzy, Gary and me.

Chapter 38

And so that's what I gave myself, time to think. Except I quickly realised the sum product of my thoughts didn't actually consume that much of my time. Maybe other people are more thoughtful than me. Like in the past when you read about certain historical figures and their occupation is listed as 'thinker' or they're described as 'one of the most influential thinkers of their time'. What a great job that would have been. I reckon as a thinker I could have wacked out a day's work in one of the ad breaks whilst watching *Good Morning Britain*, leaving the rest of the day to myself.

And so, after thinking very briefly, it became clear to me that I was now a grown up, and that I had carried around these questions and this burden for my whole life, and that now was the time to have the questions answered and to free myself of the weight on my shoulders. And if I found my mother and she didn't want to know me, then I'd be in exactly the same position I am in now. And if she happened to be deceased, I would say a prayer for her and would be in exactly the same position I am in now. And if she was alive and was willing to talk to me, then maybe I might understand more about myself, maybe I might find an answer to lifelong questions, and maybe I might bring a little more love into my life.

And although there was trepidation certainly, none of the outcomes seemed to scare me, and I think Claire was responsible for that. I felt stronger knowing she was with me.

Chapter 39

Where do you start when looking for a mother who abandoned you thirty years ago? Someone whose name you probably don't even know.

I started from basically the only piece of information I knew. Her name at one point was Maura Green. I Googled it. 383,000 results. 'Maura Green Uxbridge', 1,860 results. 'Maura Green Steve Green Uxbridge', 1,740 results. I looked at the top hits; an Austrian legislative election website, a 1995 yearbook for a school in Issuu and the definitive guide to murder in the state of Iowa from 2000-2016 being the first results. On all sites the keywords were dotted all over the place, none coming in together.

'Would you ever consider approaching your dad about it?' Claire asked as we sat on my sofa watching the *Great British Bake Off*, Claire's legs resting on my lap, after I'd explained the complete lack of success and ideas I'd had in my search. 'He's the only link you have to the person you're searching for, so it really would be the best place to start?'

'I know, I know, it just means the engaging in a particularly tricky and awkward conversation.' I replied.

'I know what you mean, but I think you need to stop underestimating your dad and, above all else, remember that you're not doing anything wrong here. You've waited thirty years, you're more than entitled at any stage to go looking for your mother, to try and find out answers about yourself, about your history.'

'I know you're right,' I replied, 'but if you'd been there in the past when I'd mentioned Mum, if you'd seen the pain on Dad's face, you'd understand why it's not something I'm relishing the prospect of.'

'Look at me,' Claire said, swinging her legs off my lap and taking my head between her hands, 'your dad will be absolutely fine, nothing will break the bond the two of you have, and if you need to provide a little assurance to him about this, then go ahead and do so.'

I pondered Claire's words. I think he would be fine. I know he would be fine. Providing assurance of our bond felt a bit much; we didn't really have the sort of relationship where we'd hug and say we loved each other. If I had to, I guess I could send him a text. Just say: 'Don't worry, Dad' or something like that. No, I could do better than that, I'm sure I could.

And so that was it. I messaged Dad and said I'd pop round to see him Saturday morning.

I didn't invite Claire with me to Dad's. I thought it best it was just the two of us. And so, on that sunny, crisp, wintry morning I jumped on the Piccadilly Line to Uxbridge and headed over to Dad's.

Dad answered the door in jogging bottoms pulled up too high and a navy t-shirt tucked into them. To be fair to him, he'd kept himself in very good shape over the years but this was not a good look.

'Hello, Jamie, come in,' Dad greeted me, pulling me in for a semi-awkward hug.

'Alright, Dad.'

'Cup of tea?' he asked, leading the way into the kitchen.

'Yeah go on then, thanks, Dad.' I stood in the kitchen, leaning on one of the work surfaces as Dad busied himself boiling the kettle and getting the mugs ready with his back to me. Just say it, I thought to myself, rip off the plaster, don't let it fester in your head any longer.

'Dad… I want to find Mum.'

Dad remained completely still with his back to me, ceasing instantly to stir the mug of tea he was making. A deafening silence filled the room, and it seemed to grow with every second that passed. My mind flashed to a scene with dad turning around suddenly and launching the hot cup of tea at me. Eventually, Dad put the teaspoon down and turned round slowly to face me.

'OK. What's brought this on?' he asked calmly, eyes fixed upon me.

'Erm…' I stumbled. 'Nothing…really, in particular. It's just something that has niggled at me throughout life – not like anything has been missing or anything,' I added hastily. 'I just sort of want to find out a bit more about me, and maybe find out some answers.'

'OK. And what if you don't like those answers?' Dad asked, again the personification of calm.

'I'm prepared for that, Dad. I'm sort of expecting that, to be honest. I can't imagine I'm going to like the reasons Mum walked out on us and never came back thirty years ago.' And suddenly a new possibility hit me. What if dad had been so keen to stop me from seeking out, even mentioning my mum for all these years because he had done something terrible to make her leave? What if that was the reason the pain was etched on his face at every mention of her name?

'OK. OK.' And with that dad left the room and headed upstairs. I stood there, wondering what was going to happen. Images of him returning downstairs having lost his mind at the mention of Mum, carrying an old World War Two pistol he'd kept in the loft in his hand, and blowing my brains out in a fit of uncharacteristic rage filled my head.

After a couple of minutes he returned, holding an envelope.

'Here,' he said, handing me the envelope, 'the last I ever heard of your mum.' And he returned to the counter to finish making the tea.

My hands shook as I struggled to remove the letter from the envelope.

Steve
If Jamie does ever ask in his older age to find me, please can you give him this address.
43 Minchistle Avenue, Woollongabba, Brisbane, QLD 4102
Thanks
Maura

I stared at the letter. Mum's writing. Mum acknowledging that I exist. The letter was dated October 1993. I'd have been three years old. Three years after mum left us. It felt good to think that she hadn't completely forgotten me three years after she'd left. The letter seemed sort of cold, blunt, to the point. Did that mean anything? Should I read anything into that?

Dad had resumed making the tea and placed mine beside me on the kitchen work surface before taking a seat at the kitchen table and having a sip of his own.

'Is this everything you have from her?' I asked, finally looking up from the letter.

'That's everything. Sorry, Jamie. I've wrestled many times over the years as to whether I should give it to you, but now that you've asked I think the time is right.'

I paused, staring down at the letter once again. Australia. Bloody hell.

'And you've not heard from her since?' I asked.

'No, heard rumours from people after she initially left, then heard she'd gone to Australia and the rumour mill quietened, then received this in the post, and then nothing.'

Silence again.

'Do you hate her, Dad?'

Dad turned in towards the table, back facing me, and took another sip of his tea.

'I don't hate her, Jamie. Because of her I have a best friend, a reason for living and the biggest source of pride and happiness in my whole life. So no, I'd find it very difficult to hate her. I wish things had turned out differently. I wish so much that things had turned out differently, but life generally doesn't go the way you want it to. If you're going from A to B you very rarely go in a straight line, you zig-zag, you go in circles, you come back to before where you started, but if you persevere you get there in the end. Sorry, I'm waffling.'

'No,' I cut in, 'I know what you mean, Dad.'

Chapter 40

The Chronicles of a Malfunctioning Male

That Saturday I turned thirty-one. As I sat at my desk at work, once again completely naked, anxiously praying that nobody would ask me to pop over to their desk and wondering where the sound of footsteps was coming from, my mind gradually recognised that I was dreaming and I slowly drifted towards consciousness. The sound of my bedroom door opening made me open one eye, as Claire entered, dressed in her white, fluffy dressing gown carrying a tray full of mugs and plates, filled with what looked like pastries and croissants and all sorts of doughnut-y treats.

'Happy birthday my lovely one' she said as she slid into bed and under the covers, perching the tray on our laps as I groggily sat up, 'Breakfast in bed for the birthday boy, one card from me and you had a card on the mat.' Claire continued, gesturing to the two cards propped up between the two mugs full of coffee.

'Ahh, thank you Claire, this looks absolutely great' I said, eyeing up what was far too much breakfast for two people and what consisted of mainly sugary, doughy treats, my favourite kind of breakfast.

'You are most welcome Mr Sweet Tooth, now come on, open your cards.' Claire said whilst handing me the two cards. I slid my finger under the envelope of the first one and pulled out a card with two large, red tomatoes with smiley faces on it. "Wishing you a Happy Birthday from my head to-ma-toes" was written in large letters beneath the smiley tomatoes.

Jamie,
Have a wonderful time on your birthday
Best wishes from
Papa Giuseppe
Pizza

And even though my custom to Papa Giuseppe had undoubtedly waned over the past year, his generosity of spirit had clearly not dipped. 'Papa Giuseppe' I said to Claire, showing her the card and smiling, 'the pizza place down the road.'

'Ahh how nice is that' Claire replied taking the card, looking at it briefly, repeating the "Ahh" and placing it on the bedside table beside her. 'Now this one' she said picking up the other card and pushing it into my hands.

"Hmm… who could this be from" I said raising an eyebrow whilst opening the envelope. Taking out the card and without looking at it I turned the card face down and opened it swiftly, 'No cash,' I said pretending to chuck the card as I said it.

'Just read the bloody thing' Claire said. I looked at the front of the card, completely white with a large red heart in the middle, the words *My Love* written beneath it. I opened the card and read it.

To my love
   I hope you have a wonderful birthday and a brilliant 32nd year ahead. Thank you for being such a genuinely wonderful man, for looking after me and for making these last six months the happiest ones I can remember.
Love always
Your Claire xxx

'Ahh, thank you beautiful one, I love you very much too.' I said, pulling Claire towards me and kissing her on the top of the head.

'And there's something else in the envelope.' I reached into the envelope and removed a folded piece of paper, unfolding it to reveal a picture of a male sportsman with short dark hair, legs astride whilst running, arms outstretched in front of him, hands grasping what appeared to be a rugby ball, wearing shorts and a strange sleeveless sports top.

'Erm… thanks Claire, is this for my bedroom wall?' I said, my brain scrambling for reasons as to why Claire considered this to be a suitable birthday gift for me.

'That,' Claire responded, 'is Jonathan Brown, and he is, so the powers of Google have led me to believe, possibly the best player to ever don the famous Brisbane Lions Aussie Rules football shirt.'

'Hmm… excellent… thank you Claire, for my picture of Jonathan Brown of the Brisbane Lions,' I said, wondering if Claire had gone temporarily insane or whether she had always been insane and I had somehow, till now, just failed to notice.

'The picture, Jamie, isn't the actual present, it's what it represents.'

'OK…' I responded still debating whether the insanity was temporary which would be good news, or permanent which would be unfortunate.

'I've booked you some flight tickets.' Claire said, taking the tray of treats off our laps and putting it down beside the bed, sitting up straighter and taking my hands in hers, 'to Brisbane. Where your mother is. Or she may be.'

'Oh. Wow. Thank you Claire.' I said, wondering whether I preferred the present when it was a random picture of an Aussie Rules footballer which indicated Claire was insane.

'Look, it's totally up to you whether you decide to go or not, the ticket is refundable, I just know you, and know that sometimes you need a little nudge to actually do things.'

'Thanks, Claire, no, this is great. Why not? Australia, Down Under, throw another shrimp on the barbie and chuck me a tinny of Castlemaine XXXX.'

'Exactly!' Claire said, pulling me in for a hug, 'And I've only booked a ticket for you as I thought it might be something you wanted to do alone, but if you want me to come too, then I'm in!'

'No, I think you're right, I think this is something for me to do on my own, find my mum, or maybe not find her, but maybe find some answers.' And Claire beamed.

So that was it, the flight was booked, Australia, mum, I'm on my way.

And so that night I put my two cards on my mantelpiece and headed for dinner to celebrate my birthday. A table for six: Claire and I, Gary and Emma, and Ozzy, bringing his friend Will from work. We sat around the table, Ozzy initially slightly quieter and more reserved than normal, but after a couple of drinks becoming more like his usual self, spouting various nonsensical anecdotes which required significant effort to believe. Gary chipping in with the odd comment which would invariably result in fits of laughter coming from the rest of the table and Gary becoming increasingly perplexed as to why we were laughing. Emma teasing Gary relentlessly before having mercy and pulling him in for a cuddle. Will, perfectly presented and being the personification of politeness and good manners, fitting into the group seamlessly. And Claire, Claire just being her wonderful self, including everyone in conversation and making a fuss over me on my birthday night out. And I just sat, soaked it all in, smiled, laughed and just enjoyed being in the presence of the love of my life, and my friends, a misfit bunch with hearts of gold, and, at that moment in time, there was absolutely nowhere else I'd rather have been.

THE BEGINNING

The Chronicles of a Malfunctioning Male

A E Bem

Acknowledgements

A huge amount of thanks is owed to my editors, Peter Robb, James Lawless and Nicola Lovick, thank you for all your feedback, comments, suggestions and editorial notes but also for your words of encouragement, they helped push me through to completion when it felt like a better idea to stop.

Thanks also to my wife Sophie, for your encouragement, your enthusiasm and your early reading of the book, it meant a huge amount to me that you were so positive about it.

Printed in Great Britain
by Amazon